"Jo Davis turns up the heat full-blast. Romantic suspense that has it all: a sizzling firefighter hero, a heroine you'll love, and a story that crackles and pops with sensuality and action. Keep the fire extinguisher handy or risk spontaneous combustion!"

—Linda Castillo, national bestselling author of *Gone Missing*

"Jo Davis . . . completely reeled me in . . . heady sexual tension, heartwarming romance, and combustible love scenes."   —Joyfully Reviewed

"One of the most exciting 'band of brothers' series since J. R. Ward's Black Dagger Brotherhood. It's sweet and sexy, tense and suspenseful."   —myLifetime.com

"For a poignant and steamy romance with a great dose of suspense, be sure to pick up a copy of *Trial by Fire* as soon as it hits the bookstores! Five bookmarks!"

—Wild on Books

"Hot, sizzling sex and edge-of-your-seat terror will have you glued to this fantastic romantic suspense story from the first page to the final word. Do not miss the heart-stopping, breath-stealing, incredibly well-written *Trial by Fire*."   —Romance Novel TV

THE FIREFIGHTERS
OF STATION FIVE NOVELS

Ride the Fire
Line of Fire
Hidden Fire
Under Fire
Trial by Fire

SWORN *to* PROTECT

A SUGARLAND BLUE NOVEL

JO DAVIS

A SIGNET ECLIPSE BOOK

SIGNET ECLIPSE
Published by the Penguin Group
Penguin Group (USA) Inc., 375 Hudson Street,
New York, New York 10014, USA

USA | Canada | UK | Ireland | Australia | New Zealand | India | South Africa | China

Penguin Books Ltd., Registered Offices: 80 Strand, London WC2R 0RL,
England
For more information about the Penguin Group visit penguin.com.

First published by Signet Eclipse, an imprint of New American Library,
a division of Penguin Group (USA) Inc.

First Printing, May 2013

ISBN 978-0-451-41500-4

Printed in the United States of America
10 9 8 7 6 5 4 3 2 1

ALWAYS LEARNING   PEARSON

To my son, Bryan. You're a smart, funny, and compassionate young man with a desire to succeed founded in a strong moral compass. Let those qualities continue to shine, to guide you, and you'll go far in life. Follow your dreams and never give up. I'm so proud of you and I thank God that you're mine.

Shane's story is for you.

I love you so very much.

1

"It's way too damned quiet around here."

Several other cops groaned and a couple of them shot Taylor Kane the death glare. Shane Ford just smirked, getting more comfortable with his booted feet propped on his desk and crossed at the ankles.

His cousin, Christian Ford, a recent transplant from the Dallas, Texas, PD, wadded up a sheet of paper and launched it at Taylor's face. "Thanks a lot for jinxin' us, dipshit," he drawled. "Even the dumbest rookie knows better than to let the *Q* word pass his lips."

Taylor slapped a file onto his desk with a grimace of disgust. "I'm just sayin' I'm sick of investigating vandalism and stolen bicycles, that's all. It's a waste of my rather large and brilliant brain. Shut up, Chris." At the other man's snort, he threw the paper wad back, missing his target.

"Hey, there's a lot of money to be had fencing bikes," Shane said, crossing his arms over his chest. "And a crime is a crime."

"I know, but it's *boring*. Since Jesse Rose and his bunch got shut down last year, nothing exciting has happened around here," their friend griped. "I'm about to lose my frickin' mind."

Shane suppressed a shudder. Jesse Rose was a homeland terrorist who had planned to blow up their fine city of Sugarland, Tennessee, and had damned near succeeded. A Sugarland Fire Department captain by the name of Sean Tanner, along with Shane and the entire police force, had been instrumental in stopping the bastard just in time. Tanner had since been promoted to battalion chief, and it was a well-deserved honor as far as Shane was concerned.

Another new hire, Tonio Salvatore, spoke up. "That case Shane and Daisy solved last month was pretty exciting. . . ." An uncomfortable silence fell over the room. "What? What'd I say?"

Shane's good mood did a belly flop and curdled in his stomach. It always did whenever someone mentioned Daisy Callahan's name and the case that had almost gotten them both killed. Or, worse, when he was forced to exchange polite, professional conversation with the stunning blond juvenile officer. Especially when all he wanted to do was bend her over the nearest flat surface and fuck her until she screamed his name.

Yeah, their passionate affair hadn't been such a great idea before, and that fact hadn't changed.

Easing his legs off the desk, he studied the other officers' faces. Most reflected curiosity, the barely disguised desire to pry. So they didn't *really* know, just likely suspected. Chris was the only one who knew, and it seemed he'd kept his promise not to say anything to the others. Their friends were merely attuned to the sudden tension that snapped like a rubber band whenever

Shane and Daisy were mentioned in the same sentence, or the two of them were in a room together.

Shane wasn't about to satisfy their avid curiosity.

"Our lack of excitement means nobody has been murdered," Shane said dryly, sidestepping the reference to him and Daisy. "Let's not borrow trouble."

"Too late for that." Their captain, Austin Rainey, swiped a trickle of sweat from his rugged face with one hand as he approached. "Goddamn, this heat is already bad enough to poach an egg, and it's not even spring yet."

Shane studied the man's grayish pallor. Austin wasn't just his supervisor; he was a good friend who'd been through a rough time in the last couple of years. The man's bitch of a wife was really putting him through the ringer lately. Shane feared for his health, as did the men and women who respected and loved him.

"You okay, Cap?" Shane asked him. "It's February and it's not that hot in here. You're not looking so good."

Austin waved off his concern as usual and addressed his detectives. "We've got a body in the gulley out on 49. White male, no ID, shot once in the back of the head, execution style." He gave Taylor a baleful glare. "Since you're so fucking bored, you can take this one with Shane. Oh, and you can do all the reports, too."

Taylor grimaced as a few others snickered. "Thanks a million, Cap."

"Don't mention it. Get the lead out. Eden and the FU are already on their way."

Shane had to smile a little at that—Eden and the FU, as though they were a rock group. But it was appropriate, since Nashville's taciturn medical examiner and the

Sugarland PD's forensic investigations unit sort of went together like a guitar and strings. Though they were employed by separate entities, they worked toward the common goal of finding and analyzing clues that would help the police locate and apprehend the bad guys.

And then there was the shortening of FIU to FU, which one of the uniformed officers had jokingly said stood for Fuck U, because the science geeks thought they were smarter than a bunch of cops.

"On it." Taylor grabbed a set of keys off his desk and jingled them, looking at Shane. "I'll drive."

As they headed out, Shane fell into step beside him. "Happy now? You got the murder you wanted, and a messy one, too."

The other man shrugged. "I'm not happy someone bought it, but it happens."

"You like solving the puzzle. A lot of us do." That might seem strange or morbid to some, but to them, the need to make the pieces fit, the satisfaction they felt when they were successful, was normal.

"For me, the seemingly random pieces are more like snippets of a story, and aren't usually random at all," Taylor said thoughtfully. "The body is the last chapter, and I have to read the story backward to find out what led up to it."

"Never thought of it like that before, like reading a book in reverse."

He pondered that as they pushed outside and the frigid air hit them, slapping them like dozens of tiny needles. But that wasn't the only reason he suddenly felt as though he were suffocating.

Daisy Callahan was striding purposefully up the steps

to the precinct house, and all the spit dried up in Shane's mouth at the sight of her. Like the other detectives, Shane included, she wore street clothes consisting of dark pants and a casual shirt, a holstered gun and badge at her hip. But there the similarities ended. Blond hair was pulled back into a ponytail, emphasizing an angular face adorned with little makeup, large blue eyes, and a wide mouth. The woman was a long, tall drink of water on a scorching day, five feet, ten inches of lean muscle and confident stride that should have made her seem mannish, except she was anything but.

Her breasts were full, and he knew from experience how they spilled over a man's hands, ripe and tasty. He knew how smooth her skin was, how small her waist was just above the slight flare and curve of womanly hips. How toned those long thighs were, just how fantastic they looked wrapped around his waist as he—

"Earth to Shane?"

He blinked, becoming aware that he and Taylor had stopped in front of Daisy. Taylor had greeted her and they'd exchanged a few words, and now they were both regarding him with two completely different expressions—Taylor with amusement and Daisy with a polite detachment he'd grown to hate.

Completely my fault. I'm a first-class jerk.

"I'm sorry. What?" He hoped his smile gave no indication of just how desolate he felt inside. Given the unnatural tightness of his face, he suspected he'd failed.

"You guys caught the body out on I-49?" Her look was cool, appraising.

"Word travels fast as always," he said, striving to keep his tone even. "Yeah, we're headed out there now."

She made a face. "You and half the county, no doubt. Good luck, once the news people decipher the dispatch that went out on the scanner. I figure you've got an hour, tops, before the real madness hits."

"Shit. We'd better make tracks." But he couldn't get his feet to move. Daisy turned to go, and on impulse, he called after her. "Wait!"

She blinked at him, surprise causing the mask to slip. "What is it?"

"Can I . . . have a word with you?" He sent a pointed look at Taylor, who nodded and walked toward the parking lot. Thankfully without comment.

Once Taylor was out of earshot, his former lover gazed at Shane coolly. "Is there something about the case that you couldn't say in front of Taylor?"

"Of course not." He ran a hand through his hair. Never had he felt more awkward around a woman, and it was his own fault. "Dammit, I hate this weird distance between us."

"Really?" She gave an incredulous laugh. "That's funny, considering distance is exactly what you wanted. And lots of it. Which I gave you." Her last words were clipped. Angry.

"We were friends before and I ruined that. You'll never know how sorry I am," he said quietly.

The blunt edge of growing hostility disappeared as quickly as it had begun to form, and her face softened. "Me, too. But I guess I can't blame our failure solely on you. I'm the dumb-ass who slept with a friend—a fellow cop—and I should've damned well known better. So, lesson learned."

A raw lump formed in his throat and he spoke with

difficulty. "I'd like to think we're *still* friends. Or can be again." He waited, but she didn't let him off the hook. "Want to grab a beer after work sometime? Or coffee? I'm free Sunday—"

"Stop." Looking away, she regained tight control of the abject misery that had flashed across her beautiful features. "Just stop, okay? I'm not there yet. Maybe I won't ever be, either. And if not, that's a loss we'll both have to own, and move on."

Oh, God. The stab to his gut was sharp. Powerful. Had he honestly thought she'd forgive him, and they'd simply go back to the place they had been? Somehow, he mastered the unexpected pain and managed a sad, lopsided smile.

"I suppose we will at that." He glanced toward where Taylor stood by the car, studying them with undisguised interest. "Better go."

"Let me know what you find," she said, all business again. "I doubt it'll overlap with any of my cases, but you never know."

"You bet."

Before Shane could say anything more, she turned and walked into the building without a backward glance. As though they'd never been anything to each other at all. Which was how he'd wanted it. Right?

Numbly, he went to meet Taylor at his friend's beat-up vintage Chevelle, a "project car" that in Shane's opinion should have been sold for scrap twenty years ago. In an effort to deflect the questions he knew were coming, he scowled at the wreck. "Why can't we drive a *cool* car, like Starsky and Hutch, or Steve and Danno?"

His friend grinned at him as they climbed in and

slammed the doors. "So buy yourself one and we'll drive it. You're the guy with all the money." He started the ignition, and the car sputtered before roaring to life. "Or, better yet, fix up this one."

Shane rolled his eyes. "First, stop saying I'm rich just because I own a nice house on the Cumberland. Second, I like my truck just fine, and even if I was into muscle cars, I'd buy my own beater instead of pouring a small fortune into yours."

Taylor rolled his eyes. "Oh, sure. Compared to the rest of us, you're shitting money. You're like fuckin' Batman—you don't need a job; you just like to play superhero," he shot back, pulling out of the parking lot.

"Nah, I don't have a really cool, snarky butler. That's a superhero requirement, in case you missed the memo."

"Good point." They rode for a couple of minutes in silence before Taylor glanced at him, his tone growing serious. "So, you and Daisy . . ."

Crap. The man wasn't going to be put off so easily. "Me and Daisy, nothing. Nada."

His friend wasn't buying. "I knew it! Christ, of all the good-lookin' ass in town, you had to tap hers?"

"Daisy is *not* just some piece of ass," Shane said in a low, dangerous voice. "So watch your mouth." Too late, he realized his friend's ploy.

The man laughed and slapped his steering wheel. "Oh, you've got it bad! You never get all protective and snarly over your random hookups. So what gives? How did you two happen?"

Shane sighed. His cousin had been bad enough, but Taylor was a pit bull. He wouldn't let this go until Shane gave him something. "We've been attracted to each other for years, but it's not such a great idea to get involved with a colleague. You know?" His friend arched a brow, waiting. "So, while we were working the case, we got a little too close to the subject we were researching . . ." He shrugged. "That's how."

Taylor whistled through his teeth. "Man, that's heavy. Something tells me it wasn't a one-time thing."

"No, but it should have been. I let the relationship go on too long, and that was wrong of me."

"Why?"

He stared at Taylor. "Why? What do you mean, *why*?"

"Why was it wrong? You're both consenting adults, and you guys clearly aren't over this thing between you."

"Um, other than the rule about not dating fellow cops, the one that could get one or both of us fired for breaking it?" he replied sarcastically. "Gee, let me think."

"Don't give me that bullshit. You wouldn't be the first couple to ever fall in love at work."

"Whoa, nobody said anything about *love*." Jesus, he should've called in sick.

"Well, then, just bang each other in secret. You wouldn't be the only ones in the department doing it, and it's not like you haven't done it before. Hellooo, remember Leslie, from patrol?"

Shane frowned. "The problem is, Daisy deserves better, you moron. Unlike Leslie, she's not a *bang-in-secret* kind of woman—which is why I had to end it." His friend just snickered, as if he knew something Shane didn't. "Taylor?"

"Hmm?" He appeared way too satisfied.

"Shut the fuck up, okay?"

"As you wish." Taylor winked.

Something told him that the matter wasn't closed. Between Taylor and Chris, they'd drive him nuts about the issue. Which, dammit, was totally *not* an issue, because it was over between him and Daisy! Shit.

After several interminable minutes, Taylor pulled the Chevelle onto the shoulder behind a couple of squad cars. Laura Eden and the FU hadn't arrived, so they'd have a few minutes to scope out the scene before the techs gathered evidence and the ME eventually took the body.

Cautiously, he got out, checking the traffic. Highway 49 might be a gorgeous drive, but it was just about the worst place in the county to work any sort of official call, whether an MVA—motor vehicle accident—or something even worse. People were killed on this curvy stretch of treacherous road all the time, and he had no wish to be the next.

The man lying in the gulley, however, had definitely not suffered an accident. As the captain had said, he'd apparently died from a bullet that entered through the back of his head and subsequently blew off most of his face. He was lying slumped on his stomach, sort of curled in a bit, as though in death he'd tried to return to the fetal position. His clothes were torn and dirty, and some scrapes were visible on his arms.

"Jesus," Taylor muttered as they reached the bottom of the incline. "What a way to go."

"At least it was quick," one of the uniforms offered.

As they stood studying the corpse, Shane nodded. "Quick and efficient. Maybe professional, maybe not. He was a problem, and somebody erased him."

"The job wasn't done here," Taylor pointed out, flicking a hand at the ground and surrounding area. "No brains or blood spatter from the kill shot. He mostly bled out before he was dumped from the road."

"The killer wasn't concerned about him being found," Shane said, glancing up toward the highway. "It was just a matter of time. How was he discovered?"

One of the uniforms spoke up, flipping through his notepad. "Teenager stopped on the shoulder to fix a flat tire. Got an eyeful of the dead guy when he happened to look over the edge, and then called us. We took his statement and let him go. The kid was really shook up, and I doubt he was anything but an innocent bystander."

Shane nodded. "I'll make contact with him later. Maybe he'll remember something important."

"I'll get a description of our dead guy out, check missing persons and see if we can make a quick ID on him," Taylor said.

They all knew the chances of that were less than fifty percent—nothing was ever that easy. Dental work, DNA, and fingerprints were useless without missing persons to compare them to, and something told him this guy hadn't exactly been flying above the radar.

"He looks like a rough character," Shane mused, studying the body.

The cop tucked the notepad back into his pocket. "So?"

"Not all of that dirt is from his trip down into the gulley." Shane crouched, peering at the dead man. "He's filthy, he stinks, and those jeans and that T-shirt have seen better days. Holes in the toes of his sneakers. This wasn't a man who sat behind a desk and shuffled papers."

Taylor crouched beside him. "So we've got a guy who was down on his luck and kept ruthless acquaintances. Backwoods killing."

"Yeah. But the bullet in the back of the head tells a story of a brutal conclusion to business, rather than a crime of passion."

"That stench isn't just from his lack of a bath, either."

Shane thought about that. "I agree. Chemical?"

"That's my thought. Can't place it, though." His friend wrinkled his nose. "It's kind of sickly sweet. Sort of like marijuana, but not quite. It's heavier."

"Hopefully, Eden will be able to tell us more in a couple of days." Shane glanced up to see the woman in question picking her way carefully down the steep slope. "Speaking of the devil, here comes his bride."

"I heard that, Ford, you asshole."

Snickering, Taylor and the two uniformed cops gave Eden their undivided attention. The tall, raven-haired ME wasn't what Shane would call beautiful, but he had to admit she was striking. Her frame was willowy and it appeared as though a strong wind would blow her away, but he knew she was extremely resilient in both mind and body. Her mannerisms were a bit tomboyish, her jokes as dirty as the most seasoned cop's, yet she was also brilliant. No-nonsense. Almost all the guys liked her, including Shane. She was one of the most genuine people he'd ever met.

"Hey, now. You know I was just teasing." Giving her a wink, he stood.

"*I* wasn't," she said dryly. Bracing a hand on her hip, she squinted at the body. "Bullet to the occipital lobe? That'll ruin a guy's day."

Pulling a pair of latex gloves from her coat pocket, she snapped them on. Then she made a slow, careful circuit around the body, stopping to crouch now and then, observing in silence for several long moments. "Young white male, five-ten, approximately one hundred twenty pounds, between twenty-five and thirty years old. Possibly transient, given his appearance."

"Right up until he crossed the wrong person," Taylor muttered.

The ME nodded in agreement, then pointed without touching. "Abraded palms. Tears, dirt, and grass stains on the knees of his jeans. Those injuries *could* be from his tumble down the slope, but it's not likely."

"How so?" Taylor asked curiously.

"Because a person would have to hit the ground like this," she said, moving into a position on her hands and knees. "You'd instantly put your hands out to protect yourself as you fell—which would be impossible to do if you're dead."

"Meaning our victim was kneeling at some point," Shane speculated. "Pushed to his hands and knees, maybe, before he was shot?"

The ME nodded. "That would be my guess. See the entry and exit wounds, the scorching of the flesh at the back of his skull?" Standing, she walked over to Shane. "The angle and the wounds themselves suggest his head was pushed down, and the killer popped him like this."

Moving quickly, she assumed the role of the killer, grabbing Shane's arm and spinning him to face away from her. Giving him a gentle mock shove, she ordered, "On your knees."

Shane went along in the role of the victim, dropping

down and bracing himself with his hands before pushing to sit up on his heels. His "murderer" placed a finger at the back of his head to simulate the gun's muzzle.

"Boom. You're dead."

Shane sighed. "Quick and easy."

"But not clean," Taylor put in. "We've got one hell of a murder scene out there somewhere."

Shane stood, brushing off his pants. "ID this poor bastard and we might locate it."

"I'll do my best." Eden turned her attention to the slope, where the forensic team was making their way down, carrying their boxes of supplies.

"Looks like we've done all we can here," Shane said, clapping Taylor on the shoulder. Then he addressed Eden again. "Call us—"

"I know, when the toxicology and all the other results come back. Don't I always?"

He winked. "You're the bomb, darlin'."

She arched a brow. "I thought I was the devil's bride?"

"Nah, just his mistress."

She rolled her eyes, remaining unfazed. "Well, you're still an asshole." She winked back and gave him a half grin. "Just for the record."

Laughing, Shane turned to go. As they trudged upward, Taylor whistled through his teeth.

"Damn, that's a fine woman. I love a lady with a brain who's not afraid to use it."

"Isn't that what you usually say about their tongues?"

"Ha-ha." He shot a glare at Shane, which went ignored.

"Seriously, you say that every time we see her. Why don't you just grow a pair and ask her out?"

"What makes you think I haven't?"

They reached the top, and Shane studied his friend as they walked to the car. "So did you?"

"Yeah," the other man replied with a grimace. "Seems she's got a thing for someone else. Not that she said that in so many words, but it's a vibe I got. Found out I might've been right."

"Shit, that sucks," he said in sympathy as they climbed in. "Any idea who?"

"Heard a rumor she's got it bad for Rainey."

Shane blinked at him. "Austin? Since when?"

"Hell if I know. Just passin' along what I heard."

He thought about that as the car started with a roar and his friend pulled onto the road. "Wonder if the captain has any idea."

"Beats me, but I'm not sure it would make a difference if he did," Taylor said. "That bitchy wife of his has him by the balls. What guy in his right mind would want to complicate his life that way?"

"He's miserable, and that's a divorce just waiting to happen," Shane pointed out. "This is Eden we're talking about, and the guy deserves to be happy."

"True. And the doc is worth the wait."

"Yeah."

Shane's cell phone buzzed in his pocket, and he fished it out, glancing at the display. *Brad.* A prickle of apprehension followed when he saw his best friend's name, and he hated that feeling. The shadow of doubt where there used to be nothing but happiness at hearing from the man he'd admired for most of his life. Lately, Brad Cooper had gone from being unpredictable to . . . what, exactly? Posing a danger to himself and others?

No. Just because Shane had a cop's suspicious mind didn't mean his best friend was traveling down the same path as so many other sports celebrities.

Feeling like a disloyal piece of crap for hesitating with his finger over the button, debating whether or not to let it go to voice mail, Shane answered. "Hey, what's up?"

"Shane, my man! You about ready to knock off for the day?"

He huffed. "I wish. Just caught a new case, and I have a feeling this one is going to be sticky."

"Damn. I was hoping you could drive out to the house, kick back with a few cold ones. It is Friday, you know. All work, no play . . ." His friend let the statement dangle as a temptation.

"I'd love to, but it's not going to be tonight," he said with real regret.

"No problem. Just thought I'd put it out there."

But it *was* a problem, Shane could tell. His guilt doubled at Brad's voice, the man's tone edged with a hint of something that ran even deeper than disappointment—though that was probably his imagination. He shoved down the mounting disquiet and tried to sound cheerful. "Tomorrow instead?"

"Maybe." Brad paused. "Yeah, that'll work." His mood seemed uplifted, just a little.

Relieved, Shane smiled. "Great. I'll bring some pretzels and stuff. Will Drew be there?"

"Yeah, most likely. All he does lately is complain that he doesn't get to see you because you're always working."

Or his dad either, because you're always out partying.

Playing the big NFL star while the kid rambles around alone in a mansion that's more like a prison than a real home.

He squashed the uncharitable thought and focused on how much he was looking forward to seeing his sixteen-year-old godson. "Great. Tell him I'll bring some of Shea's homemade snickerdoodles to make up for it." Shane's twin sister loved to spoil her husband, Tommy, her brother, and most especially Drew, nearly as much as the teenage bottomless pit loved eating her cookies.

Brad laughed, sounding more like his old self than he had in some time. "You'll be instantly forgiven. So, tomorrow, around two?"

"Wouldn't miss it." He'd allowed work to rule his life enough of late. The case could wait for a few hours while he reconnected with two of the most important people in his life.

Somehow, he'd make the time.

Shane wanted to be friends? *Friends?* After what he'd put her through?

"Have coffee with you?" Tossing her keys onto the coffee table, Daisy stalked through her living room to the master bedroom. With jerky movements, she unholstered her sidearm and unclipped the badge from her belt, then laid them on the dresser. Then she began to strip off the unflattering navy pants and boring white shirt, fuming.

"Coffee? A beer? Like I'm just another one of the guys after we were . . ." What *were* they, exactly, besides stupid? "No, *I'm* the stupid one. Damn you! Bastard!"

Unable to come up with anything else bad enough to

call him, she yanked a pair of sweatpants and a T-shirt from a dresser drawer and dragged them on. Next, she freed her hair from the tight confines of the ponytail she'd sported all day and scratched vigorously at her scalp, sighing with relief.

"I'll have a beer, but I'll very much enjoy drinking it alone, you jerk!"

She *would*. She had a good job, great friends, and her crazy best friend, Mary Anne, who always had her back, so she certainly didn't need a man. Especially one with commitment issues.

In the kitchen, she tossed a frozen pasta dinner in the microwave and grabbed a brown bottle from the fridge. Twisting off the cap, she took a long draw, savoring the bubbly, honeyed flavor of the microbrew. A pricey brand, but worth every penny at the end of a long, frustrating day.

Padding into the living room, she rolled her shoulders, trying to work out the kinks. To relax some. But unwinding always took a while. Shane was far from being the sole source of stress in her life—working with juveniles was rewarding, but terribly exhausting. As much as she loved kids, never had she dreamed that seeing them in trouble, some of them desperately lost, their futures at risk of complete ruin when their lives should just be beginning, would be so heartbreaking.

It was her job to protect them, and she didn't always succeed.

With a sigh, she grabbed the remote and turned on the television. The drone of the six o'clock news already underway assaulted her ears, and she wondered why she bothered to watch when the stories covered had a short range of bad to worse.

When did I become so cynical?

She knew the answer to that question—she just preferred not to face it.

Disgusted with herself as much as the depressing newscast, she picked up the remote, fully intending to silence the TV, when the camera switched to a live picture of one of the seasoned reporters standing in front of a residential home. A really large one.

"Chad, I'm sorry to interrupt. We have some breaking news here," the reporter said in a grim tone. He quickly consulted a sheaf of paper in his gloved hand before continuing, the cold air causing his breath to puff with frost.

"I'm standing in front of the home of the Tennessee Titans' longtime star running back, Brad Cooper. Moments ago, the Nashville police confirmed that earlier today Cooper was found dead inside the house by his sixteen-year-old son, Drew. No further details have been released at this time, including the possible cause of death, but I'll be back with more information as it becomes available. All we know so far is that tragically, NFL star Brad Cooper, much-loved sports hero and native son, is confirmed dead at the age of thirty-seven. Back to you, Chad."

"Shocking and sad news indeed," the anchorman replied as the camera returned to him. His solemn face filled the screen. "We'll give you more on that story as soon as we can. In other news . . ."

Flicking off the television, Daisy sat frozen, eyes wide. "Oh, my God. That poor kid. And . . . Shane!"

Scrambling off the sofa, she hurried to retrieve her purse and keys and dashed out the door. She was down the street before she remembered that she hadn't grabbed her gun or shield, which she never went anywhere without. But that didn't matter right now. All that did was getting to Shane, comforting him while he dealt with the blow of losing his mentor. His best friend.

God, what if he hadn't yet heard the report? She had to reach him before he saw it on television, as she'd done, or worse, some reporter showed up at his house to get his reaction as fodder for their ratings.

The drive seemed to take forever, but was in reality just a few minutes. Shane lived in a gorgeous custom home on the Cumberland River, on the edge of Sugarland, that boasted a beautiful view. She was sure the house had to cost a ton of money. Not that it was any of her business, but she couldn't help but wonder how a cop could afford such a spectacular place. Shane's twin sister and her husband had built a place next door, and it was rumored they'd inherited the land from their deceased parents. Daisy had never asked if it was true.

Pulling her car into the drive, she stopped next to the front porch and shut off the ignition. The sun was about to disappear over the horizon, and she could see lights on in the house. She could picture him inside, sipping a cold one as she'd been doing.

Or maybe grieving the man who'd been his best friend. Alone.

With a deep breath, she got out, approached, climbed the steps, and knocked. In moments, the door swung open to reveal Shane's surprised face. He was dressed in loose, holey jeans and a faded Metallica T-shirt, his chest stretching the material nicely. He was tall, long, and lean, with muscles everywhere they should be. His sable-brown hair, a little too long to be regulation, flopped over gray eyes that assessed her with very male interest — despite the fact that he'd broken things off between them.

She noted all of this in a glance, and his open, questioning look jolted her to reality, because it meant one thing: he didn't know.

"Hey," he said, clearly at a loss. "What are you doing here?"

The simple inquiry hurt, even though it was a normal thing to ask. "Can I come in?"

"Sure." Looking puzzled, he held open the door and waited for her to come inside. After he shut it again, he followed her into the big living room. "What's wrong? You look like somebody drowned your kittens."

His attempt at levity fell flat as she turned to face him. Their gazes held, and the half smile that had been forming on his lips vanished.

"You haven't turned on the news." It wasn't a question.

"No, I haven't. What is it?" He closed the distance between them, brows knitting in concern.

"Shane . . ." Swallowing hard, she gripped both of his big hands in hers. Very gently, she said, "Honey, it's about Brad Cooper."

He stared at her, uncomprehending. "Brad? What about him? Did he get another speeding ticket? Or did they arrest him this time? Damn, his manager is going to have a fit — "

"No, that's not it." She shook her head.

Sucking in a breath, he said, "Daisy, you're scaring me."

"They said on the news that Brad is dead," she whispered. "God, I'm so, so sorry."

And as he slowly processed what she'd told him, Daisy watched the man she loved shatter into a million pieces.

2

Dead. Brad was dead?

"No. That's just not possible," he said reasonably, his mind refusing to accept her crazy words. "I spoke to him not even two hours ago and he was fine. He *is* fine. I'm sure there's some mistake."

"I'm so sorry," Daisy repeated, her big green eyes filled with sympathy. And a sheen of tears for a man she didn't really know.

No one did, save for Shane and Drew.

"Drew," he gasped. "Oh, Christ . . ."

His mind reeled and he gripped the back of the sofa to keep from falling. Ice spread through his veins, the shock of the truth chilling him from head to toe, the blood draining from his face. "What happened?" he rasped.

"I don't know." She laid a hand on his shoulder. "The reporter just stated that he was found by Drew a short time ago in the house. Police aren't releasing more details right now."

"They'll damned fucking well release them to *me*."

Oh, God. Brad was dead. And Drew had found him.

Shoving his grief aside, he lurched for his cell phone resting on the kitchen counter. Right where he'd left it before going into the bedroom to change clothes. Grabbing it, he checked the display and his heart sank. Four missed calls. All from Drew.

Without listening to any of the messages, he called his godson. Waited through several rings before the teen answered.

"Shane? Where are you?" Drew sobbed.

"On my way," he said firmly, jogging to the bedroom to fetch his wallet and keys. "I'll be there in thirty minutes or less, I promise."

"Shane . . . they're gonna take me into protective custody or something! Please hurry!" His words were barely understandable.

"No, they absolutely will not. Tell them your legal guardian is on the way, okay? Tell them I have papers. Can you do that?"

"Yeah. Hurry . . . My dad . . ."

His heart broke. So did his voice as he said, "I know, buddy. I'm coming. Just hang tight."

"Okay." The kid's voice sounded small and helpless. Nothing like the normally exuberant, self-assured son of a famous man.

"See you soon."

Hanging up, he stuffed the phone in his front jeans pocket and dashed from the bedroom right past Daisy, down the hallway and into his study. There he ran to a four-drawer file cabinet, jerked it open, and rifled through the hanging files, as Daisy came inside.

"You have guardianship papers for Drew?"

The pain in his throat burned so badly, he could

barely speak. He had to keep it together. "Yes. Brad had his lawyers set it all down legally, years ago, just in case anything ever—" Breaking off, he closed his eyes to stop the tears from escaping. "Brad's estranged from his parents and would never trust them with his son, for very good reasons. Drew's mother died of cancer when he was a baby, and Drew has no one else. Jesus Christ, he's alone now."

"No. He has you," she said softly.

"Yeah." Blinking the moisture away, he finally found the right file and quickly checked the contents. Assured he had the correct papers, he pushed unsteadily to his feet. "Thank you for coming, for being the one to tell me."

She shook her head. "No thanks needed."

"I have to go—"

"I know, and I'm driving," she said in a no-nonsense voice. "You're in no shape to get behind the wheel, and you might need some backup when you get there."

In the depths of her beautiful eyes, he read the words she actually meant—*you might need a friend.*

"All right." Pushing a hand through his hair, he nodded. A wave of gratitude washed through him at the thought of having Daisy at his side, helping him face the impossible. "I might at that."

Giving him a meaningful look, she held out her hand. He relinquished his keys without argument and he led her through the kitchen to the large, attached garage where he kept his truck, motorcycle, and a bass boat. Hitting the lock, she walked around and climbed into the driver's seat of the truck, and he got in the other side.

As she punched the garage door opener and started the engine, it momentarily crossed his mind how strange it was to ride as a passenger in his own truck. But the feeling was fleeting, drowned in a wash of numbness as shock set in. Grief would come later, he knew. Would hit hard. For now, he was on autopilot, doing what needed to be done, for himself and Drew.

This wasn't his first rodeo in this sort of situation. After his parents had been killed, after years of long, hard struggle to get himself and Shea on their feet, he'd never wanted to be in this position again.

Brad was supposed to be at home, alive and well, taking care of his son.

God. What happened? Why?

"The house is in Nashville, right?"

Daisy's question brought him back to reality, and he nodded. "On the outskirts, north side. We don't actually have to go into the city."

"Okay, just tell me where to turn."

They rode in silence for a few moments before she spoke again. "Do you have a bedroom ready for him?"

So practical, his Daisy. Again he was grateful for her companionship. "There's a room he always uses when he stays with me. I guess it'll be his now." He stopped to rein in the emotions threatening to tear a jagged hole in his calm. "It needs airing out, the sheets changed, the closet cleaned out for his stuff. . . . Christ, I don't know if I can do this," he choked. "What am I going to do with a teenage boy?"

The warmth of her hand enveloped his, and squeezed. "You're not alone. I'll help you get the room ready and get him situated. The rest you'll learn. You *can* do this and you will. He's depending on you."

Clutching her hand like a lifeline, he nodded. "Okay."

It was far more than he deserved, and selfishly he wasn't about to turn her down.

He found himself wishing the drive would never end. That he'd wake up from this nightmare and be glad that none of it was real. But it did end, all too soon, as Daisy pulled the truck to a stop outside the massive iron gates of Brad's estate.

Outside it was fully dark, the night broken by the flashing of red and blue lights in the yard beyond the estate's walls—and by the frenzy of the media on their side of them. An officer was stationed at the gate, and walked over to the driver's door with an unwelcoming frown as flashbulbs created a strobe effect.

"No press and no unauthorized access to the premises," he intoned, waving a hand in motion for them to get lost. "Please turn your vehicle around—"

"I'm Detective Shane Ford, Sugarland PD, and I'm Drew Cooper's legal guardian," he barked, shoving the papers and his shield in the officer's face. "I'm here to pick up Drew, and I want to see him *now*."

Arching a brow, the officer took the papers and scanned them with his flashlight. After a few seconds, he glanced up, his manner somewhat improved. "Hang on, Detective." As he turned and walked a few feet away, Shane heard him speak into the microphone clipped to his shirt. "Got a man here, says his name is Detective Shane Ford . . ." His voice faded as he moved off.

I probably could've handled that better, Shane thought, but right now, he didn't give a shit.

A couple of long minutes later, the gate began to swing open. The officer walked back to the car and returned the papers and shield, thoroughly scrutinizing Shane and Daisy before saying, "You can go on through. The boy is outside with Officer Anita Daniels."

"Thank you."

He stepped back and Daisy pulled slowly down the drive, searching for a good place to park that would allow them to leave without being blocked in.

"I'm going to pull around back," she said thoughtfully. "That way when we leave, he can crouch down until we're out and the gawkers won't know what vehicle he's in."

"Good idea."

She found a spot in the driveway in back, and turned the truck around to face the entrance before shutting off the ignition. Glancing out the window, Shane saw Drew standing on the wide back deck with several uniformed cops, including the woman that must've been Daniels.

The boy looked so lost in the sea of activity. So alone. His shoulders were slumped, head down. And then he glanced up and spotted Shane getting out of the truck.

Drew cried out and bolted straight off the deck, running for Shane as fast as his legs would carry him. Shane met him halfway, caught him, and wrapped the boy tight in his embrace. Drew clung to him and broke down, face buried in Shane's neck, sobbing his heart out. The kid might be almost as tall as Shane, but right now he was a hurting boy. Despite Shane's effort to hold back, he couldn't help the tears that slipped down his face and into Drew's dark hair.

"I got home from school, got a snack, and messed around for a while, and—and I wondered where Dad was," he gasped between sobs. "He d-didn't come out to ask me about my day l-like he always does."

"You don't have to talk about this now if you don't want." But apparently the boy needed to get it out. Shane held him tighter.

"I walked around the house, calling him, but he didn't answer. I—I found him on the floor of his study . . . He wasn't breathing and I tried to help him! I couldn't— He wouldn't breathe!"

"I'm here," Shane whispered over and over. "I'm here, and it's going to be okay. I've got you."

Vaguely, he was aware of Daisy taking the shield and papers from his hand and then speaking softly to someone. He wasn't sure how long he and Drew stood clinging to each other, but gradually he stepped back, keeping his hands on the boy's shoulders. Even in the poor lighting, he could see that Drew's vivid blue eyes were swollen, the boy's handsome face—so like his father's—the portrait of devastation.

"There was nothing you could do," he told his new charge, and prayed that was true. That, horrible as it might sound, Brad was gone long before the boy got home. "We're going to get through this together."

Drew's chin trembled and his gaze dropped to the ground. "I don't know what to do."

"You're coming home with me, all right? I'm going to see about getting inside to pack you a bag, and the rest we'll worry about later."

"O-okay." He sniffled, looking around in a daze.

It hadn't hit Drew yet that he wouldn't be coming

back here to live. That he'd not only lost his dad, but everything familiar to him as well—his home, school, friends, his entire way of life. Shane didn't look forward to the coming explosion.

And there *would* be one, he was certain.

"Drew, this is my friend Daisy Callahan," he said, feeling self-conscious about introducing her as such. She'd been *much* more than a friend. "We work together at the police department."

"Hi." The boy tried to muster a smile, but failed.

"Hey, Drew," she greeted him warmly, placing a supportive arm around his shoulders. "I'm going to stay here with you while Shane gets your stuff and clears you to leave. Is that all right?"

"I guess."

Tossing Daisy a look of sheer gratitude, Shane squeezed Drew's shoulder. Then he turned to Officer Daniels, who motioned him several yards away from the stricken teen so they could speak discreetly.

"Your papers appear to be in order, and they support the call we received from Mr. Cooper's attorney. You're free to take Drew home."

Shane blew out a breath. "Thanks."

The officer wiped at her tired, bloodshot eyes. "I gotta be honest. If the dead guy was anybody else, nobody would give two shits about this kid or where he went." She shot a pointed glare in the general direction of the gate and the clamoring press beyond. "As it is, I hope you've got a giant set of brass balls, 'cause you're gonna need 'em to fend off the sharks. I don't envy you one single bit."

He merely nodded, not taken aback by her blunt observation. Cops tended to be direct like that with each other. But the reminder that the grieving young man would be under a microscope until the furor died down brought all his protective instincts to the fore. "We'll be just fine." *Eventually.* "Who's in charge? I need to see about retrieving some of Drew's belongings."

"That'd be Detective Lacey. Go on in, tell him I sent ya."

"Thank you, and thanks for taking care of Drew, too."

The older woman gave him a smile that didn't reach her eyes. Not an unkind smile, but one of a cop who'd seen too much. "No problem. He seems like a good kid, and I hope things turn out okay for him."

"Me, too."

He left her and made his way up the deck steps and through the French doors leading into the living room. No one spared him their attention, focused as it was on the activity in the study on the opposite side of the room. With every step in that direction, the band around Shane's chest grew tighter until he struggled to breathe.

When two plainclothes detectives and the ME parted enough to give him a full view of Brad lying on the floor, arms and legs splayed helplessly, Shane had to stop. His best friend was faceup, lips blue, eyes open, staring sightlessly in what might have been mild surprise.

Dead. Not a horrible nightmare. It was *real.*

And poor Drew had seen his dad like this.

Shane almost reached for the door frame, but ingrained training halted him from touching any part of the crime scene—if that's what they had here. Instead he bent at the waist, hands on his knees, and concentrated on taking air into his lungs before he passed out and made their work more difficult.

"Hey, man, you okay?" A hand landed on his back.

"No." He wasn't sure he would be ever again.

"You need to sit down?"

"No." With an effort, he straightened, took in the man who was studying him and seemed to be waiting for an introduction. Willing down bile, Shane offered his hand. "Detective Shane Ford, Sugarland PD. Drew Cooper's my godson."

The cop's expression cleared as he shook Shane's hand. "Detective Alex Lacey, Nashville. Daniels told us you were coming. Well, she said Drew's guardian was on the way, not who you are." The man studied him for a few seconds, working something out in his head. "I remember reading about your terrorist case last year in the paper. How do you know Brad and Drew Cooper, exactly?"

Grief threatened to strangle his response. "Brad is my best friend." He couldn't bring himself to use past tense, just yet. "I've known him since I was a kid. Hero worship on my part gradually became a solid friendship as I grew up. He's a few years older than me, and our parents were good friends back in the day."

Or had been, before things went horribly wrong.

"You know, I think I heard Cooper talk about you during an interview once." Lacey's face grew solemn. "I'm sorry for your loss."

"Thank you," he managed. Their gazes held, and they both knew the question was coming. One that Shane had no right to ask, no jurisdiction, and was going to press anyway. "Does Eden have any idea yet on the cause of death?"

"It's all speculation at this point," Lacey hedged.

Shane didn't miss how the man had placed his big frame to block his view of Brad's body. "What's she speculating?"

He sighed. "Possible OD. I'm sorry."

Shane stared at the other cop. "Drugs? No fucking way. Brad has *never* done drugs in all the years I've known him. *Everyone* knows he didn't do that shit."

The increasing volume of his protest had garnered some attention. Shane shifted, looked away, anger rising to almost override the wrenching sadness. Lacey's attempt to placate him didn't help.

"Listen, you know better than anyone that people will do all kinds of things they wouldn't normally do with the right amount of motivation. Especially stress."

"I do know, but don't write him off as another statistic."

The detective's tone softened in warning. "I know how to do my job, Ford. And I'm good at it."

Fuck! There was hardly room to swallow his pride with all the other emotions stuck in his throat. "My apologies. I'm just . . ."

"Yeah. Forget it, okay? I'll give you a call when we get the ME's report. How's that?"

"It's more than I have a right to ask," he said gratefully. "Thank you. Now, if it's all right, I'd like to run upstairs and get some clothes and things for Drew."

"Sure." Lacey called out to one of the uniforms to escort him upstairs.

Seemed professional courtesy only went so far. But

Shane couldn't blame the detective for being careful with the scene. The man didn't want anyone loose in the house, snooping—which he knew perfectly well Shane would be back to do at the very first opportunity.

With one last look toward the study, he turned and jogged up the stairs. In Drew's room, he ignored the presence of the officer at the door, grabbing a gym bag from the walk-in closet. Drew had brought it to his house many times when Brad was out of town and he stayed over. He stuffed it with socks, underwear, jeans, shirts, toiletries. Everything he could think of to get the boy through a few days. He believed he had what they needed.

Then his gaze fell on Drew's mini laptop resting on top of his desk. He really shouldn't take it until he had the okay, but the boy might like having something familiar at hand.

And if there was the slightest chance it contained any valuable insight as to what had happened to Brad, he wasn't leaving without it.

The officer at the door was now standing with his back against the doorjamb, facing the hallway. Quickly, Shane unplugged the net book, wrapped the cord around it, and stuffed it in the bag, between piles of clothes. He'd examine the contents and browsing history before giving it to Drew.

All set, he hefted the bag over one shoulder and met the cop in the hallway. "All done."

The officer escorted him downstairs, giving him a brief nod before moving away to talk to some of his colleagues. A stretcher was being rolled in, an empty black body bag on top, and a chill of horror washed down

Shane's spine. He froze and stared as it was wheeled into the study.

Lacey stepped into view, carrying a backpack. "Here's the boy's school stuff we found in the kitchen. There's nothing more you can do," he said gently. "Get the kid out of here before they're ready to take his dad from the house. I'll call you, probably tomorrow."

Oh, God. He nodded, taking the backpack. "Thanks again."

The hardest thing he'd ever done was turn and walk away. To leave Brad alone with strangers who didn't know him. Didn't love him. Who would now reduce him to nothing more than flesh and bone to be studied, dissected, even derided.

Any second, Shane was going to lose it. Fly apart and never be put back together.

Then he spotted Drew standing next to his truck and forced himself to do the impossible. To shore himself up for the boy he loved like a son and who was depending on him. "I've got you some things to hold you over. Ready to go?"

Drew swallowed hard, wiped his wet face. "Yeah."

After setting the gym bag and backpack in the bed of the truck, Shane climbed in, scooting to the middle, leaving room for Drew on the passenger's side. Before Daisy drove toward the front, they had him crouch as far under the dash as possible—not easy considering the boy's height. But it worked well enough to throw off the press, and their vehicle was hardly spared a glance as they drove through the gate and past the crowd.

Once they were on the road, Shane gestured to him. "You can get up now."

The boy scooted into the seat and stared out into the night for several minutes. "What do they think happened to my dad?" he finally asked, his voice surprisingly flat.

"They don't know yet. That's the truth."

"I asked what they *think*. They hounded me with all these questions about what kinds of medications he was taking." The boy barked a surprisingly grown-up, bitter laugh. "I'm not a little kid and I'm not stupid, Shane. Tell me."

"No, you're definitely not stupid. I just don't think this is the time—"

"It's never going to be the time. Is it?" Drew snapped.

Shane paused, wondering if the sharp comment referred to his dad's death or something else. Whatever it was, he understood Drew's need for some scrap of information that made sense now that his world had gone insane.

Christ. He cut a sharp look at Daisy, silently asking her opinion, and she gave a barely perceptible nod. Drew was smart; would be seventeen soon. One short year from being a legal adult, no matter that Shane still thought of him as a boy. If Shane treated him as less than a man when it mattered, he'd lose ground real fast.

Digging deep, he found his resolve. "They suspect an overdose, but it's early yet. We might know something more solid by tomorrow."

Drew made a soft noise of distress. Daisy reached over and squeezed the boy's knee in support, but he simply turned his head, staring out the window at the night. He said nothing more. Shane had questions of his own, but this wasn't the place and tonight was too soon. Answers, if there were any, could rest until the morning.

Finally, Daisy pulled into his garage and shut off the ignition. It seemed like a hundred years since she had shown up with the horrible news. The whole tragedy was surreal.

As they got out, Shane grabbed Drew's belongings from the bed of the truck and they filed inside. Shane carried the bags down the hallway to the spare bedroom that his godson always used and set them on the floor. Then he returned to find Drew sitting on the sofa, face buried in his hands, shoulders shaking. Daisy was sitting on one side of him, arm around his shoulders, talking to him softly.

Shane hurried over and sat on the other side, placing a palm on the boy's leg. "I wish I knew the right thing to say," he managed.

"Just don't tell me again that it's going to be okay, because it won't." Tears leaked from between his fingers, dripped onto his lap.

"All right." In fact, he'd been about to repeat that very thing. "Do you want to talk?"

The boy shook his head, shoulders hunching in. It was a posture of self-protection, and Shane could physically feel his withdrawal. Drew was fast approaching the stage where he'd want to be left alone, and Shane had no clue how much space to give him. How far was too far?

"Have you eaten?" Daisy asked the boy quietly.

"No." He sniffled. "I'm not hungry."

She met Shane's eyes, searching. "That's okay. Why don't I find something to heat up, and maybe by the time it's done you'll be able to get something in your stomach."

Drew didn't reply. Shane gave her a grateful half smile and she rose, heading into the kitchen. He couldn't believe she'd been willing to hang around, to help him deal with this sort of crisis when he'd given her no reason to care. Guilt ate at his gut. He had to find a way to express how much this meant to him, but didn't know if she'd accept anything in the way of thanks.

As Daisy made sounds in the kitchen, he sat with his godson, feeling totally out of his depth. Drew wasn't open to talking, and Shane didn't know if his presence was any comfort at all. Gradually, the boy's tears stopped and he leaned back on the sofa, eyes red and staring into space. But his expression was far from blank.

Emotions roiled there like a distant storm, a tempest the kid was barely holding back. Anger, shock, grief—all so easy to read. All would need to be purged eventually. When was the time right to push? Shane was damned good at his job, at working with people, getting them to spill secrets they didn't want to share. But his instincts failed him now. Completely.

"Come eat, guys," Daisy called from the kitchen.

Drew shook his head. "I can't."

Standing, Shane offered him a hand. "At least try, for me."

For a long moment, Shane thought he'd refuse. Then the boy took his hand, allowed himself to be hauled up, and followed him to the breakfast table off the kitchen. Daisy had three bowls of tomato soup accompanied by grilled cheese sandwiches. Comfort food. It smelled good, and Shane's traitorous belly growled.

"Looks good," he told her. "Thanks."

"Yeah, looks great if you're ten years old." Drew snorted and sat back, arms crossed over his chest.

"A person never gets too old for soup and grilled cheese," Shane said, trying to lighten things up a shade. "I practically survive off food like this in the winter."

"Then I guess I'll starve."

Silence descended, heavy, awkward. Daisy bit her lip, exchanged a worried glance with Shane, then started on her meal. He followed suit, hoping the boy would be tempted to eat at least a few bites. After five agonizing minutes, Drew pushed from the table and simply walked out without a word. Shane rose to go after him, but Daisy grabbed his wrist.

"It might be best to give him some space for a while. Give him time to process what's happening."

"Yeah? And how would you know what's best for a kid I've known all his life?" he snapped. Immediately he felt like shit.

"I'm in a better position than you because you're too close," she said, unfazed. "Working with kids is my job, and from his body language I'm reading that he needs some time alone. Just for a little while."

With a sigh of frustration, he sat down again and took her hand. "I'm sorry for biting your head off."

"Don't worry. It's an occupational hazard, so I'm used to it." She gave him a soft smile, which he returned.

As he studied her, he had an epiphany. It was like a curtain being lifted. "The kids you get are such lost souls. How do you do *this*, every single day?" he asked, waving a hand in the general direction Drew had gone.

"That's what we ask ourselves about you guys in homicide."

"Yeah, but it's different. How do you deal with at-risk children who've endured so much they're in danger of going down the wrong path, and with parents who don't care?"

She leaned forward, expression intense with passion for the subject. "That's a misconception. Most parents *do* care a great deal, just like you do for Drew. Most of them desperately want to save their kids, but don't have the skills or resources to help them. I've seen abuse, sure, and parents who couldn't care less what happens to their children, but they aren't the rule. You just hear more about them than the good ones, that's all."

"Still, I couldn't do your job. I don't see how you keep sane."

"You want to know how? Because every kid I save from ending up a statistic in *your* division makes it worthwhile."

That simple statement struck him hard. What she did was so damned important. How could he have failed to really *see* her before? To appreciate her not only as a woman, but as a friend and colleague who was making a difference?

He was humbled at his shortsightedness—and shamed.

They finished their meal and Daisy rose. "I'll clear the dishes. Why don't you go check on Drew?"

"Okay. And thank you."

She waved him off, and he went in search of his godson. The boy wasn't in the living room, so he made his way to Drew's room. Pushing open the door slowly, he saw the boy's figure curled on the bed on his side. His body was relaxed, breathing deep and even. As Shane moved closer, he saw Drew really was asleep. Probably the best thing for him right now.

Drawn forward, Shane knelt by the bed. Reached out and touched the boy's hair. Stroked gently, his heart broken for Drew. And for himself. He'd never imagined anything happening to Brad. Had never seriously entertained having children. But both had come to pass.

In the blink of an eye, Shane was parent to a grieving sixteen-year-old boy he had no idea how to raise.

Or how to protect.

3

Daisy hovered in the doorway to Drew's room, breath caught in her throat.

Shane was on his knees beside the bed, stroking the boy's hair. His expression was grief stricken, but there was such love, too. This wasn't a man fulfilling an obligation. This was a man who truly loved the people he allowed into his life, a man who would do anything for them.

And she longed to be one of those people.

How selfish can I be? It wasn't Shane's fault she'd enjoyed a couple of rolls in the sack and had gotten her heart broken when she expected more. She blamed herself. He'd made it clear she wasn't going to be someone he wanted to keep, and she had no business hanging around here longer than necessary.

Quietly, she backed away and returned to the living room to wait for him. Over and over, her mind replayed what she'd just witnessed and the fact that Shane wasn't the cavalier, happy-go-lucky slut he pretended to be. He was so much more.

He came back into the room just then, looking worn-out. "He's resting."

"He'll need a lot of that to get through the next few weeks." She paused. "Is there anything else I can do?"

"No," he said, moving to stand right in front of her. "But thank you for being here."

The clear dismissal had her throat tightening in disappointment. She shoved it down and mustered a small smile. "Well, if you need me, don't hesitate to call."

"All right."

He wouldn't, she knew. She squeezed his hand, then turned to leave. But she was brought up short when he didn't let go. Instead he pulled her back, slid an arm around her waist. Surprised, she met his gray gaze. He was staring at her like she was the last drink of water in the desert, and her heart hammered in her chest.

He was going to kiss her. He hesitated once, in silent question, and receiving no protest, lowered his mouth to hers. Every cell in her body ignited in flames, scorching her from head to toe. And everywhere in between.

No man had ever kissed her the way Shane did—with his entire being. Rational thought fled, swept to sea in a tide of desire. And just as quickly it was over. Her former lover pulled back, studying her as though he wanted to say something else.

Ask me for that beer again. This time I won't say no.

But he didn't. "Good night, sugar."

"Night."

She turned and headed down the porch steps, and the door closed with a soft *snick* behind her. *I'm my own worst enemy sometimes. Why do I let him tie me in knots?*

She'd been hung up on him for so long and finally she'd gotten him. But not forever. No more. Best to let him fade away and rest with all the other pipe dreams.

Like falling for a man who actually understood and appreciated her job. Getting along with her dad. Not feeling so alone. Not watching life pass her by. Having children of her own.

Right. With a sigh, she started the car and pulled out of the drive. Glancing in the rearview mirror, she could've sworn she saw the curtain flick closed.

But it was probably her imagination.

The day after Brad's death dawned obscenely bright. After switching on the coffeepot, Shane stood staring out the window overlooking the back of his property and the river. A couple of fishermen were trolling the bank in a boat, hoping for an early-morning catch. Birds were singing. A typical lazy Saturday.

For some, anyway. It didn't seem possible that the world could simply go on when lives were shattered. But it did, and he couldn't think what to do next. Not without coffee to revive his exhausted brain.

Drew had woken up screaming, covered in sweat, twice last night. The second time, Shane had broken down and given the boy a mild over-the-counter sleep aid to help him rest. It worked, but sleep was lost on Shane by then and, wanting to be alert in case Drew needed him, he didn't dare take the same medication. He'd been up since four, prowling back and forth to the kid's room to make sure he was all right. How did parents do this?

Suddenly it hit him that this was forever. Socked him hard in the gut and filled him with fear. This wasn't just a visit, and Brad would never come to fetch his son. Drew was *his* responsibility now, just as Brad had wanted if anything ever happened. Shane and Drew had always been close, but the rules were going to change along with their relationship. It was inevitable.

The crunch of tires outside snagged his attention. Walking to the front window, he half-expected to see Daisy returning, demanding to help in some way. Instead he was greeted by the sight of Tommy pulling up in his truck, Shane's twin sister riding shotgun. In his shock last night, Shane hadn't even thought to call them, so they'd probably rushed over as soon as they heard the news this morning.

Not wanting the doorbell or a knock to awaken Drew, he went out on the porch to meet them. Shea practically flew out of the truck and up the steps, launching herself into his outstretched arms. He caught her and held her close, burying his nose in her curly brown hair, and inhaled the familiar, comforting scent of his twin.

"Oh, my God, Shane," she breathed. "We just heard when we turned on the television this morning. Why didn't you call us?"

"It was an awful scene, sis. I wasn't thinking." He hugged her tighter, grateful for her presence. "I would have this morning after I got my head on straight."

Releasing her, he turned and offered his hand to his tall, blond brother-in-law, who promptly ignored the gesture and pulled him in for a bear hug. Jesus, he was so damned grateful for his family. His eyes stung as he stepped back and jerked a thumb toward the house.

"Ya'll want some coffee? I sure could use some."

That suggestion met with approval, and the couple

followed him inside, waiting until they had mugs of fragrant brew and were seated in the living room before beginning the interrogation.

"What happened?" Shea asked. "The news is saying some pretty wild crap about drugs." Her hubby was nestled close beside her on the sofa, every bit as intent on the answer.

Shane shifted in his chair, impotent anger clawing at his gut. "Yeah, well, it might not be mere speculation. The detective at the scene told me it looks like an overdose. They didn't let me see what evidence they had, but they've got something solid, or he wouldn't have said that much to me."

"Drugs?" Tommy frowned. "I met him only a couple of times, when he was here visiting you, but he didn't strike me as the type to dabble in shit like that."

"He wasn't," Shane said. The idea made him sick with grief, frustration. "I can't understand it. He never confided in me about a habit."

"Maybe it was a new thing," Tommy offered. "Obviously he wouldn't have been proud of it, so he wouldn't have wanted you or anyone else to know."

The three of them chewed on that for a minute, sipping their coffee. Shane didn't get any enjoyment from his brew this morning, but he could almost feel the much-needed caffeine flooding his veins.

"The detective is going to give me a courtesy call when they get the ME's report," he told them. Then his voice cracked. "I can't fucking believe I'm discussing Brad and an autopsy in the same sentence."

In an instant, his sister was perched on the arm of his

chair, hugging him tight. "We're here for you both. Anything you need."

"I know," he rasped. "Thank you."

"What about the funeral arrangements?" Tommy ventured gently. "Need any help with those?"

Shane shook his head with a sad laugh. "Brad was organized to the point of being anal. I teased him about it constantly. His lawyer has all the instructions, and all I have to do is make a few calls."

A few calls. A few days, and it would all be over. Except it wouldn't—not really.

"How's Drew?" This from Shea, who gave him one more hug and moved back to her seat.

"In shock." He took a sip of coffee. "Time will tell how he'll adjust. I don't know what the hell I'm doing, and I don't know how Brad raised a boy on his own."

"That's simple—he didn't." Tommy snorted. "He had you and half a dozen other people to bail him out whenever he needed."

Shane winced. "That's true."

"And you'll have us, plus all your friends," Shea said. "You'll both be fine. At least he's a teenager instead of a little one in diapers."

"I'm not sure that's going to make things any easier in the long run." In fact, he knew it wouldn't. "This is going to be damned hard. His dad was—is—his hero. Larger than life, famous. I'm just a cop, a regular guy Drew enjoyed spending weekends with. And that will change fast enough when I have to lay down the law for the first time."

His sister didn't agree. "I think you're selling yourself

short. That boy loves you, and you'll both be fine eventually."

Shane glanced at his brother-in-law, but noted the man wasn't quite as quick to gloss things with a rosy paintbrush as Shea. Tommy had been through issues with his own parents, and working through them to become a family again hadn't been easy. Hell, they were *still* working on their relationship, though it was much improved. The man in front of him had grown up a lot in the last year.

"You're right. It won't be easy," Tommy said seriously. "It'll get tough before it gets better, and when it does, we're here. That's what family is for."

"Thanks, you guys."

"Do you think you'll have any trouble out of James and Rhonda over custody?"

James and Rhonda Cooper were Brad's parents—Drew's grandparents. The couple had been good friends of Shane and Shea's parents, once upon a time. Before the huge falling-out between the two couples and the accident that had followed, taking Darryl and Linda Ford way too soon.

In spite of the Coopers' betrayal and the horror of the aftermath, Shane and Brad's friendship had not only survived, it had also deepened over the years. Brad had been horrified by the corrupt layers that had been revealed in his parents.

"No," he said coldly. "Not unless they want the entire country to know that they attempted to embezzle hundreds of thousands from Dad's company, not to mention being indirectly responsible for the accident. They're on a short leash, and that's where they'll stay."

They'd never met Drew, and that wasn't going to change as long as Shane was alive. He knew from Brad that should the couple survive their son, they weren't even invited to the reading of the will—they'd get not one red cent of his money.

A shuffle behind them caught his attention and he turned to see Drew standing awkwardly just inside the room. His dark hair was damp from the shower, and he'd dressed in jeans and a T-shirt. His eyes were bloodshot, his face pale.

Shea was up and across the room in seconds, wrapping the boy in her arms. Tommy got up and followed her. Shane noted that Drew was taller at sixteen than petite Shea. Not a boy for much longer, he was again reminded.

"I'm not going to ask a stupid question like how you are," Shea said, earning her a sad, watery laugh from Drew.

"I keep thinking it's not real. Right?"

"I know, sweetie. But we're all here for you, and we're not going anywhere."

"That's what Dad always said, and he's gone." They exchanged looks of concern before Drew pulled away. "Can I have some of that coffee?"

"Sure," Shane told him. "Help yourself."

He shuffled off, and once he was out of earshot, Shea scowled. "You let him drink coffee?"

"He's almost seventeen, sis," he said in defense. "Jesus, it's not like I'm letting him shoot bourbon. Anyway, give the kid a break, huh?"

"Sure." She blew out a breath, then lowered her voice as she glanced toward the kitchen. "It's just that I was thinking there's gonna be a lot of freedoms you gave him before, as a friend, that he might not have anymore. You can't spoil him constantly."

"That's the point I was trying to make before," he said evenly. "Don't you think I'm aware of how hard it'll be to walk the line between being a parent and a friend?"

"Maybe the word you're looking for is *mentor*," Tommy suggested. "A mentor can be both."

"I can hear you guys whispering," Drew said, walking back into the room. "I'm not deaf."

Shane gave him a pained look. "We're just worried about you, kiddo. Did you end up getting any sleep?"

The boy shrugged. "Some, I guess." His drawn, tired face belied his claim.

"Where's your coffee?" Shane asked.

"Didn't sound good after all."

"Are you hungry? I was about to ask Shea and Tommy if they'd stay for breakfast and—"

"I don't want anything," Drew said shortly. "Think I'm gonna crash again."

Helplessly, Shane watched him go, heart sinking to his feet. Finally, he turned to his sister and Tommy. "So, how about that breakfast?"

Tommy clapped him on the shoulder. "Sure. And if the scent of bacon won't lure him out of his cave, nothing will."

It didn't. As they ate their somber meal, talking quietly, Shane wondered whether he was making a mistake allowing Drew to hide, if he should have pushed harder.

Inevitably, his thoughts drifted to Daisy and their soul-melting kiss last night. Seemed like he was doomed to fuck up quite a bit before he got anything right.

That afternoon, he headed for Drew's room, determined to pry him out for a while. He had to keep the lines of communication open, whether the boy wanted to talk or not.

At the closed door, he rapped twice, and was met with a muffled "Come in."

Stepping inside, he saw Drew perched on the padded window seat, arms around his knees. His gaze was fixed into the distance, perhaps studying the bare trees dotting his property or the lazy Cumberland beyond. He turned his head to look at Shane, eyes dry. And terribly blank. That void scared Shane a lot more than the outward grief.

Crossing the room, he sat on the edge of the bed close to his godson. "Been awake long?"

"Yeah. Couldn't sleep anymore."

"Feel like taking a walk?"

"Not really."

"Please?"

The boy studied him for a long moment, then shrugged. "Fine."

Grateful to have won even this slight measure of ground, Shane stood. "Come on, let's get our coats."

Once they were zipped up, Shane led them out through the sliding glass door that opened onto the large back deck. When the weather warmed up, he'd have the guys from the station over, grill some burgers. Maybe Drew would've made some new friends by then. He hoped.

As they picked their way slowly down the trail leading to the riverbank, Shane struggled over how to broach the subject. But it was Drew who broke the ice.

"When do I have to go back to school?" He frowned. "And who's gonna take me if I'm staying here?"

"That's one thing I need to talk to you about," Shane hedged. "I live and work here, and since this will be your home now, too, it makes more sense for you to attend school in Sugarland."

Drew stopped walking and gaped at him. "Here? In Hicksville, USA?"

Here we go. "Sugarland is a nice city. You've always seemed to love it here."

"Yeah, to visit." His voice rose. "What about my friends?"

"They're welcome to come see you, and vice versa. In the meantime, you'll make new ones." He hated the placating parental tone of his own voice. Seemed that came naturally, no matter how much of a novice you were.

"I wouldn't need to if you'd just move in to Dad's house! It's my home!" the kid almost shouted.

"I know it is," Shane said evenly. "But living there isn't going to be feasible for the two of us."

"Why not?" Drew shook his head, becoming more upset. "It's, like, seven thousand square feet! We could go for freakin' days without seein' each other!"

"That's part of the problem, son—"

"I am *not* your son!" he yelled, jabbing his finger in Shane's face. "You're not my dad!"

"I know that." *Deep breaths. You expected this, and you can handle it.* "I'm your friend . . . your mentor. But I'm also an adult, your legal guardian, and I have to do what I think is best for you."

"Even if I fuckin' hate it," the teen spat.

"Even if you fuckin' hate it." That got the boy's attention, and he visibly struggled with his emotions. Shane softened his voice. "I know this is hard on you, so many changes at once. But I'm hoping you'll meet me halfway."

The kid tried to stare him down, but it obviously didn't take him long to realize that tactic wasn't going to work on a cop.

"Whatever." Drew kicked angrily at a rock, scowling. "It's not like I have that many friends at the academy anyhow."

That surprised him. "Why do you say that?"

"Those rich asswipes mostly just care about who's who, you know? I know they only like me because I'm Brad Cooper's son."

"That's pretty cynical for a guy your age."

Again with the shrug. They were going to have to work on that.

"You never said when I have to start school."

"I've been giving that some thought," he said carefully. "This week is going to be rough for both of us, with the funeral and getting you moved. I think next week is soon enough."

"You're not driving me, are you?"

The question was edged with such teenage angst, he almost smiled. "I take it that would be too lame?"

"Totally," the boy agreed, rolling his eyes. "I usually take the shuttle from the academy."

"Well, I'm sure the school district has a bus run out here. I'll check on the schedule this week."

"Or you could just let me get my driver's license . . ."

At the hopeful suggestion, he gave in to the smile that had threatened. "Not yet. Your dad and I specifically talked about this. I know he wanted you to finish your junior year, and getting your license depended on your grades."

"But *you're* in charge now. Remember?"

"That's right. And because I am, I'm carrying out your dad's wishes." At the boy's protest, he held up a hand. "You make good grades, then we'll sign you up for a summer driver's course, get your license, and see about getting you something to drive. Something affordable and sane."

"That sucks," the teen grumbled.

"That's the deal. Take it or leave it."

"Fine."

As they walked on, Shane felt a sense of accomplishment at winning rounds one and two. But deep down, he knew in his gut that had been much too easy. That feeling wasn't going to last.

This week would mark the start of the rest of their lives. Futures forever changed. These would be the hardest days Shane had endured since the deaths of his parents. For Drew, they'd be the worst ever endured in his young life.

Shane knew the boy was still in shock, unable to grasp that his dad really was gone. Today's conversation proved it—the boy was angry one minute, something approaching normal the next. He was struggling to make sense of a horrible, permanent hole in his heart.

He just prayed he could catch Drew when he fell.

Daisy managed to stay away all day Saturday and Sunday. She probably would have stayed away indefinitely—if it hadn't been for that kiss.

The memory of it was inescapable, not that she'd tried to run. Though she should, far and fast. However, she couldn't stop thinking of the naked vulnerability on Shane's face before she'd left. The pain. That's what lured her back now. The idea that Shane needed her, that he might not run this time.

If she escaped making a fool of herself, it wouldn't be for lack of trying.

The late-afternoon sun was slanting through the trees, sending shadows across the yard. It would be dark soon, which was why she'd taken off a little early. In the winter, it always seemed later than it was.

She rang the doorbell and waited. Voices could be heard inside from the TV, and there was a lingering aroma of something cooking. Then the door opened to reveal Drew, gazing at her, unsmiling.

"Hey," he said, stepping back. "Shane's in the kitchen."

Then he turned and left her standing there, returning to flop on the sofa and grab the remote. *O-kay.* Seemed the kid was going to be a tough nut to crack. Maybe more so than his guardian.

"Thanks." Shouldering her purse, she walked to the kitchen, where Shane was stirring something in a pot on the stove.

"Who was at the door?"

"Me."

Whipping his head around, he smiled. "Oh, hey! Sit down. Would you like a beer?"

"I'd love one, thanks."

Tapping the spoon on the edge of the pot, he laid it down and wiped his hands on a towel. Then he fished two bottles from the fridge, twisted the top off one, and handed it to her. "How were things in the trenches today?"

"The usual," she told him, then took a sip. "Two drug arrests at the high school, both of the kids sixteen. An assault—a dad who punched his daughter. Enough about that. How are you two holding up?"

His expression sobered. "Not too well," he said quietly, with a glance toward the living room. "He's slowly shutting me out, becoming withdrawn. There's a lot of anger, denial."

"If you need the name of a juvenile counselor, I've got a couple of good ones."

"I'm thinking that's not a bad idea."

She nodded. "I'll call you tomorrow with the names. Any word from the ME on Brad's report?"

"We're still waiting, but I'm expecting a call anytime. Detective Lacey from the Nashville PD phoned yesterday and said Eden had to work all weekend because of some extra stuff that came up."

"He didn't say what?"

"No, and it's driving me crazy." He gestured to the pot. "I made some chili, if I could persuade you to join us."

"I don't want to intrude—"

"Don't be ridiculous. I made way too much, and besides . . . I like having you here." A small smile curved his lips, and her stomach fluttered.

"In that case, I'd love to."

"Drew, dinner's ready," he called. Obviously worried, he stared at the doorway until the boy came in. Then he visibly relaxed some. "Would you set the table, please?"

The teen rolled his eyes but did as he was told. None too gracefully, though. He yanked three bowls and three small plates from the cabinet, then let the door slam shut. Ignoring Shane's stern frown, he slapped the dishware on the table, then went for the spoons with a noisy rattle.

"Attitude check, kiddo."

"Whatever."

Daisy could feel the tension between the two of them just about shoot through the roof. She felt sorry for them both, and could identify with each of them as well. They both looked haggard, dark circles under their eyes from little sleep. Shane hadn't shaved, apparently, since she'd seen him last, and his mouth was lined with fatigue. He carried a platter of cornbread to the table and practically collapsed in his chair.

"Let's eat," he said.

They sat, grabbing pieces of cornbread, and Shane served the thick, delicious-smelling chili. Daisy and Shane dug in, but Drew mostly picked at his. After taking a few bites of cornbread and not much more than that of his chili, he carried his plate and bowl to the sink.

"I wish you'd eat a little more—"

"I'm full. Check ya later."

After the boy left, Shane's shoulders slumped. "I'm at a total loss with him. We usually get along great, and now it's like we're strangers."

"Give him time," she said softly. "It's been only three days."

"I know. I just—" The doorbell interrupted whatever he'd been about to say. "Hold that thought."

Daisy remained where she was, figuring he didn't need her hovering over his guests. She was about to take another bite of her dinner when she heard him say hello, and two very familiar voices drifted her way.

Chris and Taylor were here.

Shoving to her feet, she hurried into the living room, where the men were standing. Her colleagues glanced her way and didn't razz her good-naturedly for being at Shane's house, as she'd thought they might. Instead their faces remained grim, and her pulse tripped. That could mean only one thing.

"We have some news about the autopsy results," Chris said, glancing around. "Where's Drew?"

"In his room, most likely." Shane sighed. "That's where he stays most of the time. Hang on, why are *you* guys here about the results of Brad's autopsy?"

"Because Detective Lacey gave us a call and figured it would be best if we talked to you in person," Shane's cousin replied.

Taylor spoke up. "It appears we might have some crossover on our cases."

Shane glanced back and forth between his friends, frowning. "So, Brad's test results warrant opening a case? How so?"

Chris gestured to the sofa. "Let's sit and we'll run through what Lacey told us." Once they were seated, he went on, bracing his elbows on his knees. "This isn't going to be easy for you to hear, cuz, so I'll give it to you straight. Brad died as the result of an adverse reaction to a designer drug."

Shane's face paled. "A-a what?"

"Designer drug," Chris repeated, expression sympathetic. "The DEA has jumped in with both feet and all sorts of tests are being done, but the preliminary consensus is that this drug is something nobody has seen before. It's illegal as hell, with traces of amphetamines mixed with a bunch of other shit, likely performance enhancing, or at least that's how they feel the drug is being marketed on the street. A pick-me-up, iron-man drug that makes steroids look like aspirin."

"Jesus, Brad. Why?" Shane's eyes closed and for several long moments he said nothing. When he opened them again, it was apparent he was holding it together by a thread. "Official cause of death?"

"Heart failure due to adverse drug reaction," Taylor said. "Not technically an overdose."

"The shit stopped his heart."

"Yes. I'm sorry, man."

Shane grappled with that, blinking moisture from his eyes. "What does that have to do with one of our cases?"

"It connects with the one we just caught the other day," Taylor told him, leaning forward to hand Shane a file folder. "The dead guy in the ditch with the hole in the back of his head—remember him? He was identified as Larry Holstead, age twenty-eight."

"Who'd he run with?"

"We're working on it. The interesting thing is the compound that the ME found on his clothing."

Shane paused in the act of flipping through the file, snapping his head up. "Traces of the designer drug that Brad took?"

"Bingo."

"What the fuck does this mean?" Shane asked, shaking his head. He flipped the file closed. "What the hell had Brad gotten himself into?"

"I don't know, but we're going to find out," Chris said firmly. "Hang in there, all right?"

"Yeah."

Daisy's heart twisted at the devastation etched on Shane's face. But there was also a new determination that hadn't been there before, and she knew that look.

It was the look of a cop who would go through hell to find the answers he needed. And he might have to do just that before he had them.

Unseen and unheard by the group in the living room, Drew crept back into the safety of his room.

On shaky legs, he wobbled back to his window seat perch, shaking hand pressed to his heart. Tears welled in his eyes, spilled unchecked down his face. Their words haunted him, scored themselves into his soul.

Designer drug.

Heart failure.

"Dad," he sobbed. "I'm sorry. It's all my fault."

Lowering his head, he cried until he was sick. And wished he was being buried next to his dad.

Right where he deserved to be.

4

On a cold gray afternoon in February, the heavens wept as Brad Cooper was laid to rest. Sleet struck the protective canopy hard, nearly drowning out the mournful words of the elderly preacher. But not quite. Each syllable rocked Shane like a physical blow.

Fine man.

Good, loving father.

Will be missed by all.

Safe in the hands of God.

Ashes to ashes, dust to dust.

Shane sucked in a harsh breath at the dreadful finality. He could only imagine how Drew was really feeling as he stood stoic and silent next to him. His back was straight, eyes dry. Was that normal? Everyone was worried about the kid. No one more than Shane. In his line of work, he knew that sometimes once a person broke inside, he might never be fixed. It scared him to think of Drew losing his way.

But the boy was stronger than that. Had to be.

The graveside service that had seemed to take forever was suddenly over, and he and Drew had to suffer through the line of their friends and Brad's who'd come to pay their respects. There was a healthy contingent representing the NFL, including coaches, scores of players, and sportscasters. Any other time, for any other occasion, Shane would have been thrilled to meet some of his idols. Though his heart ached, it was good to see them, and also see some of the guys from the station, ones who'd met Brad and Drew, come to give their support.

Especially Daisy. She was there for them both, and as she stepped up and wrapped Drew in a hug that the boy didn't return, Shane's throat burned. She didn't have to come, yet here she was, comforting a boy she barely knew. She was a damned fine woman—and Shane was an idiot for pushing her away.

After kissing Drew on the cheek, she moved to Shane and hugged him, too. Wrapping his arms around her, he held on tight and swallowed a sob. He wouldn't lose it. Had to stay strong. But she knew it was a front, and clung to him. Held together the broken pieces.

Finally, she pulled back. "I'm here for you both, okay?"

"I know." Now wasn't the time to get into an intense conversation, but he had to find out something. "Will you come to the house?"

She looked surprised and pleased to be asked. "Of course I will. About an hour?"

"That sounds about right."

"I'll be there."

After kissing him on the cheek, she moved on to allow other guests to pay their respects. He watched her go, a tall, gorgeous figure in her dark pantsuit, blond hair pulled back into a sedate twist. Then she raised an umbrella, and he lost her in the crowd. A pang lanced his chest that had nothing to do with the day's sad event. He truly was a fool.

Chris, Shea, and Tommy stepped forward to give them both bear hugs, promising to meet them at the house. Everyone was bringing food, as was the tradition in their family. He was already tired simply thinking about it. But maybe Daisy really would show, and that brightened him some.

The next half hour became a blur of visitors. Once they were all gone, Shane and Drew stood watching as the cemetery workers lowered Brad's casket into the ground. Drew walked to the edge, bent, and scooped up a handful of dirt. Then he tossed it in, stood again, and turned to Shane.

"Can you wait for me?" He swallowed hard.

"Sure," he said softly. "Take your time."

Shane walked slowly back to the limo, where the driver was inside, waiting patiently. The Nashville police were gone now, along with almost all of the uninvited gawkers they'd been hired to keep out. The sleet, thankfully, had ceased. Shane arrived just in time to see one last reporter lean over the private wall and snap a photo of Drew, alone and mourning by his dad's grave.

That private sorrow, intruded upon and soon to be splashed everywhere, broke his heart all over again.

Snarling, Shane started for the gate, but, seeing him, the reporter vanished from view. He continued on, making sure the man left. Just as he reached the gate, the reporter fled the scene in an SUV. There was no one else.

As he trudged back to the limo, he spotted Drew sitting by his dad's grave, face in his hands. He longed to go to the boy, scoop him up, and herd him away, but he couldn't. Drew deserved to be left alone to grieve.

To say goodbye.

Well more than an hour had passed by the time Drew rose and returned to the car. The boy's face was no longer stoic—it was a portrait of such complete desolation that Shane couldn't help but pull Drew into his arms. Hold him tight.

To his surprise, Drew didn't pull away as he'd done with Daisy, but held on to him like he was a life raft in a storm. "I can't b-believe he's gone," the boy whispered.

Oh, God. "Me either, son." He hoped he hadn't made a mistake calling Drew that when it had upset him before, but the boy either didn't notice or didn't care at the moment. He went on, addressing what Drew had overheard a couple of days before about his dad taking the designer drugs. Shane had found him sobbing, and discovered the boy had heard it all.

"I'd do anything to bring him back, you know that. But I *am* going to find out who's responsible for selling your dad that shit, and that's a promise."

In his arms, Drew shuddered hard. "Okay."

Pulling back, he cupped the boy's face, wiping the tears with his thumbs. "And when I catch them, they'll go to jail and nobody else will be hurt by that evil drug." Drew sniffed, nodding. He looked as beat as Shane felt. "Come on. Let's get you home."

Another hot-button word, but, thankfully, Drew accepted it. *Home.* Shane had initially found it was strange that, after that first heated discussion, the boy hadn't mentioned living at the mansion. But after he thought about it, he figured maybe Drew didn't really want to live in the house where his father had died. With the terrible memories. It made sense.

But the cop in him wondered.

He didn't like loose ends, and Brad's death was no exception. He'd said his goodbyes at the funeral home, in his own way. But the most fitting tribute he could pay to his friend would be to find the bastards responsible for selling him a handful of death in the disguise of pretty pills.

Since Shane and Drew had caught a ride with Shea and Tommy to the funeral home, the driver drove them to Shane's house. It was nice of the director to arrange the transportation, but he was a big supporter of the Sugarland police. He'd insisted, and Shane didn't resist.

There were a bunch of cars in the driveway when they arrived, everyone already inside, since Shea had a spare key. He owed his sister for organizing the food and guests. They got out, and the limo driver pulled out with a last wave.

"Do I have to talk to everybody again? I don't think I can listen to one more person say how sorry they are." Drew grimaced.

"No, I think you've done your part. Why don't you change into something comfortable and take a nap?"

The relief on the boy's face was palpable. "Thanks."

Once they went inside, he didn't get away quite so easily, however. Guests came at him from all sides, and he nodded, responding as expected, until he was able to make a break for it.

Shane shrugged off his jacket and ripped off his tie. He carried both to his own bedroom, unfastened the top couple of buttons on his dress shirt, then returned to the gathering. He scanned the crowd, not surprised to see Brad's coaches and some of his best friends from the team among the guests. "There you are."

He turned to see Daisy standing there, and suddenly the day didn't seem quite as gray as before. "Hey, you came."

"I promised, didn't I?" Lowering her voice, she asked, "How's Drew?"

"Wrecked. He went to get some rest."

"And you?"

"I'm holding up." He looked around. "I'd offer you a seat, but the house is packed. Too bad it's too cold today to sit on the deck."

"Yeah. A few more weeks, though, and it'll be warm again."

"Maybe . . . Would you like to come over for a cook-out one day when the weather is nice?" This invite was different than a simple social call, and they both knew that. It was Shane reaching out after hurting her so badly. His pulse thudded, waiting for her answer.

Slowly, she nodded. "I think I'd like that."

"And maybe, since the weather doesn't look like it's going to cooperate anytime soon, you'd like to have dinner with me?"

"I'd like that, too." She smiled. "Very much."

He smiled back, some of the misery lifting from his soul. They'd never really dated. Months ago, during a dangerous case, their passion had exploded, taking them along for a hell of a ride. Then Shane had gotten cold feet and blown it. Big time.

He liked to think he learned well from his mistakes.

"Great. How about next Saturday, after Drew's been in school a week and is settling in?"

"Sure. Just call me."

"Think about where you'd like to go. The sky's the limit."

"Okay. In the meantime, I'll be checking on you guys. I worry about both of you."

Emotion clogged his throat. He didn't know what to say, so he just pulled her into a hug. It lasted only a few seconds; then he let her go. Not that he cared about who might be watching, but he was mindful of the occasion.

But he knew Brad, of all guys, was looking down on them, getting a laugh out of Shane making a date at his freaking funeral repast. The man would think it was great.

"Are you okay?" she asked in concern.

"I'm fine. Really."

"All right." She looked doubtful, but relented. "Then I'll let you get to your other guests. Talk to you tomorrow."

Leaning in, she reached to give him a kiss on the cheek. But this time he turned his head so that it landed on his lips instead. She pulled back in surprise that he'd made the move here, with their colleagues nearby. Then her mouth curved in a slow smile as she walked off.

Shane's insides were quivering. The woman got to him as no one else ever had. He hadn't been able to forget her, and God knows he'd tried.

Now he had to figure out how to woo the woman he'd once so carelessly thrown away.

And how to piece back together some semblance of a family for a heartbroken boy.

*   *   *

Friday arrived all too soon, and with it the reading of the will in the conference room of Albert G. Farnsworth, Attorney at Law. One week to the day after Brad's funeral.

It seemed like yesterday. And a lifetime.

As expected, Brad had provided generously for his driver, housekeeper, and a handful of acquaintances. Then came Shane's turn, and he sat uncomfortably next to Drew, not knowing what to expect.

"To my best and oldest friend, Shane Andrew Ford, I leave the sum of five million dollars."

Several in the room gasped, and Shane swayed in his seat. Drew grabbed his hand and squeezed it tight, shooting him a look of satisfaction as Farnsworth continued.

"I would've left you more, because you're priceless to me. But the truth is, you're a tight bastard and probably won't spend a fraction of it. At least quit that sucky job now, for God's sake, before you get shot again." Soft laughter met those words, as Brad had intended. Even the stuffy attorney's lips twitched. "You probably won't do that either, so please be careful. Take care of yourself, because I'm trusting you with what means more to me than all the riches in the world—my son. Never forget that I love you, brother. I'll see you again."

Shane hung his head as Farnsworth paused before the next section. There was no help for the tears that escaped to stream down his face. Hearing one last personal message from his best friend shattered his resolve to hold in his grief. He struggled to collect himself as the attorney finished.

"And finally, to my son, Andrew Cooper, I leave my estate, including my home, cars, and personal possessions. I also leave to him the remainder of my money, a total sum of more than fifteen million dollars, to be held in trust by his legal guardian, Shane Ford, until he reaches the age of twenty-five."

Another pause while the murmuring died down. It was no less than Shane had expected, and was what Drew was entitled to.

"Son, if you're already an adult by now, then I know you've grown into the fine man I always knew you'd be and will use your inheritance wisely. If for some reason I've been taken too soon, look to Shane for the example of what a real man should be. After all, you're his namesake, if I never told you. If you let Shane guide you and be your second dad, you can't go wrong in life. I'm so proud of you. You're the best son a dad could ever have been blessed with. Remember I love you, always and forever."

Except for Farnsworth, there wasn't a dry eye in the room. Thank God the reading was over. *You really know how to rip my guts out, don't you, old friend? And oh, yeah—set the bar so high in Drew's eyes I can never hope to reach it.*

Why did you do something so stupid? Did you know the possible price?

Drew was bent over now, weeping quietly. Shane laid a hand on his back, rubbing, trying to give what comfort he could. This had been a god-awful week for them both, especially Drew. And he was supposed to start at his new high school on Monday. So many changes in such a short time.

Once they were finished at the attorney's office, Shane steered his godson out, a copy of the will in hand.

They met with the expected throng of reporters who, in turn, met with all the police that acted as a barrier between them. Though there would've been a few on hand anyway, Shane suspected he had Detective Lacey to thank for the extra show of force from his brethren. Cops protected their own.

The reporters had been relentless once they figured out who Shane was and that he was now legal guardian to Brad's son. They were playing up the "working man inherits big" angle, but for the most part had portrayed Shane in a kind light as the bereaved cop who now had to raise his best friend's son. Surprising, but true.

Shane just wanted them all to go away. The next big story couldn't happen soon enough, as long as nobody was left grieving like he and Drew were.

Once they were safely in Shane's truck, pulling out of the underground parking garage, he glanced at Drew. "What do you say we go get something to eat?"

A shrug.

Shane tried again. "Where do you like to go?"

"Dad and I never went out to eat much." The boy wiped his reddened eyes and turned his gaze out the window. "Always said wading through the fans made it too much trouble to go out."

"I know." That struck him as sad, but he didn't say so. "Well, I *do* like to go out, so I hope that's okay with you."

Another shrug. "That works."

He bit back a sigh. At least he'd gotten an actual answer with the shoulder movement this time. "Where to? You pick."

The boy gave it some thought. "I like those restaurants along Second Avenue, by the river. Dad never wanted to go down there because it's so touristy."

"Okay. Second Avenue it is. How about the spaghetti place? Or there's a brewery that has good pub-style food."

"Spaghetti," he said without hesitation.

Shane smiled. Maybe they could do this. They would be okay. "You got it."

Parking was a bit of a pain, but he managed to find a spot in a prepaid lot not far down the street from the restaurant. To coax a smile from Drew, he'd park in Alaska.

After a short wait, they got seated. Shane was relieved to see that nobody seemed to recognize them. If anyone did, they were left alone.

The waitress came and took their drink order. That simple question gave him pause. Typically, he'd order a beer, but for some reason that didn't seem right today. Drew was his responsibility from now on, and he had to set a good example. No alcohol if he was going to drive with his godson in the car afterward, period. He ordered tea, and Drew gave him a funny look as the waitress moved off.

"Tea? Dude, I've never seen you touch a glass of tea."

"Well, I'm thirsty."

The kid rolled his eyes. "You are so full of crap. When you're thirsty, you always drink water. You're trying to be a *parent* now, right? Jesus, get over yourself."

Shane blinked at him. "What?"

"You want a beer, have a beer. Who fuckin' cares?"

"Language." That earned him a snort. "And *I* care, very much. You're not just visiting me, you're my kid now."

"Don't remind me," he shot back sarcastically.

That stung. "The point is, it's been a long, rough day for us both, and I don't feel right about being this wiped out, having a beer at lunch, and then getting behind the wheel. The brew can wait until I get home."

"Fine, whatever."

"And it would be nice if you could learn some new vocabulary words besides those two."

"Christ, you sound like Dad."

I'm not your dad, as you've pointed out before, hovered on his tongue. But he squashed the urge to kamikaze their lunch outing by uttering it. Just barely.

"Then I'm doing my job," he said instead.

Suddenly serious, Drew leaned forward, elbows on the table. "What if I just want you to be Shane?"

He had no ready response for that one. Giving it some thought, he said, "I want to be, but I'm more than just your friend now. Give me a chance and we'll figure it out together."

"Then let me breathe, dude. Don't ride my ass like a virgin nun and we're good."

In spite of himself, Shane laughed out loud. "I'll try. That's all I can promise."

"Fair enough." He paused. "So, I was named after you? Dad never told me."

"I thought you knew."

"Nope. I didn't even know your middle name is Andrew."

"Guess it just never came up."

"'S pretty cool."

Pride surged in Shane's chest. "Really?"

"Yeah."

Still no smile, but that was okay. Baby steps. They spent a few moments looking over the menu. The waitress came back and they ordered, then Drew changed the subject.

"So, what's the deal with Daisy Duke?"

Shane almost choked on his tea. "Do *not*, under any circumstances, call her that within a mile of her earshot. She hates that nickname. I'm surprised you even know about that old TV show."

"Are you serious? *The Dukes of Hazzard* is a classic, man." He shook his head. "Is Daisy her real name?"

"It is, and she's pretty sensitive about it."

"Gotcha. I *can* keep my mouth shut when I want. Honest." But there was a gleam in his eyes that indicated trouble on the horizon.

"It's your hide if you mess up around her."

"I have been warned. Is it serious between you guys?"

"That's a none-ya." At the boy's puzzled look, he clarified, "None-ya biz-ness."

"Ha! It is serious! Is she good in the sack?"

Shane's eyes widened. Now, here was a subject he'd completely forgotten he'd have to tackle with a young man of almost seventeen—that of women. And sex. *Jesus Christ!*

"That is *really* none of your business," he said firmly. "Ask me anything you want about women, men, and sex, but under no circumstances will I discuss me and Daisy in that regard, as a source of amusement. I'll only talk about us in the most general of terms, as it affects my relationship with you."

"Don't get all bent out of shape," Drew muttered. "I was just curious. Lately, Dad had loads of women in and out of the house, all the time. It's no skin off my nose what you do. Just let me know when you need to scratch that itch, and I'll make myself scarce."

Brad had behaved that way around Drew? Shane stared at the kid, stunned at the blasé way he'd revealed that tidbit. He didn't want to make the boy feel bad about Brad's habits, but he had to let Drew know where he stood on the matter.

"I will not have loads of women traipsing in and out of the house. For one thing, I don't date that much, and for another, yes, I'm serious about Daisy. Or I want to be, if she'll eventually take me back."

"Ahh. You messed up, huh?"

"Big time. Now I've got to crawl on my belly for a while."

"Sounds like you're totally gone over her."

"That's about right." No point in denying it.

"Can I ask you a question?"

"Shoot."

"When do you know . . . you *know* . . . when it's right to be with a girl?"

Kill me now. Did you not discuss anything *meaningful with your son, Brad?*

He cleared his throat. "You mean to, uh, have sex?"

The boy nodded earnestly. "Exactly! I mean, I want to, but I don't want to do it with just anybody. That doesn't seem right, unless you're a *lot* older. Like you and Dad."

Thank God! "You're absolutely right to wait. And it's never a great idea to just go around doing it with who-ever. Having sex, even once you find a girlfriend you love and are convinced you can't live without, is a huge step. You can only have one first time, and you both deserve for it to be special."

Like a long, long time from now. When you're in college and I don't have to know about it.

"I know you're right. It's just that it's all I can freakin' think about sometimes."

This is my punishment for being a free and easy bachelor for so long. Cosmic justice.

"We're guys. That's the way we're wired."

"So, I guess it's best just to keep taking things into my own hands, so to speak."

"Um, well, it's safer that way."

The boy definitely didn't have much of a filter. He was a lot like his father in that respect. Shane about fell to his knees in thanks when the food arrived and the conversation turned to another subject. Specifically, Drew's future car.

"You don't have to get me a car, you know. I can just drive Dad's Mustang Boss 302."

Give me patience. "Forget it. That's way too much muscle for a novice driver to handle."

"Dude, what *century* are you from?" The boy gave him an incredulous look. "Come on, man! The cars are mine anyway, so why should you buy me a different one?"

"Because the first thing you'll do is go out and wrap it around a tree."

Congratulations, Shane. You've become your father.

"Jesus, I thought you were cool." This, stated with such disappointment.

"I'm smart, and that's better than cool."

"Whatever."

When Drew arrived at his fallback word, Shane figured the in-depth part of the conversation was over. Which was more than okay, since he needed time to recover from talking about sex and how much his teenager wanted to do it.

Lord help them both. They were going to need all they could get.

Monday arrived all too soon, and with trepidation, Shane watched as Drew slung his backpack over one broad shoulder.

"Are you sure you don't want me to go to the school with you just this once, get you settled in and meet your teachers?"

"Sure, if you want to ruin my social life." He snorted.

Shane sighed. "Well, have a good day, then. I love you, kiddo."

"Yeah." Relenting some, the boy gave him a one-armed hug before heading out the door. "See ya."

Worried about any last lurking reporters, Shane went out onto the front porch and watched Drew walk down the drive to wait at the end. Five minutes later, a Sugarland ISD school bus pulled up, and the boy hopped on and disappeared.

As it rumbled away, he couldn't help but feel a tug in his chest. That odd sensation lasted all the way to work, into the building, and was still hanging on as he sat at his desk.

"Hey, cuz!" Chris called out. "Welcome back!"

This attracted the attention of the rest of the gang, who swarmed his desk, doling out backslaps and shaking his hand. You'd think he'd been gone for a month instead of a week.

"Thanks, guys. It's great to be back, though I'm not looking forward to reducing the pile on my desk." There was a round of agreement on the general shittiness of being absent and having to deal with the load.

"How's Drew?" Austin asked, joining the group. His captain hadn't attended the funeral, but had called several times to check on them.

"As good as can be expected, I guess. I sent him off to the high school this morning, and I have to admit, it was kind of weird watching him go. I can't help but worry, you know?"

That met with a bunch of sympathy as well. The consensus was that he'd better get used to worrying. That's what parents do.

"The thing is, since the reading of the will, he seems to be doing fine, considering. I keep waiting for the other shoe to drop."

"He's a sixteen-year-old boy, so it comes with the territory," Austin said. "But he'll adjust fine. You're gonna be a great dad."

"Thanks, Cap," he said, touched.

"Okay, get your lazy asses to work." The captain ambled off, presumably to his office.

When the crowd parted and he saw Daisy approaching, a little smile on her gorgeous face, Shane's heart gave a little jolt. "Like the others said, welcome back."

"Thanks. I missed being here among the action. And I'm ready to resume my life."

"Sounds promising."

"I certainly hope so." He leaned forward, speaking for her ears only. "Still on for Saturday night? Drew is staying with Shea and Tommy."

She arched a fine blond brow. "Is he, now? A girl might think you're awfully sure of yourself, detective."

"I'm not—just hopeful." He gave her his sweetest look, which earned a laugh.

"Hold that thought." She patted his cheek. "Until Saturday."

"Can't wait."

"I hope you love a challenge, because this time? I don't plan to make it so easy for you."

With that, she turned and walked off. He ogled her high, round ass until she was out the door. Hearing a snicker, he looked around to see Taylor smirking at him.

"Shut up, asshole."

"Hey, I didn't say a word!"

Shane reached for a file, hardly able to keep the smile off his face. She planned to give him a challenge, did she? Well, he was up for one.

Game on.

5

Drew walked into third-period English and took his seat just before the tardy bell rang. He typically didn't stress about being Mr. Punctual, but he didn't want to stand out too much. Not before he'd scoped out this place.

So far, he wasn't impressed. The building had to be fifty years old, and it reeked of the musty smell of dirty socks. It was clean enough, but it was shabby, in need of new paint and carpet. And a lot of the teachers were so freakin' old, they must've worked there since the dawn of man.

The worst thing of all was the kids here sucked. They were loud and rude, shoving each other, insults flying on a regular basis. Okay, not all of them, but plenty. The ones that weren't assholes just kept their heads down and tried to present a smaller target.

Fuck that. Drew Cooper wasn't about to play anybody's bitch.

But the whispers were getting to him, and it was early yet. By third period, word had gotten around. Didn't matter that the teachers must've decided not to make a big deal of Drew's arrival—everybody knew who his dad was and what had happened. He hated feeling like a circus freak.

Even at his old school, he was just one of a crowd of rich kids. Everyone had idolized his dad, even though most of them were the children of sports figures, politicians, scientists, and famous musicians. He wasn't stupid—he knew the real world wasn't made of the elite. But it was what he knew. He wanted to jump on a bus and get the hell away from here.

"Hey, Cooper."

Two desks over to his right, a boy with shaggy brown hair was sneering at him. Tall, built. Drew pegged him as a jock. The Big Man on Campus, from his football-field-sized attitude.

"That's me." He kept his tone uninterested in whatever the jock might be about to say. But that didn't stop the jerk.

"You're not such a big shot now, are ya?" A few of his buddies snickered. "You like slummin' with the rest of us?"

The taunt wasn't too far off the mark, so he said nothing.

"You're livin' with some cop now, right? What's up with that? You his little butt buddy or something?"

"Why, you want to watch?" he shot back.

The jock's face reddened as his friends laughed. It obviously pissed him off that he'd lost the advantage. "Figures that Brad Cooper's son would be a faggot. Hey, did he drop dead when he found out his kid is a little homo? Is that what happened?"

He sucked in a breath. Guilt stabbed him in the gut, made him sick. No one knew it was Drew's fault his dad was dead. But he never forgot for a minute.

Rage boiled, slow and dangerous. It shocked him how much he wanted to physically hurt this prick. "Why don't you drop your pants and bend over for your friends so they can see who's queer?"

Now his buddies cracked up. The jock bolted to his feet, ready to lunge for Drew, but the teacher's sharp reprimand halted him.

"Alan, sit down and stop making a nuisance of yourself." The teacher glared until Alan did as he was told, then pointed to the board. "Open your literature books to page one thirty-eight."

Groans sounded all around, but most followed the directions, including Drew, but that didn't mean he planned to listen. After twenty minutes of lecture, the teacher assigned the class to read the story and answer the questions at the end. Then he parked his skinny ass behind the desk and started grading papers.

"That was pretty impressive, how you smacked Alan down," a voice said from his left.

Glancing over, Drew eyed the speaker. His shoulder-length hair was straight and dyed jet-black, to match his death metal T-shirt and skinny jeans. He wore silver studs in both earlobes, and a strip of black leather around his neck with a silver skull dangling from it. His dark eyes stared impassively back at Drew.

"He seems like a real dick," Drew ventured, testing the water.

"Class A. He's like a stray dog—feed him scraps and he'll keep comin' back." The kid smiled, and his teeth were straight and white. "But you handled him fine. I'm Ty Eastlake. You?"

Seriously? "You don't know who I am?"

"Uh, no," he drawled. "Am I supposed to?"

"I'm Drew Cooper." Nothing. "Brad Cooper's son?"

"Who?" Ty's brows furrowed.

Now, there was a refreshing change. But the explanation still hurt like hell. Always would. Especially when he could've prevented it. He swallowed the guilt.

"My dad played for the Titans. He died, like, a week ago."

"Oh, man. I'm sorry to hear that." He seemed sincere. "I'm not a sports fan, and I don't watch the news 'cause it's all just depressing shit. Ya know?"

"I *do* know."

He regarded Drew for a minute, and Drew got the strangest impression that for the first time, someone his own age saw *him*, not the famous player's kid. "What do you have seventh period?"

Opening his notebook, he glanced at his schedule. "Physics with Mr. Brenner."

"Me, too! Hmm. Well, I'm not planning on being a rocket scientist, are you?"

He gave a short laugh. "Hardly."

"Me neither. I'm in a rock band and we're gonna be famous, so screw science. What do ya say we meet after sixth and walk to my house? I'll show you my guitars."

A slow smile spread across Drew's face. It felt alien. And damned good.

"I say you're on."

On Saturday afternoon, Daisy changed clothes four times before settling on black capri pants and a black-and-purple patterned blouse. The outfit was nice enough to pass muster in a pricier restaurant, but not too dressy for most casual places. It would have to do, since Shane hadn't said where they were going.

Pausing, she studied herself in the mirror. Was she being an idiot? Probably. As excited as she was about their date, she had to admit to being afraid.

I'll call you. Maybe we'll go to dinner sometime.

That's what he'd told her, months ago. And he had called—to tell her that he couldn't see her anymore. Just like that. And his rejection had hurt so badly, she'd cried for days. She'd believed they had something real, and he'd dumped her.

Could she trust that he wouldn't do it again, even if he swore to it? True, he'd made no promises before. But the about-face had been so sudden, she had been left reeling. He had yet to give her a real reason for doing it, just some lame apologies.

Maybe tonight he'd come clean.

The doorbell interrupted her musings, and her heart jumped. "It's stupid to be nervous." Taking a deep breath, she went to open her door.

As always, Shane took her breath away. He was six feet of tall, lean, melt-your-panties yumminess in jeans that hugged his thighs and ass just right, and she was human. She wanted more.

"Hi," she said, smiling at him. "Come in."

"Been a while since I was here. The place looks nice."

"Thanks. I painted and put up some new curtains. It seems to have helped some."

"Well, maybe these will add a touch of color." From behind his back, he brought forth a bouquet of flowers, grinning like a boy.

"They're beautiful," she said, taking them and inhaling the fragrant scent. "Let me put them in some water. Would you like a drink?"

"I'll wait until we get to the restaurant, thanks. I'm cutting back some." He trailed her to the kitchen, where she fetched a vase from under the sink.

"Really?"

"Yeah. I'm trying to set a better example for Drew."

Setting the vase on the counter, she began to cut the cellophane from the stems. "Well, I don't think you drink too much, but that's very admirable. Good for you." He seemed pleased by the compliment. She eyed him as she arranged the flowers in the vase. "So, where are you taking me?"

He leaned against the counter. "There's a brand-new seafood restaurant a few miles outside Sugarland, right on the Cumberland. It's a little more upscale than the one here in town, and I heard it's good. I thought you might like to try it."

"Sounds great. Let me grab my purse."

She locked up, and he rested a hand at the small of her back as they crossed to his truck in the driveway. He helped her in, then went around to his side, climbed in, and started it.

"You look beautiful, by the way," he said, gray eyes devouring her. "I'm going to be the luckiest man in the place."

She warmed with pleasure from the inside out. "You're looking pretty darned edible yourself."

"Maybe you'll save me for dessert?"

She grinned at him but didn't give him the satisfaction of an answer. He winked and pulled onto the street, apparently not bothered by her silence. Getting along, not to mention being totally in sync when it came to sex, had never been their problem. Perhaps it was timing?

In part, maybe. But that wasn't all of it.

The drive along the river was leisurely, and they chatted along the way, mostly about work. She figured they'd start light, get into the more serious stuff later. Which suited her fine. Twenty minutes later, he pulled into the parking lot of a nice restaurant that was built in a rustic lodge theme, with the river-side wall made almost completely of glass.

Inside, Shane gave his name and they were whisked to a secluded table with a gorgeous view. The waiter immediately came and offered them wine lists along with their menus.

"Get whatever you want, sugar."

Shane took one, so she did the same, looking it over. "I'll have a glass of this cabernet, please."

"Make that two."

The waiter moved off, and she looked at him in surprise. "I didn't think you were much of a wine drinker."

"I like it now and then. A country boy *can* be cultured."

She smiled. "I wouldn't change a thing about you."

"Oh, I can think of one or two things about me that need work."

She let that slide and changed the subject. "How's Drew?"

"Quiet. Withdrawn." He thought a minute. "The only time this week he's perked up some is when he mentioned this new friend at school. His name is Ty. They've been spending a lot of time together, but I haven't met the boy yet."

"I'm glad he's met someone he clicks with. Maybe you could suggest inviting the kid over?"

"Actually, that's a great idea," he said slowly. "I'll suggest that to Drew when Tommy brings him home tomorrow."

"Glad I could help."

Their wine arrived, and Shane picked up his glass. "A toast. To new beginnings."

"I like that." After clinking glasses, they sipped. She observed him, thinking he seemed so sincere. Then again, he had before. She squashed the thought, determined not to let fear ruin the evening.

"Then what's with the sadness on your gorgeous face?" he asked, setting down his glass.

She shook her head. "It's nothing."

"That wasn't very convincing." He paused. "It's me, isn't it?"

"Maybe we shouldn't get into this right now. . . ."

"I hurt you, and you want to know why," he guessed. "Where my turnaround is coming from."

If he was willing to open up, then she knew she needed to hear it. "Okay. Yes, I'd very much like to know. Was it something I did?"

"God, no." He gave a rueful laugh. "You're perfect to me. I was the problem."

The waiter interrupted to take their order, and they quickly made selections. When he was gone again, she urged him to continue.

"So, is this the old 'It's not you, it's me' speech?"

"I promise it's not a line. But for it to make sense, I have to start at the beginning, when I was eighteen." He paused, fiddling with his menu. "That's the year Shea and I lost our parents. But we'd already been through a hell of a lot of trauma as a family before they were killed."

She took a deep breath. "I know your sister was date-raped when she was in high school and got pregnant as a result. She confided in me a few months ago."

He looked relieved not to have to broach the subject and possibly break his sister's confidence. "Then you know a little about what those months were like, she and my parents arguing all the time, and me in the middle, trying to mediate. Then they were killed, and she lost the baby."

"And you were a heartbroken eighteen-year-old who was suddenly forced to become a man." She began to see where he was going.

"It was the hardest thing I'd ever done." Old sadness and regret shadowed his striking eyes. "Our parents had money, and we were left with enough from insurance and the sale of their business to be able to stay in our house and take care of expenses while we figured out what careers we wanted to pursue, but that wasn't the biggest mountain we had to climb. Shea was almost destroyed by what she went through, and I took care of her. Got her back on her feet and into nursing school. For years, I was her protector, her champion."

"And you never stopped being that for her. Did you?" she asked quietly.

"No, not really. Even when Tommy came along, I wasn't sure how to relinquish the role I'd had in her life for so long. But somehow, I started to learn to let go. And gradually I found that it was nice, having nobody to take care of but myself." The last he admitted with such guilt, as though it was the most terrible confession he could've made.

"I think that's a completely normal feeling to have after being so strong for so many years. Now add your job to that. And as much as you love being a cop, serving the public and protecting others is stressful."

"Then you came along." He fell silent for a moment.

"What happened? Did you feel that I was one more person you had to take care of?"

"At first it seemed that way," he admitted. "I got scared. I thought to myself that maybe my life wasn't ever supposed to be my own. That I would be taking care of people until the day I died, with never any time for myself. Does that sound selfish?"

She gave him a half smile, though the first part of what he said hurt. "It might if I didn't know the whole story. But I understand where you're coming from, why you must've felt like you couldn't breathe."

"That's it exactly. But what I learned was that I can't breathe without the people I love in my life. That letting them in, taking care of them, isn't an obligation, it's a joy. I'm just sorry it took Brad's death to open my eyes," he said hoarsely.

"Oh, honey." Reaching across the table, she squeezed his hand. He gripped hers tightly, and they didn't speak as the waiter served their dinners. Once he was gone, she asked, "When did you change your mind about *me*?"

"I was already close to giving in, if you must know.

Having you nearby and knowing I couldn't have you, that I'd screwed up so badly, was driving me insane."

"And then?"

"Then I had that horrible call with Drew. When we rushed there and I pulled him into my arms, right then I was reminded that time was precious and never guaranteed. That I'd do anything at all to protect the ones I love, and that it's my calling. It's what I was born to do." He cleared his throat. "And that's when I knew, deep down, I'd do whatever it took to earn your forgiveness."

"Those are some beautiful words."

"I can back them up, I promise you."

She really wanted to believe. But although she understood where his head was when he broke things off, it still hurt. "Why don't we take things one day at a time?"

Disappointment flashed in his eyes, but he quickly recovered. "I'll gladly accept whatever you're willing to give me."

The man was saying all the right things. Time would tell if he could walk the walk.

She enjoyed the meal, which was exceptional, and he vowed to bring her back as often as she wanted. After sharing a crème brûlée for dessert, he paid the check and guided her to the truck.

He opened the door for her, helped her in. But this time he didn't step back. Instead he leaned inside and cupped her face in his hands. Their gazes met, and he simply stared at her as though she held all the secrets to his universe.

He smelled so good, and she loved his strong hands on her. She was addicted to his touch, his warmth. When he lowered his mouth to capture her lips, she moaned, pushing into him. She snaked her arms around his middle, clutching the shirt at his back. His tongue tangled with hers and she relished his taste, wine and sweet cream. And all Shane.

He pulled back with a smile. "If I don't let go, I'll end up ravishing you right here and now."

"That doesn't sound so bad."

Chuckling, he kissed her cheek and shut the door. He climbed in the other side, and they took the long way home, enjoying the sight of the river in the moonlight. She knew they both wanted this night to end the same way, but she was glad he didn't rush the trip. One thing Shane was very good at was savoring a moment.

Half an hour later, they arrived at her little house in town. "May I come in for a while?"

"I'd be sad if you didn't."

"We can't have that."

She let them in, only bothering to turn on a small table lamp in the living room so they could see well enough on the way to her bedroom. She took his hand, leading the way. Once there, she began to unbutton his dark shirt.

"I've missed you, my sexy cop."

"God, I've missed you, too."

She parted the material and he hissed as she bent and licked one of his nipples. Took it in her teeth and worried it, making the nub stand out proudly. His fingers combed through her loose hair as she gave the other equal attention. Then he went to work on her blouse.

"My turn."

He pulled it over her head and then unclasped her

bra. She let the straps slide off, and the garment fell to the floor. She loved being bared to him, because he always gazed at her as though she was the moon and stars. As if it was more than lust between them. As though he truly cared for her.

And it showed in his lovemaking. Like now, the tender way he guided her to the bed to lie on her back, never breaking eye contact. How he slowly unzipped her capris and made sliding the material down her legs seem like an art. Then he hooked her panties, taking them down as well, making male noises of appreciation in his throat. She loved those sounds.

"Can I taste you, sugar? It's been so long."

"Too long. Please . . ."

Parting her thighs, he dipped his head. One flick of his tongue and she melted, opening for him with an abandon she'd never felt with anyone else. Shane made her fly.

He licked and sucked, causing little tremors to zip to every nerve ending. Until she was squirming underneath him, practically begging. "Tell me you came prepared."

That sexy grin showed his white teeth against his tanned face, feral in the darkness. Exciting. "I brought the gun, the bullets, *and* the holster, baby."

She laughed as he fished a foil packet from the front pocket of his jeans and tossed it onto the bed. Then he stood and toed off his shoes and hiked up one leg of his jeans to remove his weapon and ankle holster. After placing it carefully on the dresser, he quickly removed the rest of his clothes.

The man was quite simply beautiful. Sable hair fell around his angular face in layers, covering his ears and brushing his neck. His gray eyes were large and stunning, framed by thick, dark lashes. His chest was sculpted but not too muscular, as was the rest of his tall, lean body. His sex was long and thick, heavy balls nestled underneath.

As she ogled him, he retrieved the packet and tore it open, then rolled the condom down his straining shaft before joining her again.

"Where were we?" he murmured, slipping a hand between her legs to finger her mound. "Right about here, I think."

She wiggled, needing him. "I want you inside me."

"I need you, too."

Covering her body with his, he positioned himself between her thighs and used a hand to guide the head of his cock to her entrance. Then he slowly pushed inside, giving her time to adjust. The stretch and fullness of him were wonderful. She opened farther and arched her back, wanting him deeper.

Taking his cue from her, he rose to a kneeling position, cradling her thighs and taking her with him to keep them connected. She loved when he thrust in as deeply as possible, and he knew this. He gave it to her just how she wanted.

He began to move, using a slow, steady rhythm at first. Slide in, balls to her ass. Then out, his rigid length glistening. In again, a bit faster. Harder. Out again. Repeating the thrust over and over until she was moaning, writhing, lost in his body owning hers, taking her to greater heights.

Now he was fucking her, hard and deep, and she couldn't hold on much longer. It was so damned good.

Fire spread from her sex to her limbs, and her body quickened. Ready for release.

The orgasm burst over her, wave after wave of ecstasy as she cried out for him. Rode his cock. In the next moment he stilled, burying himself to the hilt with a hoarse shout as he filled the condom. She experienced a moment of regret that he wasn't spilling inside her, but pushed it away. If all went well, maybe someday.

Rolling to the side, he gathered her in his arms, kissed her long and sensually. Then he tucked her against his chest, where she was quite happy to snuggle and listen to the strong beat of his heart.

"You're incredible," he whispered. "And I don't just mean in bed."

She smiled, kissed his chest. "How so?"

"You're brave and smart. You take care of people, too, and you love what you do."

The praise wrapped around her heart. "I love kids, and I hate seeing people hurt or neglect them. Someone has to show them there's a better life, and sometimes I'm the only role model around." She flushed. "Listen to me, getting all preachy."

"You're not. You're passionate, and I admire that. You're an amazing woman, Daisy Callahan."

"And you're an amazing man."

He rolled on top of her, pinning her underneath him, suddenly playful. "Then it stands to reason that we'd make a superamazing couple that would have all of our friends bowing down in awe at our awesome mojo."

"You're crazy." He nibbled at her neck, and she giggled. "Stop! That tickles."

The nibbles became kisses that trailed to her breasts.

Her stomach and beyond. Gasping, she gripped his hair as he pleasured her with his mouth, licking and sucking until he brought her to a second shattering orgasm. She bucked, clinging to him, crying out with her release.

He kissed her tummy. "Rest here."

He was gone for a few minutes, splashing and making noises of washing up. When he returned, he brought a washcloth and cleaned her between her thighs with such gentle care it almost brought tears to her eyes. He disappeared for a few seconds to get rid of the cloth, then he was back, holding her close, spooning her from behind.

"Can I stay tonight?"

Stay forever. "Yes."

She was still frightened by how much she wanted this man, needed him.

But just maybe not quite as frightened as before.

Drew lay wide awake in the guest room at Tommy and Shea's house, tense and waiting. He still wasn't too sure about this harebrained scheme of Ty's, but he was committed. If he backed out now, his friend would think he was a chickenshit.

Ty had texted him earlier, asking for the Skylers' address, because he was planning to show at two in the morning and they were going to have some fun. Who'd be awake to spot them?

"Um, the police for one, dipstick," Drew had pointed out. "And my adopted Daddy Dearest is a cop, remember?"

"Relax, man, or you're gonna get wrinkles before your time. We'll keep to the shadows, like ninjas. We won't get caught."

So, despite the warning in his gut that screamed it was a bad idea, Drew had given Ty the address. Like a pussy, he was hoping his friend was home in bed, snoring away. A tap at the window a few minutes later proved he had no such luck.

Crap. Padding to the curtains, he parted them to see Ty grinning at him. He held up a finger for his friend to give him a minute, then searched for his clothes in the dark. After getting dressed, he shrugged on his jacket and returned to the window. He'd already tested it earlier, and knew it would slide up easily.

In seconds, he was out, standing on the ground. Ty helped him put the window back down all but an inch, just enough to get his fingers under it when it was time to sneak back in. *Sneaking out, and anything could happen. What the hell am I thinking?* His heart pounded painfully against his sternum at the thought of Tommy catching him—and, worse, telling Shane.

"Man, this is gonna be awesome," Ty whispered excitedly.

"Jesus, what're you on?" he muttered. "It's the middle of the frickin' night and you're jumping around like a flea."

"Nothin' but a natural high. Chillax, my friend. Come on, let's get going."

He followed Ty to the street—and was brought up short by the sleek black SUV parked by the curb. "An Escalade? Is that yours?" he asked, incredulous. By the state of their run-down little house, he'd figured Ty and his dad didn't have two nickels to rub together.

"It's my dad's. Sweet ride, huh?"

"Ty, he's gonna freak if he wakes up to find this gone!"

"Nah. My old man doesn't give a shit what I'm doing as long as I show up before he has to leave in the morning."

"What does your dad do?" he asked as they climbed in, admiring the plush leather interior in spite of himself.

"Hell if I know. He's all mysterious and crap when I ask, but I intend to find out soon," his friend said with a grin.

"You don't *know* what your dad does for a living?" That didn't sound good. In fact, this whole scenario was giving him a stomachache. Still, he didn't want to wimp out. "What's on the agenda?"

"Look." He pointed to the floorboard at Drew's feet.

There was a plastic sack. A quick inspection of the contents revealed two cans of red spray paint. *Fantastic— not.* "What are we decorating with those? The train trestle or the bridge?"

"Even better. I'll show you."

They drove for a while, to the eastern outskirts of town. Before long, Ty pulled the SUV onto a small county road and parked off to the side. Grabbing both cans of paint, he handed one to Drew and said, "Come on."

"Where to?"

"Up ahead is Franklin Johnson's place. Yesterday he called my dad a worthless fucker and a cock-suckin' son of a bitch," Ty spat. "So we're gonna make sure he gets a little payback."

"Ty, I don't think this is a good idea. My dad would've killed me if he ever found out—"

"Well, he's not here, is he? And if he cared so much, why'd he stuff his body full of drugs and leave you all alone?" The boy's dark eyes gleamed in the interior lights of the SUV. "We doin' this or not?"

Drew's face burned as the rage welled up inside him again. Thick and hot. Anger at his friend for spouting off his big mouth. Even more rage that what he'd said was true. He was sick with resentment at his dad for not being here. For being a goddamn drug addict. For leaving Drew alone. And all that rage needed somewhere to go.

"Yeah. Let's rock."

6

The night was cold and dark. Drew couldn't see his breath forming little clouds, but it must've been.

The cold couldn't combat the anger and the over-whelming need to release it. He followed Ty through the brush, stumbling over a fallen tree. Then he almost caught a branch in the eye as it whipped his cheek.

"Too bad we can't use a flashlight. I can't see a frea-kin' thing."

"It's not much farther, just through this crop of trees."

"You say that like you've been here before." A non-committal grunt was his answer. "Ty? Have you been here?"

"I might've yanked Johnson's chain a time or two. So what? He deserves it."

Reason belatedly began to return. He didn't like the sound of that. With Ty, he was beginning to understand there was always more to the story than he was telling.

"There's the house. Look."

He came to a stop beside his friend and peered through the trees. The white wood-frame house was bathed in the glow of a single light high on a post—a security light. The house and yard were modest but well-kept. The pool of light didn't quite stretch to the barn that was partially visible behind the house.

"Does this guy have any dogs?" Drew eyed the perimeter and noted there was no fence.

"Nah. Not since I poisoned the last one." Drew whipped his head around and saw Ty's grin in the darkness. "Gotcha. No animals were harmed in the making of this mischief," he quipped.

"Very funny."

"Come on."

He trailed his friend around the perimeter until they were behind the barn and away from the damning glow of the security light. Making as little noise as possible, they crept up to the building. It wasn't easy to be quiet this time of year, given all the dead leaves and brown weeds. Each crunch under his tennis shoes went off like a bomb and ratcheted up his tension. He just wanted to do this and get the hell out of here.

At the back of the barn, Ty uncapped his can of paint and Drew did the same. His friend went right to work, but Drew stood in indecision. "What do I write?"

"What do you mean, 'What do I write?' It's not a freakin' English thesis, just start spraying!"

Feeling stupid, he got started, making random patterns. Geometric shapes and swirls. He couldn't see well enough to write actual words, and this Johnson dude hadn't done anything to him, anyway, so he wouldn't have known what to say. In fact, he was starting to feel sort of bad for messing up such a nice building. The owner obviously cared for his animals, since the barn was just as nice and well kept as the house.

Strange that the odor coming from inside didn't smell much like horses or cows. Wasn't there supposed to be an earthy scent of manure? Instead the smell was sort of . . . chemical. He was about to mention it when Ty got his attention.

"Let's do the side facing the house," Ty said, starting in that direction. "That way he'll have a nice surprise when he wakes up."

"I don't know," he replied worriedly. "What if he wakes up and looks out the window?"

"He won't. Stop worrying."

He didn't like it, but once again followed along. They repeated the process, and all the while, Drew cast nervous glances toward the house. When nobody came storming out to confront them, he relaxed a bit and finished his task.

"One last thing," Ty said. "Then we'll be done."

"What else?"

"I want to get the side of his house."

"What? No way! That's too risky!"

"Then go on back to the Escalade and I'll see you in a few." Making a few clucking noises, he sauntered off.

"Shit." Huffing, Drew hurried after the other boy. He didn't want to tag the house, but he wasn't about to walk back through the creepy woods by himself, either. Screw that.

Ty settled for doing the back of the house, since it wasn't directly in the light. They could remain mostly in the shadows, then retrace their steps to the SUV. At least that's the way it should have worked. Halfway through their dubious artwork, a deep voice almost made Drew wet his pants.

"Drop the cans." They whirled to see a man roughly the size of a tank standing not twenty feet away. And he was wielding a shotgun. "Hands over your head, boys, and stay real still."

Oh, fuck. Drew did as he was told, and Ty did, too. He also noted that all of the bravado had deserted his friend. Drew's anger was a distant memory by now, and terror had taken its place. This man could shoot them both, throw them into a ravine, and their bodies would never be found.

"I've been watching you two ever since you got here. Made for some entertaining viewing, too."

"You knew we were here?" Ty sputtered. "Why didn't you stop us sooner?"

The man gave them a toothy smile. "Because my house and barn could use a fresh coat of paint," he drawled. "And now I've got free labor."

"You can't make us do that!" Ty exclaimed.

"Sure I can, Eastlake. That's the deal that's going to keep you two shitheads out of jail—as soon as the police get here to arrest you in, say, one minute. Now, that's what I call ironic."

"Oh, God," Drew moaned. Shane was going to find out, and when he did, he was going to freaking *flip*.

"Gotta say one thing, you're a chip right off the old block," the man said to Ty with a smirk.

Drew didn't have time to ponder that statement because just then a squad car rolled into the yard. His life was over.

Shane awoke to a persistent buzzing coming from somewhere in the vicinity of the floor. The floor? His foggy brain tried to make sense of why the floor was buzzing, and hoped it would stop so he could go back to sleep. It did, for about fifteen seconds. Then it started up again and kept right on until he finally latched on to the meaning.

His cell phone. The phone ringing in the middle of the night—and his, in particular—was never a good thing. He came awake as only a seasoned cop can do. Abruptly and unhappily. He slid from the bed and fished the thing out of his jeans, hoping to answer before it woke Daisy. As he squinted at the bedside clock, he saw that it read 4:17. *Damn!*

He stabbed the touch screen and started down the hall to talk in the living room. "Ford."

"Hey, Shane? This is Cunningham, from the night shift."

Parking his naked ass on Daisy's sofa, he rubbed his eyes and tried to process that. Cunningham. Brian Cunningham, from nights, was a big, tall, redheaded uniformed cop. Nice enough guy, if a bit of an ass kisser with the brass. Had his eye on making sergeant and probably would. If his puckered lips didn't fall off first.

"Brian," he said in greeting. "Don't tell me we've got another body."

"We don't have another body. But you've got a problem, and it's sitting down here at the station as we speak."

"What are you talking about? What kind of problem?"

"The Teenage Boy Sneaks out in the Middle of the Night and Is Caught Doing Criminal Mischief kind."

"I don't— What?" Now he was fully awake, eyes widening in dread. "Explain."

"Your kid was caught out at Frank Johnson's place, along with a friend of his. They did a number on his barn and house with a couple of cans of spray paint and—"

"Wait. Hold up." He shook his head in disbelief. "You've got Drew there, at the station? That's impossible! He's spending the night with my sister!"

"Yeah, well, I don't doubt he was, right up until his friend helped him sneak out to go joyriding and tagging."

"Goddamn it," he groaned, slumping back on the sofa.

"Sorry, man. It sucks. Say, I'm having trouble reaching Callahan, and I know she'll want to talk to these two."

"I'll get in touch with her," he managed. "I'll be there in half an hour at the most. And Brian?"

"Yeah?"

He hated to say it, but it was for the kid's own good. "Do me a favor and take a hard line. It won't do him any good if he's treated with kid gloves because of what he's been through, or given preferential treatment because he's mine. Scare the crap out of them both."

He chuckled. "My pleasure. See you soon."

Ending the call, he blew out a deep breath and stared at the ceiling, trying to gather his thoughts.

"Shane? What's going on?" Daisy padded into the living room and switched on a lamp. She had slipped on a large T-shirt and was standing there looking worried.

"Drew and a friend of his got arrested. I cannot fucking believe this." He swiped a hand down his face in frustration.

"Oh no. What happened?" She sat beside him.

"Apparently, a friend of Drew's went over to Shea

and Tommy's house a while ago, and Drew snuck out. Then they ended up tagging Frank Johnson's house and got caught."

"Damn." She frowned. "If this friend knew he was at your sister's and how to get there, they must've planned this in advance."

"That hadn't occurred to me, but you're right." Anger took root and bloomed. "I'll bet it's this new kid, Ty, that I told you about. He's the only one Drew talks about. Whoever he is, I'd like to wring his scrawny neck."

"Down, tiger. Getting mad isn't going to solve anything."

"Maybe not, but neither will coddling Drew. I've already told Cunningham not to go easy on him until I get there."

She frowned. "Are you sure that's the answer? He's been through a lot in the past couple of weeks, Shane."

He gave a humorless laugh. "Do I look like I'm sure? I said from the start I had no idea how to raise a teenager, and evidently I was right."

"You're doing the best you can, and he's going through a rough time. Give yourselves a break."

"For how long? How long should I give him until Brad's death becomes an excuse and not a *reason* for him to act out?"

"Honey, this is his first offense, right?"

"Yes," he admitted. "As far as I know. Honestly, from this incident and some things Drew has said, I have to wonder what sort of stuff Brad let him get away with."

"But you and I know he's a good kid."

"He is, and I don't want to see him go down the wrong path—that's all." His hands clenched into fists. "And he had to cross Frank Johnson, of all scumbags. If that ass-hole touched my boy, I'll skin him alive."

Daisy made a face. "Johnson's too smart to do that, which is why we haven't caught him at a felony yet. Un-fortunately, he has the upper hand here."

"Yeah. Now I've got to get dressed, go downtown, and make sure Drew doesn't end up where that slime deserves to be." Leaning over, he kissed her on the lips. "And you're coming, too, since they're already trying to call you. Bet you've got a few missed calls on your cell."

"I wouldn't be anywhere else," she told him. "To me, Drew is more than just another kid to deal with on the job."

Emotion welled in his chest and he gave her a smile. "I'm glad to hear you say that, because he's a permanent part of my life now. I love that boy."

And I think I love you, too. But that was a big step after the way he'd treated her before. Would she even want him for keeps? He had a lot more thinking to do.

"I know you do." She patted his knee. "Why don't you jump in the shower? I'll take mine after, and arrive a few minutes behind you."

"Why don't you take one with me? To conserve wa-ter, of course."

"Nice try," she said, kissing him on the lips. "Now go. You don't want to show up at the station, reeking of sex."

"True." He sighed. "But I demand a rain check on that shower together."

"You've got it."

As Shane jumped into the spray, he knew she was right—he needed to get to the station soon, and that wouldn't happen if she joined him. He wasn't capable of keeping his hands off her wet, slick, sexy body.

He toweled off and dressed quickly, wishing he had a different shirt to wear. This one wasn't too wrinkled, but it looked a little too nice for being pulled out of bed at just after four in the morning. He definitely appeared as though he'd been on a date, but there was no help for it.

On the way out, he stopped by the bathroom, leaned into the shower, and gave Daisy a lingering kiss.

"Out, horn dog," she teased. "While you still can."

"Spoilsport. See you soon."

One last kiss and he forced himself to leave, grumbling all the way. What should've been a nice, relaxing day alone with Daisy was shot to hell, and he was pissed. Her caution to go easy on the boy faded more into the back of his mind with every passing minute. He couldn't believe Drew would abuse his trust this way, no matter what he'd been through.

At the station, he parked in front and jogged inside, to the room where they kept the detainees for questioning. Through the observation window, he saw Cunningham and another officer sitting across the conference table from Drew and a black-haired boy who looked like a Steven Tyler wannabe, without the mojo. Schooling himself to refrain from charging in like a raging bull, he reached for the knob and walked inside.

Drew's expression when he looked up to see Shane was priceless. His eyes were wide, face pale. It did Shane's heart good to see that he was properly terrified, because maybe that meant he wouldn't be making a repeat performance. The other kid, however, was a different story.

The boy was slouched back in his seat, skinny arms crossed over his chest, an expression of what he could only describe as insolent boredom. The classic *I don't care and you can't make me* face that Shane had seen thousands of times on career criminals. This one appeared to be well on his way to that status, if looks were anything to go by.

"I reached Daisy," he told the officers. "She's on her way."

The boys exchanged a look, and the raven-haired one smirked. This did not go unnoticed by Cunningham, who arched his red brows, and Shane fumed inwardly. *Little shit.*

The second officer, who apparently had done the arresting, rose. "Since Mr. Johnson is willing to cut a deal with these two young men, I'm going to get back on the street. Good luck," he said to the boys by way of excusing himself.

Cunningham stayed, since it was their policy to always have two people in the room with juveniles. Despite the security cameras, the police couldn't be too careful when it came to shielding themselves against accusations.

Calmly, Shane rested his arms on the table and pointed a finger at Drew. "Start talking."

His Adam's apple bobbed. "We—we just wanted to ride around for a while, a-and Ty said, 'Let's do this guy's barn,' that we wouldn't get caught."

He directed a glare at the other boy. To Ty's credit, he flinched. Shane cut him no slack. "This was your idea, the sneaking out to go tagging?"

"Yeah. So?" He shrugged, mask slipping into place again.

"All right. Continue," he ordered Drew.

"There's not much else to tell," the boy said nervously. "We sprayed the barn, then Ty wanted to do the house. We did some of that, and the owner came out with a shotgun and—"

"A *what*?" he snapped.

Cunningham nodded. "Yep. Scared the shit out of 'em on purpose. Said he knew what they were doing the whole time. Evidently our friend Ty here has made a nuisance of himself in the recent past, and this time Johnson was waiting."

Shane's blood boiled. The man could've hurt them with the gun, or worse. Even if he didn't mean to shoot, so many things could have gone wrong, it made him sick. "Then why didn't he stop them right away?"

"Said he needed a new coat of paint on both the barn and house, anyway, so he figured he'd let them get in trouble and save himself the work. That's why he's not filing charges—if they agree to his terms."

"Of all the—" Cutting himself off, he shook his head angrily. He was still struggling for words when Daisy walked in, looking cool and confident. He could have kissed her.

"Someone care to fill me in?"

Shane repeated what everyone had told him, and she nodded when they were finished. "It seems like you boys were very lucky. Mr. Johnson was generous in offering to drop the charges in exchange for repair of the damage you caused. Since I doubt either of you are eager to face juvenile court, I think it's a deal you should both accept."

Shane knew she was being professional, and none of them could very well express their low opinion of Johnson in this setting or in regard to this situation. No matter what sorts of nefarious dealings the man was involved in, the boys were in the wrong. Shane just hated that the asshole was probably getting a good laugh out of this.

Drew agreed, though sullenly. "Whatever."

Shane was going to carve that word out of the boy's vocabulary if it was the very last thing he did.

"Fine," Ty said with a shrug.

"What is your name?" Daisy asked the boy.

"Ty Eastlake."

"Has your father been notified of what happened tonight, Ty?"

"Sure. He said he'd come get me as soon as he picked up his SUV from Mr. Johnson's house."

She looked to Cunningham. "And is Mr. Eastlake planning to press charges for theft of the vehicle?"

"No," the redhead stated. "But he was pretty angry."

Ty paled at that. Seemed he wasn't as nonchalant as he appeared. In spite of his dislike of the kid, Shane found himself worrying over how the father might punish Ty.

Daisy returned her attention to the two miscreants, her expression serious, tone even. "I want you boys to understand how serious your actions were tonight. It goes beyond some paint on a wall. Do you realize that if you'd written anything that could be perceived as slanderous or targeting an individual because of his race, beliefs, preferences, or anything else personal, you could both be charged with a hate crime?"

"We didn't!" Drew blurted. "We just scribbled stuff that didn't mean anything!"

"I'm glad to hear that. But do you understand what could've happened to you?"

Drew mumbled, "We could get more jail time or higher fines, I think."

"That's right. Some offenders don't make it that far, though. Especially when citizens wielding weapons take matters into their own hands. The two of you easily could've been shot by an overexcited or angry citizen."

Ty scoffed. "Johnson wouldn't dare, or my dad—" Abruptly, he broke off what he'd been about to say.

"Or your dad would what?" Daisy asked with interest.

"Nothin'."

"Are your dad and Mr. Johnson already acquainted?"

The boy clamped his lips shut and looked away. That was interesting. And worth looking into later.

"In any case, since you both have agreed to repair the damage you've done tonight, we're finished here," she said briskly. "Detective Ford and Mr. Eastlake will set up dates for the repair work. Detective, you can take Drew home. And, Ty, you'll need to wait here for your father."

"Let's go," Shane told his boy, standing. Then to his colleagues, "Thanks. Talk to you both later." He caught Daisy's eye, hoping she got the silent message. He'd talk to her sooner rather than later. She gave him a slight smile as he walked out, Drew on his heels.

He remembered her earlier advice to be calm and understanding, but it was pretty damned difficult in light of being dragged out of bed—his *lover's* bed—in order to deal with this bullshit. This was not what he'd signed up for, and he had a perfect right to be pissed about it.

He waited until they were in the truck before speaking. "Do you have any idea how disappointed I am in you?"

Shane's own father had said that to him more than once, when he richly deserved it. At the time, however, he'd believed it was just something adults said to guilt-trip a kid into better behavior. Now he had a whole new appreciation for how much his father had meant what he said.

Drew hunched his shoulders, pressing himself as far as possible into the corner of the seat and door. "I said I'm sorry."

"No, actually, you *didn't*."

"I thought I did." The boy squirmed in his seat, looking everywhere but at Shane. "Fine. I'm sorry."

"I don't want to hear it if you don't mean it."

"What do you want from me?" Drew's voice rose as he finally met Shane's eyes. "I'm sorry, and I'm gonna fix the guy's damned walls. Okay?"

"Watch your attitude. What would your dad say if—"

"Fuck you, Shane!" he exploded. "Don't tell me what Dad would think or feel! You don't know anything about what it was like to live with him!"

"Then tell me! How am I supposed to know anything if you don't talk to me?"

Drew's lips pressed into a thin line and he shook his head, glaring out the window. His chest was heaving with pent-up anger, but he offered nothing more. Shane gripped the steering wheel, a thousand remarks running through his head to sling back at the kid, none of them productive.

He settled on the truth. "Okay, since you don't want to talk, I have a couple of things to say. I love you as though you're my own, and I hope you truly know that. I apologize if it seemed like I was throwing your dad in your face, because that wasn't my intent. I'd never intentionally hurt you."

Silence. But some of the anger drained from the boy's expression.

"But I have to say, I don't deserve being cursed at, and that's not the way we're going to speak to each other. If you have something to get off your chest, talk to me like the man you want to be."

Anger became misery as Drew hung his head, resting it against the window. "I'm sorry, for that and the thing with Johnson's place."

The statement, though still sullen, rang true this time. "All right, I accept. So, tell me why you did it."

"I don't know," he said quietly. "It was stupid."

"Yes, it was. And dangerous, too. The outcome could've been much worse, and that scares me more than you know." He paused, wondering how much to say without violating policy. In this case, however, educating Drew was more important.

"We've suspected Franklin Johnson of various illegal activities for a while now, and we haven't come up with the evidence to catch him in a felony yet. That man is dangerous, kiddo."

"What, like a psycho?"

"Not exactly. More like a man capable of taking care of potential problems—like a witness who might stumble onto something he'd done. He could have killed you boys and none of us ever would've known what happened to you, and I'm not kidding. Johnson is unpredictable and totally capable of murder, given the right motivation. Son, what you two did is like walking barefoot through a nest of cobras and somehow managing not to get bitten. Do you understand why I was so upset and afraid?"

The kid licked his lips nervously. Apparently, the warning had sunk in. "Yeah. I won't screw around with anybody's property again, so can we drop it now?"

"For the time being. What is Ty's connection to Johnson?"

"I'm not sure. He hates the man, but he wouldn't tell me any details." He thought a second. "Except his dad and Johnson got into it recently. Johnson called his dad a bunch of names. That's why Ty wanted to tag his place, because of what the man called his dad."

An argument that could have started over business. Interesting. "Have you ever met Mr. Eastlake?"

"No, he's never home. To hear Ty talk, he sounds like a real asswipe."

"How so?" He already suspected he'd find out plenty if the man had a record—and he likely did, if he was acquainted with Johnson—but he wanted to hear about Eastlake from Drew's perspective.

"Ty's pretty casual about his dad's temper, his drinking and knocking Ty around. Stuff like that, when the man bothers to come home. And it's funny, they don't seem to have much money, and their furniture is old and ratty, but he's got this big new Escalade."

Definitely worth looking into. "I don't think I want you hanging around with Ty anymore."

The defenses shot back up. "You can't dictate who I can be friends with."

"You're right, I can't. But I hope you'll make some better decisions, especially when you're with him. And it wouldn't hurt to make *more* friends."

"Whatev—"

"*And* learn some new words."

Drew huffed, slouching in his seat again. "Are we done now?"

"Not quite. There's someone else you owe an apology."

The sun had risen by the time Shane pulled into Shea and Tommy's driveway. Drew appeared properly repentant as they trudged to the front door, as he damned well should. Shane rang the bell and waited. It took a couple of minutes before Tommy swung open the door, wearing flannel sleep pants and no shirt, blond hair sticking in every direction.

His puzzled squint at seeing Shane on their doorstep so early was replaced by sheer bafflement when he spotted Drew hovering at Shane's side. "What the heck? What are you doing out there, kid?" He glanced over his shoulder toward the direction of the bedrooms, as though wondering how the boy could be in two places at once.

"Can we come in?" Shane asked. "Drew has something to tell you."

"Uh, sure." Opening the door wider, he stepped aside and let them in. In the living room, Tommy yawned and scratched at his chest. "What's going on?"

Shane nodded to Drew, who sucked in a deep breath. "I left your house when I shouldn't have," he said contritely. "I'm sorry."

Tommy took a few seconds to process this. "You snuck out?"

"Yes. I— It won't happen again."

"I see." Tommy mulled that over. "You ever done anything like that before?"

The boy flushed but shook his head. "No, I've never snuck out in the middle of the night before."

"Before I worked for the Sugarland Fire Marshal's office, I was a firefighter there. Did you know that?"

Drew nodded. "I remember. You had an accident in a fire and almost lost your hand."

"That's right." The man paused, not bothered anymore by the story. He had another point he was trying to make. "In many ways it was a rewarding career, but there's a part of that job I don't miss at all. We got calls all the time to respond to all sorts of accidents involving young men and women, and many of those happened when those kids were out places they shouldn't have been, especially after curfew."

"I know where you're going with this—"

"No, I don't think you do. Your safety is one issue, but what about us?" He gestured between himself and Shane. "What about the folks who'll have to scrape you off the pavement when you get yourself killed? How do you think we sleep at night after we see something like that?"

Drew stared at him.

Tommy went on, as serious as Shane had ever seen him. "A couple of years ago, when I was a brand-new paramedic, we got this call about a boy who'd touched a live power line while walking home from school. He wasn't supposed to be on that street, taking the long way home, but he made two bad decisions that ended his life."

"That wasn't your fault," Drew pointed out.

"No. But that call ended up being my very first attempt at performing CPR on an actual victim." Tommy's voice grew husky, his blue eyes bleak at the memory. "I'll never forget the feeling of his chest under my hands, the blank look on his face. I had his life in my hands, and I couldn't save him. It doesn't matter that it wasn't my fault. That boy's death is something I'll have to cope with for the rest of my life."

Bless Tommy. Shane could've kissed him.

Drew studied his tennis shoes. "I get it."

"Do you? I sure hope so. Every decision a person makes affects someone else eventually. I can't tell you how many people I've seen at the end of their road because of bad choices. They all hurt not just emergency workers, but the countless loved ones they leave behind."

"I never thought of it like that before." The boy met his eyes again. "I guess you won't want me staying at your house anymore, and I don't blame you."

The other man gave him a smile. "Hey, my lecture aside, I'm still pretty young myself." Drew snorted at that as he went on. "Seriously, I'm a big kid at heart. Once is a mistake, and you've promised it won't happen again, so we're cool."

"Really?"

"Yeah."

"Thanks, Tommy."

Shane rose and gestured toward the bedrooms. "Go get your stuff together so we can get out of their hair."

His brother-in-law stepped in, clamping a hand on Drew's shoulder. "I don't want to end our visit on that note. Why don't you let him hang with me for a while? I was about to get up, fetch my fishing pole, and go down to the bank to see what I can catch, if Drew wants to join me."

"Do you mind? Please?"

He was about to say no, but the boy suddenly seemed excited, despite his lack of sleep and all the drama. Tommy was a good role model, and God knows Drew needed as many of those as he could get. And this would show the boy that the man truly had forgiven him for the stunt he'd pulled in sneaking out. "I guess that would be all right. As long as you send him home the second he wears out his welcome."

Tommy laughed. "I doubt that'll be a problem. Go on. We're good."

He turned to Drew. "I do want you back this afternoon so we can talk about when you and Ty are going to start your repair work."

"Yes, sir."

Well, that was more like it. As he pulled out of the drive to return to his own place next door, he couldn't help but worry about Drew. Despite everyone's support, the boy was lost. He'd prayed love and firm guidance would be enough. Now he wasn't so sure.

One thing he *was* sure of—Ty Eastlake's father was getting a visit from him very soon. Shane smelled a big rat.

And, eventually, he'd make it squeal.

7

He'd been awakened so damned early, Shane flopped on his bed the minute he got home around seven and immediately fell into a deep sleep.

When he woke up later that morning, he was disoriented and not much better rested than before. His dreams had been strange and disturbing. He had one where he'd been running, but he couldn't see what was behind him. He just knew he couldn't let the beast catch him, or he was dead.

He hated nightmares. He always wondered if they meant something prophetic, or if they were just the product of a brain that ran in fast-forward all the time, unable to rest even in sleep. Whatever the cause, he felt off-kilter.

A cup of coffee helped regain some of his equilibrium. A second cup while reading the morning paper and he was approaching human. He could pay a visit to Carl Eastlake now and hold his own. Briefly, he thought about taking Chris with him, but that would probably tip off the man that he was being watched. No, best to keep the visit from one father to another. Even though the bastard was a joke of a human being, much less a dad.

But it would give Shane the opportunity to glimpse the man's private space. Something the police hadn't been able to do before on their brief visits, at least not out of uniform, as a regular citizen. There had been plenty of official visits, though, with the police called by neighbors to break up domestic disturbances where Carl had been hitting his son, screaming at him day and night. A few had resulted in arrests, but not for battery, since the boy wouldn't speak against his dad. No, the busts had been for public intoxication, minor possession of controlled substances, petty stuff. Nothing that kept him in jail for very long. The police knew he was into bigger shit; they just hadn't been able to catch him. There wasn't enough to hand over to the detectives in Shane's unit to even begin to make a case.

Punching the address into his GPS, Shane set off for Eastlake's place. It wasn't hard to find—all he had to do was look for the mangiest, most weed-choked yard in the neighborhood and he was there. As he pulled up and parked at the curb, he grimaced. There was no sidewalk, and the dead brown weeds were thigh high. If it wasn't the middle of winter, he'd probably end up with chiggers and ticks all over him. Hell, he might, anyway.

"Great."

Wading through the mess, he stepped onto the front porch and hoped it would hold his weight. By some miracle it did, and he knocked, since the bell was broken. He waited for a couple of minutes and knocked again. When there was no response, he turned and stepped off the porch, deciding to have a look around the back of the house.

The driveway, and that was using the term loosely,

was rutted and muddy, more weeds poking valiantly between the tire grooves. A detached garage was out back, so he headed there and wasn't surprised to see the big, shiny new Escalade Drew had mentioned parked inside. So, the bastard was home and was either sleeping or ignoring Shane. He was betting on the second option. Which meant he was likely being watched.

"Hello? Mr. Eastlake?"

Acting as though he wasn't snooping, he made a show of looking for the man, calling out his name occasionally while scoping out the place. The garage was the typical jumble of auto parts, paint, tools, and a lawnmower and cleaning supplies that had obviously never been called upon to serve their purpose. Nothing stood out as a red flag, but then, he hadn't exactly expected to find bags of cocaine lying around in the open.

"Hello?"

The backyard wasn't much of one. Half the fence was gone, and the one poor tree looked dead. Again he wondered why the hell Drew was hanging out with this kid, Ty. What was he getting out of this friendship? Nothing positive so far.

"Can I help you?"

Turning around, he pasted on a friendly smile. "Oh, hey. You must be Mr. Eastlake." Moving forward, he extended his hand. As the man grasped it with a hand that couldn't have seen a bar of soap in a week, Shane vowed to douse his own with bleach at the first opportunity. "I'm Shane Ford, Drew's guardian."

In a glance, he took in an older version of Ty, without the black hair dye. The man was about four inches shorter than Shane and wiry. His shoulder-length hair was dark brown and streaked with premature gray from presumed hard living. His jeans and T-shirt hung off his frame, but for all that, he didn't look weak.

He appeared mean and tough, like a half-starved Doberman.

The man dropped his hand, giving him a blank look. And didn't return his smile. "Who?"

"Drew, from the high school," he said, carefully avoiding the boy's last name. "Our boys seem to have become friends, and they got into some trouble last night."

Eastlake's expression cleared. "Oh yeah. Ty mentioned once that he had a new friend, but I haven't met him. I'm not home much."

You don't say. He was glad, though, that the man didn't appear to know who exactly Drew was. "Oh. Well, I just thought I'd come over and introduce myself, since Drew can't stop talking about Ty." Jesus, he sounded like the president of the PTA. "And I wanted to find out when you think is a good time for them to start on the painting they need to do for the man whose barn and house they tagged."

He was careful not to mention Johnson by name. Wouldn't do any good to put Eastlake on alert. *Remember, you're a dad, not a cop.*

Eastlake peered at him, scratching his chin as though observing a strange species of father—one who gave a damn. "Beats the hell out of me," he said with a shrug. "I don't care if they do it or not. Johnson's an asshole."

"But if they don't, he'll press charges."

He chuckled at that, then spit on the grass. "Nah, he won't. He knows I'd kick his fuckin' ass."

"So he's a friend of yours?" he asked, pretending ignorance.

"Wouldn't call him that, exactly. More like an acquaintance who doesn't want to screw with me."

"Is that so? I'll bet he knows who's boss." Shane chuckled as though commiserating with the prick when what he wanted to do was punch him in the face. The man actually smiled at that, so he played it up a bit more. "In any case, my boy could use the practice with that brush arm so I can put his lazy butt to work at home next. If you want yours to do the same, I'd be glad to give them a ride out there and back until they're finished."

"You know, that's a good idea you got there. The place could use a fresh coat of paint. I'll take you up on that, Ford."

Paint, hell. It could use a bulldozer.

"Great. I figure they can work after school this week and this coming weekend. Give them something to do besides get in our hair. Right?"

"You bet." Eastlake waved a hand in dismissal. "Pick the kid up whenever, I don't care. He gives you any lip, just remind him what'll happen if daddy gets pissed off."

Bastard. "Sure thing. Nice talking to you."

The man grunted and turned back to the house. Shane wondered as he returned to his truck whether Ty was inside, nursing the effects of *What Happens When Daddy Gets Pissed Off*, and it made him see red.

He was cursing as he pulled away. Sooner or later Eastlake would get what he had coming.

Shane hoped he'd be around when that happened.

Daisy sat at her desk, reviewing case files of the juveniles she was currently working with. Or trying to, anyway.

It was only Monday, and her concentration was shot. She had a sexy cowboy of a cop to thank for that, once again. She hadn't really come to terms with the first time he'd screwed her over—in every sense—and she'd gone and fallen for his smooth talking again.

She was more than a little angry with herself, too. Sure, his sad story had touched her. Who could hear of his parents' deaths and how he had to take care of Shea in the aftermath without understanding where he was coming from? He didn't want responsibility for anyone but himself, and who could blame him?

There was Drew now, though, and while she knew Shane loved the boy, he couldn't possibly want to take on a relationship with Daisy, or any woman, on top of that. The man's fatal flaw was that he was a serial bachelor.

Except now he was chasing after her like a hound dog on a scent. The first time he'd turned on the charm months ago, she'd lapped the attention, and *him*, like cream. Then he'd broken her heart and sent her reeling. And damned if she hadn't fallen right back into bed with him at the first crook of his finger!

"I'm an idiot," she muttered.

But a sexually satisfied one.

Opening another file, she attempted to keep the moodiness off her face. Unlike Shane and a couple of the other senior detectives, peons like Daisy were assigned a desk out in the main room among all the other desks. When you worked with people every day, you learned how to read their moods, and these guys were like vultures. They'd pick her clean in seconds if they smelled blood.

She was managing her calm facade pretty well until she heard a familiar, hated whine of a voice—and Shane's answering laugh. Her fingers tightened on her file as she looked up.

Shane was in his office, leaning against his desk as he smiled at something Leslie Meyers was saying. Leslie was a uniformed officer who'd worked for the department for a long time. She was short, redheaded, fit, and good-looking enough—thanks to a nip and tuck job that removed a few years from her face. But every time she laughed, Daisy thought a goat had somehow found its way into the station.

The female officer leaned toward him, laying a hand on his arm as they yukked it up. Leslie trailed a finger down his chest playfully, and Daisy started to feel more than a little homicidal. A few seconds later, the woman winked and sauntered out.

"It's a date!" she called, making certain the entire squad room heard. Or probably just Daisy, if the smirk she shot in her direction was any clue.

Daisy fumed silently, glaring back. *A date? What the hell?*

Leslie made a point to walk by her desk, and paused. "How's kiddie patrol, Daisy Duke?"

She gave the woman a sweet smile. "Same as slut patrol is for you, Leslie Botox."

The cop's mouth dropped open. That was mean, but the woman deserved it. She walked around the department like she ruled the roost, and many of the guys who hadn't slept with her were intimidated by her. *Not me, bitch.* Everyone knew that if you called Daisy by that hateful nickname, the gloves were off.

The other woman quickly composed herself, though her cheeks sported red flags. "Men appreciate a woman who takes care of herself. Especially Shane."

Daisy lowered her voice in a conspiratorial manner and winked. "Oh, I know."

A flash of anger went across Leslie's face; then she recovered, snorting. "Right. Gotta go. I have *real* work to do—before I have dinner and a nightcap with a certain hot detective. Guess he's wanting a repeat performance, and I can't wait."

As she strutted away, Daisy wanted to tear off her head. Then Shane's balls. *Dinner? Nightcap? Repeat performance?*

Shane chose that unfortunate moment to leave his office and appear at her desk with a smile on his face. "Hey, sugar. I really enjoyed Saturday ni—"

"As much as you're going to love *dinner* with Leslie?" she asked coolly.

His smiled faded. "What?"

"Dinner. You know, that thing a man and a woman do when he's feeding you a total line of bullshit to go with dessert?"

"What are you talking about?"

"Don't play dumb with me," she hissed. "Have you or have you not slept with that ho?"

"Whoa! Lower your voice," he said, glancing around. The few officers around were studiously pretending not to listen. "What's gotten into you? Did she say something to you?"

She stared at him. "Nice work, Detective. Of course she said something! You have a lot of nerve. You know that?"

"What do you mean?" To his credit, he appeared at a loss.

Gathering her purse from the floor, she stood. "After Saturday, I had hopes that you'd change, that things would be different. Then I told myself how stupid I was, and it turns out I was right—I'm a moron. I come running every time you beckon, and yet you still can't let your poodles off their leashes."

"Leslie?" he asked, looking dumbfounded. "She's not my poodle, or my anything else! I mean, yes, a couple of years ago we— we—" He broke off at her murderous glare. "Well, that doesn't matter. The point is, I'm not interested in her!"

"Then why is she gloating that you're taking her out? I believe a nightcap and a repeat performance came up." *I will not throttle him.*

"It's lunch, not dinner!"

She could tell that the instant it left his mouth, he knew that was precisely the wrong thing to say. He stammered as she stabbed his chest with one fingernail.

"You know what? Fuck you, Shane! Fuck you!"

"Wait! It's not what you think!"

As she swept past, the others were done pretending not to stare. They goggled openly, glancing between the woman who'd dressed down the golden boy of the department, and Golden Boy himself. Let them—she didn't give a crap!

As she stalked past Chris and Taylor she heard a snippet of conversation.

"You owe me twenty bucks."

"Twenty more says they make up."

"You're on!"

Fuckers. Every one of them. She heard Shane call out again for her to hold up, but she kept going. Where, she didn't know or care. Maybe she'd swing by the high school, check on a few of her juvies. Look in on Drew while she was at it, make sure he was in attendance and behaving himself.

She cared about that boy, even if she was never destined to be with his guardian. That thought hurt badly, but she wouldn't try to change any man. He had to want to be with her, and he must be faithful. That was a deal breaker. She didn't deserve less than what her own parents had—a solid marriage of almost thirty years.

Trust. Dedication. Love.

Daisy Callahan didn't cling to any man. She refused to be *that* girl.

And she refused to shed another tear over that man. Really.

Shane stared after Daisy, mouth open.

"You're gonna let the flies in," Chris said. "You look shocked, though I can't imagine why. Man, you really know how to screw things up with her, don't you?"

"What did I do?" He was completely baffled. "She's acting like she's jealous of Leslie."

"You think?" Taylor snorted. "You banged Leslie, man."

"Two years ago!"

"That don't matter to women. Especially when they've got their claws out and their sights on the same guy."

"But Leslie's not interested in me," he insisted. "She

just asked me to be on the committee for the police department ball this spring, and I told her I wasn't sure I wanted to put in the time."

Chris smirked. "Let me guess. She offered to give you the deets over lunch."

"Well, yeah. Except she suggested dinner first, but I said lunch because that felt too much like a date." He frowned. "Why is that a big deal?"

Both of his friends laughed, and his cousin smacked Shane in the side of the head. "Because, you big dumbass, she doesn't give a rat's hairy ass if you join the committee! She's trying to get into your jock again!"

"No way."

"He's hopeless," Taylor said.

Chris finally looked sympathetic. "Cuz, it's a female thing. They toss out a line and use ordinary excuses, like meeting about the policeman's ball, to reel you in. The fact that you were either stupid enough to fall for it or insensitive enough not to care told Daisy that she can't trust you."

"What? That's crazy," he protested. "I've never cheated on a woman in my life! I can't help the mean little games they play with each other."

"Sure you can, by being aware and not falling for them."

He thought about that. Dammit, the guys were right. Leslie had been after him for a while now, wanting another round. And he'd handed her the ammunition to piss Daisy right the hell off. "Shit. What should I do?"

Chris propped his feet up. "Cancel this lunch with Leslie and tell her to find someone else for the committee, pronto. Then go to Daisy and beg. If you really want her, that is."

With a sigh, he went back to his office and buried his face in his hands. He'd laugh if it wasn't so damned sad. When he'd opened up to Daisy on Saturday night, he'd thought she had understood him. He'd never told a woman some of the painful things he'd shared with her about his family and their losses. How he felt. Wasn't that what women wanted? Truth and sharing from their lover?

He'd done that and she still didn't trust him. Disappointment squeezed his chest. He didn't know what to do other than what Chris suggested. He'd keep trying because Daisy was worth the fight. He'd hurt her once, and it seemed she wasn't going for a second round of heartache so easily, no matter how good in bed they were.

He'd just have to make sure she knew, once and for all, that he wouldn't break her heart again. Because that would be the same as breaking his, too.

Carl pulled his ride into Johnson's yard and shut off the ignition. The prick had better be home, because they had things to discuss.

Climbing out of his SUV, he strode to the front porch, glancing around. All was quiet out here, but that was about to change. On the porch he knocked and waited.

The door swung open, and the man stood staring at him balefully. "Carl. Whatcha want?"

"What do I want? What do you think I want, you moron?" Pushing past the man, he stomped into the living room. Frustrated, he spun to face his partner. "Has the product been moved?"

"No. Why?"

He pinched the bridge of his nose and counted to ten. "Because you got two nosy teenage boys on their way out here this afternoon to paint the barn! And what's *in* the fucking barn, stupid?"

"Don't bitch at me, Carl! It's your fault that useless little sperm deposit of yours came snooping around here in the first pl—"

Grabbing Frank by the front of his shirt, Carl walked him backward and slammed him into the wall, shaking the framed pictures there. "My boy was defendin' his daddy like he ought. Which he wouldn't have been forced to do if you could keep your mouth shut and do as I say. You dis him again and I'll gut your fat fucking carcass from your dick to your neck. Got it?"

"Yeah," he whispered. "Sorry."

"You are sorry, that's for sure." With a last shove, he let the other man go. "Get that shit moved, and do it fast. I don't care where you put it, just do it. Let me know when it's done, and give me the new location."

"You're not gonna help me? This is your operation!"

"That's right, I'm the boss. And you're the lab rat, so get movin'. Call Irvin if you need a hand."

With a last glare, Carl stomped from the house. Johnson was getting to be too much trouble. If he kept on, he'd end up right where Holstead had.

In a ditch with a hole in his head.

8

Daisy walked through the halls at the high school, dodging students rushing from one class to another, plus the ones hanging in groups, clogging the flow of foot traffic.

The place hadn't changed much. Just the hairstyles and the technology. It was familiar, yet made her feel old at the same time.

The office had told her this was Drew's lunch period, so she headed for the cafeteria. The big dining area was packed, and it was hard to tell if he was there or not. So she went down every aisle of the long tables, scanning each kid. No Drew, and she was starting to get worried when she glanced out the wall of windows to her left and spotted a familiar figure hunched over a picnic table in the outside commons area.

As she moved to the door leading outside, she saw that Drew was alone, the table he'd chosen off in a corner by itself. She hated to see him isolate himself this way. He was staring at the table, head down, the picture of misery. As she approached, a tall brown-haired boy walked up to him.

"Hey, why don't you come sit with us? Or are you too good to be seen with us?"

Daisy recognized it for the invite it was, even if it was thrown out like a challenge.

"Fuck off, Alan." Drew didn't even look up.

"Dude, you're a head case. You'll hang with that creep-azoid, but not us? Whatever, man."

The boy returned to his table and said something, making the others laugh. Drew folded in even more, if possible. Daisy slid onto the bench opposite him and rested her arms on the table.

"Rough day?"

"How'd you guess?" At least he raised his head, giving her his attention. "Shane send you here to make sure I'm being a good little scout?"

"No, he didn't send me. Doesn't even know I'm here." At his expression of disbelief, her lips curved up. "It's true. Not *every* adult was put on the earth for the sole purpose of giving Drew a hard time."

"There's a news flash." He eyed her warily. "So, why are you here?"

"I just wanted to see how you're doing. Why aren't you eating lunch?"

"Not hungry."

"You should eat something."

"Why? Are you the health police, too?"

"I just care about you, that's all."

Drew sneered at her. "You have the hots for Shane and you think getting close to me will help you snag him—that's what I think."

Her brows shot up. "That's pretty cynical. You don't believe anyone can like you simply for who you are?"

"Nobody ever has before," he snapped. "Why should anyone start now?"

"Maybe if you open your eyes and look around, you'll find plenty of people who'd like to get to know the real you, if only you'd give them a chance."

He rolled his eyes. "Like who?"

"That boy who invited you to sit with him and his friends, for one. Why not give new friends a try?"

"Oh, I don't know," Drew replied sarcastically. "Maybe because that same guy gave me all kinds of shit my very first day here, called me a faggot. And he hasn't left me alone since."

"You know what I think?"

"I'm sure you'll tell me."

"I think he wants to get to know you. I think he and his friends were just feeling you out, trying to get your attention. Why not say yes the next time they ask? Or better yet, just go over and sit with them."

He was silent for a long moment, mulling that over.

"I don't want people looking at me like I'm a freak, or worse, pitying me because of what happened to my dad."

"So don't accept their pity. If they try that, give it right back to them." He sat up, interested. "Everyone has a story, Drew. Many of your peers are going through a rough time because of all sorts of issues. You're Drew Cooper, your own person, and you don't have to answer to them or justify anyone's choices but yours. Hold your head up when people speak to you, and be confident. Be honest. You'll be surprised by the positive responses you get."

"That's a nice speech."

"It's the truth."

The bell rang just then, and the teen got up from the table. "That's my cue. Don't want to be even a second late, considering."

She stood, too. "Very true."

He eyed her, posture tense. "See you around, I guess."

Before he could leave, she put a hand on his arm. "I care about you," she reiterated. "If you ever need to talk, I'm a phone call away."

"Sure," he said awkwardly, glancing toward the doors. He appeared ready to make a break for it. "I've got to go."

The boy left, and she stared after him, worried. Drew was a great kid, but he was struggling. Even if she and Shane were done, she wouldn't desert him.

How to avoid his sexy guardian, however, was going to be almost impossible.

Drew rode in the truck between Shane and Ty, casting furtive glances at his friend. There were bruises on his left arm and a matching one on his jaw. Shane had noticed, too.

"What happened to your arm and your face, Ty?"

"Fell down the stairs."

"That's not possible."

That earned the cop a startled look. "How would you know?"

"I was at your house yesterday. I dropped by there to speak to your dad about picking you guys up for the repair job." He paused. "Your house is one story. It does not have any stairs inside."

"Doesn't have much of a dad, either."

After that, the ride was silent and tense. Drew knew how Shane hated to give up on someone he didn't know how to help. Didn't matter if he actually liked that person or not—that was how Shane was wired. He caught criminals and rescued people for a living. It was kind of cool, the guy being a real-life hero. Drew loved his dad, but . . .

Nobody ever died of not watching football.

He hated comparing the two men, even in the privacy of his mind. But Shane was a stand-up guy, and he didn't get a lot of recognition for what he did. What you saw was what you got. Shane was kind of awesome.

Most of the time. Not that Drew was about to admit it.

All too soon, the truck pulled into Frank Johnson's driveway. The man ambled outside to meet them, a smirk on his face. God, this was going to suck.

"You got your cell phone?" Shane asked.

Drew patted his pocket. "Got it."

"Call me if you boys need anything." The way he eyed Johnson as he said it told Drew he didn't trust the man one bit.

"We will."

"I'll pick you both up around seven."

"Can't come fast enough," Drew muttered.

Shane let them off, waved at Johnson, and drove away. It might be childish, but he wished Shane had stayed. He didn't want him and Ty to be alone with Johnson.

In the end, he needn't have worried. The man took them to the back side of the barn, where he'd set out the supplies they'd need to paint.

"Here you go. Need anything, holler."

Then he was gone. Drew doubted they'd see him again—unless it was on the porch with a beer in his hand.

"How the hell do we start?" Ty asked, eyeing the materials as though they were an ancient mystery waiting to be deciphered.

"Beats me, but it can't be that hard." He pointed. "Rollers, paint. Dip and repeat. How tough can that be?"

An hour later, he regretted those words. His shoulders and neck were killing him from holding the roller on the rod high above his head to spread the paint. His arms were about to fall off. And still two hours to go!

"Damn, this blows," Ty said.

"Tagging was your idea, remember?" He cut his friend a filthy look.

"Never again."

"What, is that regret I hear?" he teased. "Ty Eastlake is actually sorry he did something bad?"

"Nope, just sorry I got caught."

They laughed. Drew lowered his arms and rolled his shoulders. "Let's take a break. I've got sodas in my backpack."

"Dude, you rock!"

Setting their rollers aside, they found a grassy spot and sat. Drew fished in his pack and brought out two Cokes. "Brought something else, too." Pulling out two ham sandwiches and two bags of sour cream and onion potato chips, he tossed one of each to Ty.

The boy tore into his bag and dove in, crunching. "Thanks, man. I'm starving."

"No prob. Shane bought them for us."

The boys ate and sipped their sodas for a few minutes.

"Your cop seems okay."

"Yeah. He's cool."

"Wish my dad was more like him."

That was the most honest statement he'd ever heard Ty make. He eyed his friend. "Why weren't you at school today? Because he hit you?"

The other boy shrugged. "Doesn't matter."

Something else occurred to him. "You must be sore after getting knocked around like that. I can take over the painting for today if you want."

"Nah, it's not so bad. Besides, one of these days I'll be big enough to hit back. Then it won't be a problem anymore."

Drew wasn't so sure that was the answer, but he said nothing. He didn't have to endure Ty's life. Who's to say what he'd do?

As they ate, Drew could've sworn he caught a whiff of something. Frowning, he sniffed his sandwich, but it was fine. The odor tugged at his memory, and he realized it was the same one he'd smelled the night they'd tagged the barn.

"You smell that?"

"What?"

"A weird smell. Kind of like weed, but not."

His friend sniffed a few times. "Yeah. Wonder what it is?"

"I dunno. But I was thinking it sure doesn't smell like animals. Why would a guy who's not keeping animals have such a nice barn?"

"Come to think of it, you're right. There's not a single cow or horse to be seen." He studied the barn. "Wanna look?"

"No. That's how we got in trouble before."

"Then why'd you bother to bring it up?" Polishing off

the rest of his meal, Ty stood. "Come on, let's take a quick look. This time we're supposed to be here, remember?"

"Outside the barn, not inside."

"He didn't say we couldn't stretch our legs, right?"

The guy was relentless. Ty wandered casually toward the barn. With a sigh, Drew stuffed the remains of their food into his backpack and tagged along. One day, the spaz was going to get them into a bigger mess than they could get out of.

Ty walked to the end of the barn where the two large double doors were located. Of course, they were clearly visible from the house, and Drew had no doubt Johnson was watching them even now. Probably waiting to drop on them like a snake from a tree branch the second they screwed up again.

Pushing hard, Ty slid the door open just enough to let them in. Once they were inside, Drew saw why the owner wasn't too concerned about their presence. The place was pretty much empty, though not quite.

"Bummer," he said to the other boy. "Nothing but a few tools and some junk."

"It does stink like ass, though." Ty wrinkled his nose. "What the hell has he been doing in here? Burning a combination of weed, rubber, and turds?"

"Seriously."

They drifted apart, examining what little junk there was. Drew was about to leave when something caught his eye. There was a large bare spot at the far end of the barn where some items had been sitting. There were impressions in the dirt, then scrape marks, as though whatever had been there was dragged out through the far doors. Nothing interesting.

"This was a bust," Drew told his friend. "Let's get out of here before we choke."

They went back to their job, and managed to get almost the entire back wall painted before Shane came to get them. Drew started to mention the odd stink, but they got to talking about Shane's day and he eventually blew it off.

Wasn't like it was all that important, anyway.

It turned out that the boys got the painting done during the week. Unfortunately, Shane knew it was time to face an even worse task.

He needed to take Drew to pack his stuff from the mansion.

It was going to be a horrible, emotional task for both of them, but it had to be done. There wasn't any sense in putting it off any longer. Shane let Drew sleep until nine, then knocked on his door. When there was no answer, he opened the door and saw the boy sound asleep, curled on his side.

"Drew?" A muffled response was his only answer. He went over and touched the boy's shoulder. "Hey, buddy, rise and shine."

"Ugh."

He smiled a little. "Get up, we've got some things to do today."

"Go away, Shane."

"I will, soon as you get up."

With that, the teen sat up, peering at him blearily and scowling. "I'm up already. Jeez." He yawned. "What the heck's so important, man? It's Saturday!"

"Come eat breakfast, and I'll tell you."

"Breakfast?" A glimmer of interest became a smile. "I smell bacon."

"The universal lure for sleepy teens everywhere. I've got pancakes, too. Up you go."

"Oh. Well, in that case . . ."

Chuckling, he left the room to set breakfast on the table. In less than two minutes, Drew came padding out in his bare feet, wearing sleep pants and a T-shirt. For one second, Shane remembered the tiny little sprout he'd been so long ago, coming into Shane's parents' kitchen just this way, smile on his face, ready for the pancakes Shane's mom used to make for them. It was a tradition Shane had kept up when his folks were gone.

"Looks great!" The boy plopped down and began to fork his breakfast onto his plate.

"Your favorite."

They tucked into the meal, slathering on butter and using plenty of syrup. As they started eating, Drew gave him a sad smile.

"Dad always loved coming over when you cooked. He craved homemade stuff, but he wasn't a very good cook."

"I remember." He was glad the boy could mention his dad without falling apart. "I'll never forget when he set my kitchen on fire. I never let him near it again."

"I know! Even I knew not to throw water on a grease fire." His smile was wistful, his eyes shiny. "I wish he were here."

"Me too, kiddo." Might as well yank off the bandage. "That sort of brings me to what we need to do today. I think it's time to go get the rest of your belongings."

He wished he could erase the pain from Drew's face.

The boy sucked in a sharp breath and nodded. "No sense in putting it off," he said. His voice quavered and he was obviously struggling to be brave.

God, give them the strength to get through this.

"I've got plenty of boxes and I rented a small enclosed trailer, so I think we'll have room for whatever you want to bring back. The rest, the stuff you don't want, I'll have someone take care of donating it."

"Okay," he said quietly. "I don't need much except my laptop, CDs, and clothes. Oh, my stereo for my room. It's not very big."

That reminded Shane that he'd borrowed the boy's laptop the night Brad died. He'd looked through it and found nothing but the usual social teenage stuff. "I already have your laptop. I brought it the night you came to stay here."

"Translation, the cop in you couldn't help but snoop." The teen looked annoyed.

"Guilty. But the better word is *investigated*. I'll give it back to you when we're done this afternoon."

Drew pushed his plate away. "Sure. It's not like I've missed it, anyway. I'm going to take a shower."

"All right."

After finishing the last of his breakfast, Shane rose and began to clear the dishes. Dare he hope things were improving with him and Drew? Now, if he could fix his relationship with Daisy as easily. It seemed her bullshit meter was fine-tuned these days, and he'd played a big role in that. He could hardly blame her, but damn. How did he convince her he was sincere when he was the reason she was gun-shy?

He loaded the dishwasher, then washed up the skillets and utensils. Once he was finished, he went and parked on his easy chair and dialed Daisy—for about the fifth time that week. He was fast reaching stalker status. Wouldn't that be a fun write-up if she complained to the captain?

The message signal beeped and he actually left one this time, injecting as much sincerity into his tone as he could. "Hey, it's Shane. I know you don't want to speak to me, and, hell, I don't blame you. Please give me a chance to prove I'm not the same jerk who hurt you before." He paused.

"I wasn't going out with Leslie, and that's the truth. She asked me to be on the policeman's ball committee, but I turned her down *without* meeting her for lunch. Just FYI. Anyhow, please call me." Punching the OFF button, he slumped. "Shit."

"Trouble with Daisy?" Drew asked, walking into the room. He'd showered and dressed in his jeans and a flannel shirt.

"You could say that. She thought I was going out with another woman, and now she won't speak to me."

Drew winced. "Ouch. It's not true. Right?"

"No. I'm not the least bit interested in anyone else. I haven't even dated anyone since Daisy and I were, um, together before."

The teen grinned. "Since you had wild monkey sex, you mean."

"None of your business, kid. Haven't we been through this?"

"Yeah, okay. Don't get bent. So, what? She doesn't believe you about the other chick?"

"I don't know if it's that so much as she was already

having second thoughts, and the stunt the other woman pulled, making her think I was taking her out, just gave her the shove she needed to pull away."

"She got scared," he said wisely. "That blows."

Shane laughed in spite of himself. Teenagers had such a way of simplifying things. "Yes, it does."

"If it helps, I think she has the hots for you."

Shane's eyes widened. "What makes you say that?"

"She's been checking on me during my lunch this week, and she sort of asks about you a lot. Like, I don't think she realizes how often she mentions you. Keep after her, and she'll cave. If you want my opinion, she's making you suffer, but she wants to get caught."

"How did you get to be so smart?"

"I just am. So, we ready?"

"Yeah." Shane grabbed his keys off the kitchen counter. On their way out he locked up. "So, she's been visiting you?"

The boy nodded. "Every day. Yesterday she brought pizza for me and Ty."

"That's really great of her to do. You like her?"

Drew's expression clouded some. "Sure."

"The way you say that, you don't *sound* sure."

"I think she's making nice with me because she likes you—that's all."

He shook his head. "Daisy isn't that kind of person, son. She has a soft spot for kids, which is why she's good at her job."

"So, I'm just another *job* to her," the boy said bitterly.

"That's not what I meant," he said, frowning. "You're more than that to her. In fact, she's told me how much she cares about you. She truly likes you."

Following him to the truck, Drew fell silent on the subject. Shane bit back a sigh and let it go for now. He couldn't force the boy to accept Daisy. Did Drew fear that she would replace Drew in his affections? That wasn't going to happen. Hopefully, the boy would come around.

They made good time getting to the mansion. Shane pulled around back and went in first, making certain the study door was closed before letting Drew come in and go upstairs. No need to be reminded of the room where he'd found his dad.

Shane went into the kitchen and looked around. There wasn't much in the way of perishables in the fridge. The cooking pans and utensils looked barely used. He decided he'd simply hire someone to pack up the kitchen and sell the furniture and anything else Drew didn't want. The majority of Brad's personal things could wait until another day. He knew Drew would want his dad's football trophies and mementos. Especially his two Super Bowl rings.

Jesus. Is that all a man's life boiled down to—a bunch of keepsakes that could be stuffed into a drawer?

Shaking off the depressing thought, he walked upstairs with a few packing boxes in hand and found Drew folding clothes. Pitching in, he helped until they'd packed the contents of his closet, dresser drawers, and bathroom. The personal items were last, and they filled two boxes with those, not counting the stereo in the corner. Had he ever had this much crap as a kid? Probably so.

Two hours later, they had Drew's stuff loaded. Drew was standing uncertainly in the foyer, and Shane laid a hand on his shoulder. "Is there anything else you want to take? Maybe something of your dad's?"

"Actually, I'd like to take his Super Bowl rings and a few other things." He frowned. "I'm worried that some jerk's gonna break in and take all his stuff now that there's nobody living here full-time."

"I was thinking about those. Good idea. Let's just go ahead and get them so your mind will be at ease."

"They're in the study in a safe." He swallowed hard.

"I can get them if you don't want to go in," Shane said seriously.

"No, I need to. I want to look around."

He searched the boy's face for any sign that he wasn't ready. But he really did seem to need the closure. "Okay. But I'll go with you."

Crossing to the study doors, Shane opened them and stepped aside. Drew went in slowly, then stopped and looked around for a long moment. His eyes eventually found the spot on the floor where he'd discovered his dad, and his body shook.

"I felt so helpless," he whispered. "I didn't know what to do. But I tried. I called 911, did CPR forever. Everything I could. CPR doesn't always work the way it does in the movies, did you know that? I thought it should work. But it didn't."

Tears were streaming down the boy's face, and he wiped them away. He was still mourning, but it was goodbye, too. An end of a chapter for both of them.

"You did everything just right, Drew. But I think he was already gone, and nothing you did would've helped."

"That's what they told me, but it didn't seem real. It

felt wrong, like I'd stepped into somebody else's nightmare. I was supposed to wake up and find him there, happy and alive." He turned to face Shane. "He's not coming back."

"No, son. I'm sorry." Sweet heaven, the look on that boy's face.

Drew fell into his arms and cried. For the longest time they stood there, and this time the grief was different than before. This was the soft, bittersweet sorrow that was finally edging into acceptance. That period of realizing death was final, unchangeable. That their lives would go on, but they would never be the same.

Drew pulled back and used a tissue from the desk to wipe his eyes and blow his nose. Then he walked to the wall safe, punched in the digital code, and opened it. Then he removed a box and some papers. Shane had seen the rings before and knew they were in the box.

"I want his trophies, too."

Shane fetched another moving box, and they took every treasured item from Brad's office. When they were done, Drew took one last look around.

"I'm ready."

They pulled out of the gates that afternoon, changed in unfathomable ways.

And just maybe a little stronger than before.

Daisy was outside, working in the backyard, when she heard a vehicle pull into her driveway out front. Immediately she tensed, half-hoping it belonged to Shane. The other half dearly prayed it wasn't. She wasn't strong enough to withstand him in person. Not yet.

She walked around to the front and a wave of disappointment washed over her. Instead of Shane, his sister was getting out of her car. Shea smiled at her and started across the yard.

"Spring cleaning?" she asked, pointing at the rake in Daisy's hand.

"A little early, but yes. I've been pulling weeds and cleaning up the leaves and dead things from winter. March is around the bend, and I'm eager to plant flowers."

"Wait until after spring break. Otherwise we're bound to get one last cold snap that will kill them."

"Good advice. I'll probably wait until then, at least." She eyed the other woman. "But I have a feeling you didn't come here to discuss gardening."

"No. I dropped by to tell you that Tommy and I are having a cookout next weekend, since the weather is supposed to be sunny and warm, and we would love it if you would come."

Drat. She loved the couple and their friends, but . . . "Will Shane be there?"

"Most likely. Why?" She appeared completely innocent.

Daisy wasn't so sure. "I got kind of upset with him and haven't spoken with him this week."

"What did the idiot do now?" Shea asked. "I'll skin him alive!"

"He didn't really do anything," she admitted. "It's me. Guess you could say I got cold feet."

"That's understandable, knowing my brother the way I do." She looked like she had more to say, and she did. "But, honey, I've seen the way he is around you, how he talks about you. He's got his flaws, but I honestly believe he's totally gone over you."

"You really think so?" She bit her lip. "He's been calling all week, and this morning he left the sweetest message, but I'm not sure. He hurt me really bad before, and I don't want to be the dumb-ass who goes back for more and ends up crying again."

"I get that. Tommy and I had our issues, too. But I think if you give him one more chance, you won't be sorry." She cocked her head. "Let him stew another week, just to drive him bat-shit crazy with wanting you. Then come to our party and knock him for a loop."

Daisy grinned. "That sounds like a good plan."

"Then you'll come?"

"You bet. I wouldn't miss it." The two women hugged, and Daisy invited her inside. "Would you like to come in, have something to drink? It's Saturday afternoon, and I have rum and Coke. . . ."

"I'd love that." She giggled. "I don't have to be on shift at the hospital until Tuesday, and I think I'm in the mood to be just a bit naughty today."

"Great! Let's go."

In the kitchen, Daisy fished the rum from under the cabinet while Shea got Cokes from the fridge. In minutes they were seated in the living room, giggling over stories of Shane that would turn his sexy face beet red if he knew his sister was spilling them. They were having a pretty fun time, and then Daisy got another idea.

"Let's go dancing!"

"What? I'm a married woman! I don't dance very well, anyway."

"You don't have to dance. Just come. It'll be fun!"

"I don't know." The gleam in her eyes said different.

"I can tell you want to. If it'll make you feel better, call Tommy and ask if he cares."

"Well . . . okay," she said excitedly, and dug out her cell phone. "Where are we going? The Waterin' Hole?"

"No, that's basically just a bar with some pool tables. How about Boot Scootin', down by the river? They have live music and a big dance floor."

"Sounds good." Shea made the call, and after a brief conversation, she hung up. "He says that's fine with him, as long as we let him drop us off at the club if we're going to drink. He said call when we're ready to leave and he'll pick us up, then take you home. I need to go home and change before we go, so you can ride back there with me."

"Aww, how sweet!" It was, and Daisy couldn't help but be jealous. A little. She had known Tommy from high school, and at one time last year, Shea even thought Daisy and Tommy were dating. She was mistaken, though — Tommy was just a friend of hers, and had just been trying to make Shea jealous. It worked.

Daisy was glad she and Shea were friends now. A night out was just what the gals needed.

And for one night, she planned to forget all about a certain sexy cop.

9

Daisy and Shea visited for a while until it was time to get dressed, going easy on the rum and Cokes since they'd decided to go out. No sense in getting faced before they stepped out the door. Then Daisy took a shower to wash off from working outside, and dressed in her best jeans and green T-shirt with spangles on it to make her eyes pop. Her brown boots completed the outfit.

Instead of her purse, she simply took her house keys and a small black leather wallet that held her badge, license, and money. She opted to leave her gun at home, something cops rarely did, even off duty. But it hardly seemed like a good idea when going clubbing.

Daisy rode with Shea to her house so her friend could change into something appropriate. Tommy got a kick out of the ladies rebelling, going out on the town, and teased them the entire time about getting in trouble. As he dropped them near the door, he reminded them to call, and Shea gave him a kiss before driving off.

"You have one great guy there," Daisy said with a sigh.

"Isn't he a sweetie? Then again, he gets his guy time, too."

"What's he doing tonight?"

"Just hanging at the house. I think he was going to give a couple of his friends a call, see if they wanted to come over and have a few beers. He finally wore me down about getting a pool table, and he's been itching to try it out."

"See? It's just as well that I rescued you from having to listen to their BS all night." She winked at her friend.

"And keep them supplied in munchies. Without me there, they'll actually have to find the kitchen themselves."

In good spirits, they paid their cover charge and went inside. The place was large, with the promised big dance floor surrounded on three sides by bars and tables, and the stage on the fourth side, facing the crowd. A band was already warming up, and the crowd was gradually starting to arrive.

They headed to the bar and ordered a couple of drinks, then found a table near the dance floor. It had been a while since Daisy had been out to a nice bar like this one, mostly a country and western dance hall, and she sipped her drink while checking out the scenery. Mostly the tall, lean male variety.

And she wasn't as impressed as she used to be.

Glancing at Shea, she gestured to the male populace in general. "The eye candy is nice, but why doesn't it get my motor revving the way it used to?"

"Because you're already in lust with a hot guy who does it for you in every way?" Shea teased. "And you just might love him, too?"

"Damn! There's no *might* where that man is concerned," she grumbled. "I just don't have a clue what to do about it."

"Well, you can't shoot him and hide the body. And I guess simply forgetting about him is out, since we're here with a hundred eligible men and you can only think of him. So the question is what do you *want* to do about him?"

"I want to make him mine for keeps," she admitted.

"And the problem is?"

Her jaw dropped. "Seriously? Hellooo, the man dumped me after taking me for a couple of test drives! He has a string of female admirers a mile long, and every one of them wants back into his Levi's! I'm nothing but a notch on his bedpost."

"Is that really what you think?"

"I don't know. There's this cougar at work who's doing her best to get him back in the sack, and he claims he had no idea what she was after. I mean, come on. Nobody is that clueless!"

"Honey, he's a man," Shea replied, as though that in itself provided the explanation. But she explained, anyway. "They have filters in their brains that immediately delete any information deemed irrelevant to their essential needs at the moment. And this frequently gets them into trouble."

"While women overanalyze everything to the point of a nervous breakdown." She sighed. "It's a miracle people ever get together."

"Or remain together." She smiled at Daisy. "But something tells me you're going to give in to him and give him another chance."

"I shouldn't."

"Why? You don't believe he's learned his lesson about pushing you away? That he's basically honest?"

"I *want* to, but I don't want to get hurt."

"Nobody does. But if you don't trust somebody, it's going to be a long, lonely existence. Believe me. I nearly made that mistake, and I'm glad Tommy pushed me not to give up." Her eyes grew warm at the memory. "My life would be so different now, and not in a happy way."

"Oh, my God. Sugar-coma alert!"

Shea laughed. "Okay, no more philosophy. Let's just have a good time."

"I agree with the pretty lady," a masculine voice said. A large hand touched Daisy's shoulder. "Would you like to dance?"

Daisy turned to see a nice-looking cowboy hovering with a smile on his face. He seemed polite, and there was no reason to refuse. She *had* come out to dance, and it wasn't like she was being unfaithful to Shane. It irked her that she would even think that way.

"Sure, I'd like that."

Shea saluted her with her glass, and Daisy left her to take a turn or three around the floor with the nice cowboy. So what if he didn't turn her crank?

Dammit, it seemed only Shane could do that.

Shane was pretty well wiped out, and was sprawled in his easy chair, watching his favorite police drama—so what if the writers had the facts all wrong?—when his cell phone buzzed on the coffee table. Looking at the display, he saw it was Tommy. He almost let it go to voice mail, but then thought, *Why not?* It could be important.

"Hey, what's up?"

Tommy's cheerful voice sounded in his ear. "Just playing some pool and drinking some beer with a few of my old crew. Why don't you come on over and relax for a while?"

"Man, that's what I was already doing. Drew and I packed up his things at his house and brought them here, and it's been a bitch of an afternoon."

"Well, that's exactly why you should come! Bring the kid, too. The guys would love to see you both." Tommy paused, sensing his friend was on the fence. "Come on, big guy. Don't sit home all alone on a Saturday night like an old man, 'cause that's just freaking sad."

Jesus, the guy was right. And it might help take his mind off how very different tonight was than this same night one week ago.

"All right. I'll ask Drew, and if he wants to come, we'll be over in a few. He might not, though—" He broke off when he saw Drew standing in front of him mouthing, *Yes!* "Never mind, we're on the way."

"That's my man! See ya soon."

Hanging up, Shane gave the boy a half smile. "I thought you were tired."

"I was, but now I'm bored. It's, like, *way* lame to sit around on a Saturday night." This said like it was the end of the world.

"You sound like Tommy."

"That's who was on the phone?"

"Yep. Ready to go, then?"

He didn't have to ask twice. Shane smiled at the teen's exuberance when ten minutes ago he'd been moping in his room. Maybe a guys night out was what they needed.

The night was cool and it would've been a bit of a walk in the dark, so they drove down the road to Tommy and Shea's place. Before they were even out of the truck, Tommy was on the porch, waving them inside.

"Thank God for you, or Shane would be one big party pooper, huh?" Tommy slung an arm around Drew's shoulders, making the boy smile.

Seeing the kid happy was worth just about anything. Shane trailed them inside to the kitchen, where he found a couple of the firefighters from Tommy's former team at Station Five. Howard "Six-Pack" Paxton had taken over as captain when Sean Tanner had been promoted to battalion chief in January. Shane had first met Six-Pack when the firefighter was being terrorized by a stalker, and Shane had been assigned to work the case. The huge man was raiding the chips and dip and sipping a soda. Six-Pack didn't drink alcohol, but nobody cared. Shane thought that was admirable.

"Shane!" he called, moving forward to give him a one-armed hug. "Where have you been hiding?"

"Working, taking care of the place. The usual."

They all knew that was an understatement—his responsibilities now extended far beyond his norm. Of course, they were all wondering how the serial bachelor of Cheatham County was faring in his new role. Thankfully, no one mentioned Brad's death in front of Drew.

"How are Kat and the new baby?" Shane asked.

The captain beamed. "My wife is as beautiful as ever, and Ben is the smartest, most perfect little boy in the world. Not that I'm biased or anything."

"I'm glad to hear it."

Six-Pack merely smiled and turned to Drew. "I'm Howard, or you can call me Six-Pack, like most everyone else."

"I'm Drew," he said, suddenly looking a little shy. He was used to his dad's larger-than-life athlete friends, but these men were much different. They were real-life heroes, and he simply didn't know them.

"Good to meet you, Drew." Six-Pack gestured to a dark-haired man wearing glasses. "This is Zack Knight, my lieutenant at the fire station."

"Hi, Drew," Zack said warmly. "Welcome to the nuthouse. The rest of the guys are in the game room, shooting pool, and shooting even bigger bull."

Drew smiled at that and visibly relaxed. Shane figured the boy would be fine after all, but, then, how could he not be among this group? These were the finest men Shane knew, and he'd take a bullet for any of them. He had done exactly that, in fact, last year when Tommy got himself into a scrape with one of Jesse Rose's minions.

Shane turned to Zack. "And how's Cori and your new little one?" Last year had been busy for the men of Station Five.

"They're both doing great! I can't wait to get home to my women," he enthused. "And Evie is the smartest little girl in the world, so she's going to give Ben a run for his money someday."

"As if," Six-Pack snorted. "But she is cute."

"Speaking of, is Eve here?" Shane knew Cori and Zack had named their baby Evie after Eve Marshall, Zack's best friend and his teammate at the station.

"No, she and Sean had other plans tonight. But Clay and Julian are back there with a couple of guys from the Fire Marshal's office."

"Great, it'll be good to see them." He clapped a hand

on Drew's shoulder. "Come on, kid. Let's go see if we can whup some butts at pool."

Shane gratefully took a beer Tommy handed him, and then they all went back to the game room. A fairly competitive match was in session, with Julian Salvatore yelling as Clay Montana sank two balls at once.

"Dammit, you fucker! I'm gonna kick your skinny, lyin' ass! *I can't play pool*," he mocked in an exaggerated falsetto voice.

The other three howled with laughter, but the merriment was tempered when they spotted the teenager in their midst. "Oops, language check," Clay said with a smirk aimed at Julian.

The man glanced between Shane and Drew and gave them an apologetic smile. "Sorry, amigo. Didn't know we had kids in the house."

"Dude, I'm almost seventeen," Drew said in an affronted tone. "Besides, you think firefighters are bad? I grew up around football players."

And there it was, the elephant in the room. The others shifted uncomfortably, apparently not knowing how to respond. Shane was about to change the subject when Drew tackled it himself.

"Yeah, I'm Brad Cooper's son, and I'm proud of it. Now I'm Shane's son, too, so save your condolences." He gestured to the pool table. "So, who thinks they can beat me?"

Just like that, the ice was broken and they had a good time. To Shane's surprise, Drew was a pretty good player and held his own. He'd almost won one game and was well on the way to trouncing one of the guys from the Fire Marshal's office.

On his second beer, Shane asked Tommy, "Where's Shea? Tucked in the bedroom with a book, trying to ignore the noise?"

"Hardly." Tommy looked a bit uneasy for some reason. "She went out tonight."

"Out? Like, to dinner?"

"No, she went to Boot Scootin' with a friend." Tommy called out to Drew, "Nice shot!"

The man was trying to avoid the subject. Shane frowned. "Isn't that the country and western dance club on the river? Why the heck did she go there without you?"

"She and her friend wanted to kick up their heels, I guess. I'm not too worried, since I'm picking them up later."

"Who's the friend?"

"Jesus, Ford, don't you ever turn off the detective mode?"

Suddenly he knew. "She and Daisy went out, didn't they?" The man's sympathetic expression said it all. "Son of a bitch."

The idea of Daisy drinking and dancing the night away with anyone but him . . . God, it made him crazy! Mad enough to break someone's face. Preferably whoever she was laughing and partying with right now.

It disappointed him, too. She'd run so far from him that she was going out, searching for someone else? Was that it? The pain in his heart was so damned bad, he wanted to die.

He was honestly falling for Daisy, and he had no idea how to convince her.

Or whether there was any point in trying any longer.

*   *   *

Daisy returned to their table and to Shea, who hadn't danced to anything but line dances. It was sweet how her friend was so completely committed to Tommy that she wouldn't even entertain the idea of a harmless one-on-one turn with another man. Then again, Daisy would be, too, if she had a good reason waiting at home.

Every man she'd danced with tonight had come up short in comparison to Shane. It was damned annoying as hell. The guys were attractive, a couple of them jaw-droppingly gorgeous, but none of them lit her fire. Not a single one.

The situation was hopeless. She was officially ruined for any other man except her sexy cop. That really sucked.

A burst of raucous laughter got their attention just as Daisy sat down. The two of them glanced over at a table of guys who'd gotten progressively drunker as the night went on. Not in the way of good-natured boys out having a good time, but in a way that put all of Daisy's cop senses on alert. This was part of what was not fun about going clubbing—she was always an officer, no matter where she went.

The table she and Shea were watching was different than the others. Daisy had seen their kind all too often on patrol—guys who'd had a few too many and were getting loud. Their jokes were tinged with potty humor, and the tone was getting mean.

"Those jerks have obviously had enough," Shea said, wrinkling her nose in distaste.

"Too much. I think— Oh, crap, here comes one."

Damn, one of the jerks had caught them looking, and

from his swagger and inebriated smile, had gotten the wrong idea about why. The man wasn't very tall and was sort of average-looking with a bit of a beer gut and brown hair. He was maybe in his thirties. What wasn't average was the cruel hint to his mouth and the gleam in his eyes. It made her nervous, and she worked to keep her poker face.

"Hey, pretty ladies," he slurred. "How about a dance?" He looked to them both as if either one would do.

Charming. Not.

"I'm worn out," Daisy said. "Taking a break. But thanks for the offer."

"Me, too." Shea's smile was flat, a clear dismissal.

"Aw, come on," he wheedled, sidling up to the table and slinging an arm around Daisy's shoulders. "I'm short a dance partner. Let's go."

"No, but thanks." Her words were clipped, less polite now.

The man didn't take the refusal well. "I think you gals ought to loosen up and have some fun. Me and my boys will help you get that stick outta—"

Daisy shot to her feet and shoved him hard in the chest. "Fuck off."

The man goggled at her for a moment before he realized his buddies were hooting with laughter at his expense. His expression morphed into ugliness. "You bitch. Think you're better than me?"

"What the hell is going on here?" A big bouncer wearing a black T-shirt with the club's logo on it stood there, scowling at the man. "You again?"

"This loser doesn't know what the word *no* means," Daisy informed the bouncer.

"That's it—strike three. Get out and take those assholes with you." He jerked a thumb at the man's friends, who immediately began to moan about it being unfair. The group started to get loud, but three more bouncers joined the first one. All of them were huge, plenty big enough to kick ass and take names. That pretty much ended the confrontation. The original offender shot Daisy a venomous look as if his being ousted was all her fault, and then stalked off with his posse in tow.

"Sorry about that," the first bouncer said with a grimace. "We have so much trouble with that shithead, the management is about to bar him from coming back. They will for sure after this."

"It's no problem," Daisy assured him. "He's gone now. No harm done."

"Can I get you ladies a drink on the house to make up for the unpleasantness?"

Shea looked at Daisy. "We should probably go. It's getting late."

"Can I call a cab for you?"

"My husband is coming as soon as I call him, but thanks," Shea told him.

The bouncer nodded. "All right. But here, let me give you this." Digging in his jeans pocket, he fished out his wallet and removed a business card belonging to the club. Printed on it was a ticket for two free drinks. He gave them each one. "Just show this to the bartender next time you stop in, and they're on us. We don't put up with jerks like those—we want you to come back. Want me to walk you out and wait for your ride?"

"No, we're fine," Daisy said with a smile. She refrained from telling him she was a cop and could take care of herself. Too often men thought she was bragging or lying.

They thanked the bouncer and pocketed their cards. As they walked out under the awning, both of them shivered as the cold night air slid over their heated skin. Shivering, Shea took out her cell phone and made a brief call to her hubby, then hung up.

"He'll be here in a few. He's only had a couple of beers all night, so he's fine to drive."

"We could have cabbed it."

"He doesn't mind."

"He spoils you," Daisy teased.

"And I love letting him." Shea gave her a hug. "I had fun tonight."

"Me, too. I—"

A shout interrupted what she'd been about to say. Peering into the parking lot, she didn't see who'd made the noise. Then a scuffle caught her attention at the corner of the building. It wasn't as well lit over there, so it was hard to see, but it appeared that two men were getting into a fight.

"Shit," she muttered. "I'd better see what that's about."

Shea looked worried. "Let's tell that bouncer and let him deal with them."

"I've got this."

Daisy headed for the men, who were making a show of shoving each other, hurling insults. She walked faster, closing in on them, and then groaned when she recognized the jerk from the club as one of the men doing the pushing and cussing. Great.

"Hey, knock it off!" she called, going into cop mode. "That's enough!"

"Daisy—"

"Look who it is," the man sneered. "The stuck-up bitch wasn't good enough to talk to me, and now she's buttin' in our business."

"*She's* the reason we got thrown out," his friend accused, pointing at Daisy. Clearly he planned to take advantage and shift the blame. "It's her you should be mad at, Len, not me!"

"True." Len cocked his head at Daisy, stumbling to within a few feet of her. "I could be persuaded to forgive and forget, though."

"Don't come any closer," she warned. Angry drunks were unpredictable. "I think you boys should get a cab home and forget all about this place for a good long time."

Len shot an incredulous look at his friend and they both laughed. Len waved a hand at her. "She thinks we should shut up and go away. Is that what you heard?"

"Yep, 'bout right."

"I think I should shut *her* up, and I know just how. Come here, sweet thing, and let Len give you something productive to do with your mouth."

Moving faster than she'd given him credit for being capable of, he grabbed her arm and shoved her against the wall, pinning her against the brick with his body.

"Get off me!" she hissed, fumbling in her back pocket for the leather wallet. Dammit, she should have identified herself sooner. "I'm a—"

Just as she brought out the wallet, Len knocked her hand aside, causing her to lose her grip on it and sending it skittering on the pavement. Shea dove for it at the same time Daisy kneed her assailant in the groin and shoved him forcefully. He shouted and was sent off balance, stumbling backward. Unfortunately, the knee to his balls didn't hurt him—only sent his temper over the edge.

Len's friend egged him on with vulgar insults at Daisy, and Len lunged. Shea screeched as Len grabbed Daisy again. She gave him a punch to the ribs just as Shea yelled.

"Stop! She's a police officer!"

But the two were too far gone for reason. Daisy fell to the side, unbalanced by his weight, and the man hit the pavement with her. She winced as her palms scraped the concrete, and was about to push to her feet when she was wrapped around the waist with a beefy arm. She elbowed him in the stomach, and he released her with a vicious curse.

"Daisy! Look out!"

Again, she began to push up, and just had time to hear Shea yell before something hard smashed into the side of her head. Pain exploded through her skull, and she slumped to the ground, something wet and acrid flowing over her face.

"I'm calling the police!"

Then Shea's shouts were joined by others, and the world disappeared.

Shane hadn't wasted a second thinking about it when Tommy said the girls were ready to leave and asked if Shane wanted to ride along.

He wanted to see Daisy's face when he showed up with her ride. And he also wanted to find out if she'd had too good a time with some fast-talking cowboy. Yeah, he wasn't too proud to admit he was seething with jealousy.

If she'd hooked up with someone else, he'd lose his damned mind.

So he'd left Drew having fun playing pool with the guys who were still there, and headed out. Now he was nervous as well. What if she resented him butting in on her evening? What if she honestly didn't want to see him?

In just a few minutes, Tommy pulled his truck up next to the awning. The parking lot was still pretty full, the club in full swing. His friend frowned as he scanned the front.

"They were supposed to wait right here. I don't see them. Do you?"

"Not yet."

But then a movement ahead of them caught his eye. There appeared to be a fight going on in the shadows at the corner of the building, not quite out of sight. A chill slithered down his spine.

"Is that Shea?" he asked.

"What the fuck?" Tommy breathed. Putting the truck in gear, he sped to the corner. As he slid to a stop, they jumped out.

Shane jogged around the corner to see Shea yelling at two burly men who were apparently wasted. One was egging on the fight, and the other—

His gaze found the struggling pair on the ground at the very same moment the man found a beer bottle at hand. And smashed it into the side of Daisy's head. She went limp, and Shane's vision became a red haze.

In a few strides he caught her attacker in a flying tackle, taking him down. Straddling the man's bulk, he pulled back his fist and let it fly into the bastard's jaw, snapping his head back.

"You like hitting women, you motherfucker?" he snarled. "Make you feel like a real man?"

Before the drunk could answer, he hit him again. And again. This slime had hit the woman he loved. Yes, loved. His Daisy.

"Shane, that's enough!" Arms wrapped around him, pulling him off the assailant. "He's down! Don't get in trouble because of this scumbag. Daisy needs you."

Shaking himself back to reality, he looked for her. Shea was crouching next to her, helping her to sit up, examining her head. Shane hurried over to the women and his heart lurched. Blood was streaming down the side of her face from a nasty cut near her temple, and she had glass in her hair.

Dropping to his knees next to her, he pulled her into his arms. "Baby? Can you hear me?"

She moaned, head lolling against his shoulder, and tried to reach up and touch his face. He stopped her, pulling down her hand, and glanced up at Tommy. "Did someone call an ambulance?"

"I just did."

"I called the police," Shea said. "Just before you got here. Daisy, can you hear us?"

"Yes," she whispered. "I'm dizzy."

"Easy, baby. Help is on the way."

He cradled her against him, never wanting to let her go. If this was what happened when she got loose for a night of so-called fun, he'd never let her out of his sight again.

Red and blue lights cut through the darkness, and Tommy waved them over. The police arrived first, and Shane wasn't sure whether he was relieved or not to see Brian Cunningham get out, along with another officer.

"Ford? Hell, boy, you're just a magnet for trouble lately."

"I didn't start any of it," he pointed out. "I just got here in time to see that asshole assaulting Daisy and breaking a beer bottle over her head."

"Shit, that's Callahan? What happened here tonight?" Brian glanced around the group for an explanation.

Shea explained, starting when they were inside and the bastard, Len, wouldn't leave them alone. They'd decided to leave, and then Daisy tried to intervene outside when Len and another man in his group were fighting over being kicked out. The other man had slipped away, not bothering to help his buddy once assault and cops became involved. The rest Shane and Tommy had witnessed as they drove up.

Shane wanted to kill Len. The fucker tried to get Shane in trouble for hitting him, but that argument went nowhere. Len had attacked a woman, and a cop on top of that. It didn't matter that he didn't realize she was a police officer—he could cry to the judge about it. Brian advised Len of his rights, cuffed him, and put him in the back.

"You came to get me." Daisy clung to Shane.

He held her tighter. "Yes, and I'm glad I did."

"Me, too. Shane?"

"Yeah?"

"I'm gonna be sick."

"It's okay, baby. I'm here." He held her so that she could heave if she needed to, but she didn't throw up. Thanking heaven for small favors, he was also glad when the ambulance showed up. He didn't know anyone on this crew, but that didn't matter.

Tommy knew some of them and they greeted him before making Shane move aside so they could work. He hovered like an angry grizzly, doing his best to remain calm as they checked her vitals and started an IV.

"We think it's best to take Miss Callahan to the hospital to get that head wound checked out," one of the paramedics said. "I suspect she's got a mild concussion, what with the dizziness and nausea."

Shane nodded. "Can I ride with her?"

"Sure. Let us load her first, and then you can climb in back."

While they got her ready, Tommy spoke up. "We'll follow you to the hospital."

"No. I appreciate that, but I think it's best to get Shea home." He held up a hand at her protest. "I know you want to be there, but it's bound to be a while before we're done. You can help me the most by letting Drew spend the night, if that's all right. He won't sneak out again."

"Sure, no problem. I know he won't. I'd hog-tie him if he tried. How will you two get home?"

"I'll call a cab and take her to my house. Chances are she's going to need someone to watch her because of the concussion."

"Okay. But if you need anything, don't hesitate to call."

"I promise."

Shane could tell they didn't want to leave, but there wasn't anything they could do. They also understood he needed their help with Drew more.

The ambulance was ready to roll, and he climbed aboard, taking Daisy's hand.

He studied her pale face, blood smeared on her creamy skin and in her shiny blond hair. It frightened him to think what could've happened to her if he and Tommy hadn't showed up. That bastard could've killed her, and then Shane would be the one headed to jail.

Never again. He absolutely could not let her out of his sight.

And if she had a problem with that? Tough shit.

10

The ride to the hospital was a weird kaleidoscope of sounds and images.

In the back of her fuzzed mind, Daisy knew her attacker must've hit her pretty damned hard with that beer bottle. She got that she was on the way to the hospital and there were paramedics talking to her. But not much else made sense.

Except Shane. Somehow he was there, and she'd never been more relieved to have him at her side. Even though she couldn't process most of what he was saying, his presence was a soothing balm. He clung tight and kept saying something about never again. Whatever that meant.

He had to let go when they arrived, and she didn't like that. They whisked her off to a white room that was so bright it hurt her eyes, so they turned the lights down some. Then she was transferred onto a traylike bed thing and shoved into a tube that started to whirr and make strange knocking noises. She didn't like that either.

A CAT scan. She remembered that and shuddered, hoping she never had another one. The scanner around her head was kind of scary. When she was all done, they put her back on a rolling bed and moved her down the hallway again. The motion made her sick, so she closed her eyes.

Then she was in the ER, in a cubicle, and Shane was waiting. He had blood all over his shirt, and she frowned, trying to reason out why, then realized it was from her head. He'd been holding her on the ground. If she could recall that, maybe she wasn't so bad off. Now if her brain would quit spinning.

"How are you feeling, baby?"

"Not so good. Hurts."

"I know." Taking her hand, he sat beside her bed as the nurse fiddled with her IV and checked her vitals. "I paid him back for you, though. And his ass got arrested."

"Good," she murmured with a faint smile. "You rescued me."

"I wouldn't have needed to if you two hadn't gone to that stupid club to begin with. Do you have any idea how much worse—"

"You're making my head hurt more," she whimpered.

"Sorry." Contrite, he bent and pressed a kiss to her lips. "I'll save the lecture."

"Thanks."

"You still have glass in your hair. You're filthy."

"He'll have sore balls tomorrow."

He laughed softly. "Good. They'll go fine with his broken nose."

She was savagely glad about that. "Sleepy." She yawned.

"I don't think you should go to sleep yet, sugar. Stay awake for me, okay?" His handsome, worried face hovered above hers.

But try as she might, her lids wouldn't stay open.

The next time she awoke, she blinked, trying to figure out where she was. The space around her looked different, and she realized she'd been put into a regular room. She didn't recall leaving the ER, and hated that she'd apparently lost a few hours.

The room was almost dark, except for a dim light on near the door. In the shadow, she could make out Shane beside her bed, asleep in a fold-out visitor's chair. The fact that he'd stayed touched a spot in her soul. He looked young and vulnerable and tired, with dark smudges under his eyes, his tall body sprawled uncomfortably in the horrible chair.

Someone must've brought him a clean T-shirt, because this one was free of the bloodstains she remembered. She didn't see a clock, so she couldn't tell how long she'd been here, but it must've been the middle of the night.

Lying there, she simply observed him for a while. He was so beautiful. He had a good heart, even if he'd run from a relationship the first time. And he'd begged for another chance. He'd rescued her and hadn't left her side. That had to mean something, didn't it?

Didn't everyone deserve a second chance?

Soon her brain couldn't cope with the drama anymore. The uncertainty. So she gave in to sleep, her heart a lot lighter than it had been in months.

The next time she woke, sunlight was streaming through the cracks in the blinds. Her brain was still a little sluggish, but the confused fog seemed to have lifted. The side of her head hurt a bit and there was a strange tug at her temple, though. Reaching up, she found a bandage and worried it with her fingers.

"Hey, don't mess with that, sugar."

Shane captured her hand and brought it to his lips. "How are you feeling?"

"Better. I can form a coherent thought now." She studied him. "You didn't have to stay here all night."

"I wouldn't be anywhere else." He kissed her forehead. "You can't get rid of me, either, so don't think about trying."

She smiled, or tried. "I wasn't going to. But you do look like you could use a shower and your bed."

"I'm planning to do that as soon as they release you."

"Which will be when?"

"This morning. The CAT scan came back fine, but the doctor kept you overnight for observation. When you get your walking papers, I'm taking you home with me."

"Oh, there's no need—"

"I wasn't asking," he said firmly. "You obviously need a keeper, and I'm the man for the job."

"I do not need a keeper, and we were having a perfectly nice time until that jerk and his buddies had a few too many and got obnoxious." He smirked and she blinked at him. "What?"

"You said you had a *nice* time. Not great, fantastic, or incredible, but *nice*. That's the kiss of death word for all things social."

She wanted to be annoyed with him but couldn't work up the effort. Besides, he was right. "It was something to do on a Saturday night besides stay home." *And pine over you.*

"Last Saturday night was much more fun, as I recall."

"Until a certain teenager went joyriding and got arrested for vandalism."

"We both know that's not the reason you pulled away." His thumb brushed the back of her hand. "I think us getting close again was too much reality for you. The question is, do you still feel that way?"

"I don't know," she said honestly.

"Are you still willing to take it one day at a time with me, or was that canceled out because you *thought* I was going to do something wrong?"

She hadn't been fair to him. "I want to be with you. I just got scared. I ran."

His sexy mouth quirked up. "You'll fight a man twice your size who's drunk and wielding a beer bottle as a weapon and not bat a pretty eyelash, but the idea of being with me scares you?"

"He only hurt my head," she said softly. "If you break my heart, the recovery time is a hell of a lot longer."

His gaze warmed. "Then I guess you have to ask yourself if we're worth the risk. But don't say anything now. Come home with me and let me take care of you. Let me show you how serious I am about making us work."

Looking into his face, so hopeful, she didn't have it in her to refuse. "Okay."

His smile transformed his face and erased the shadows. "Fantastic. Now we need to get you sprung, head home, and get some real rest."

"Sounds great."

Two hours later, Daisy was being wheeled out to a cab waiting at the curb. If she'd had any idea that last night would turn out the way it did, she never would've gone. But, then again, her mishap had brought Shane to her side, fussing and fretting over her every second. It was kind of awesome.

He held her hand in the cab, and when they arrived at his place, helped her up the porch steps as if she'd received major trauma instead of a mild concussion. He settled her on the sofa with a sweet kiss on her lips.

"Would you like something to drink? Do you have a headache?"

"Just a slight one, not bad enough for a painkiller. But I wouldn't mind some juice or something."

He plumped the pillows around her head. "All I have is orange juice, and that might not settle on your stomach right now. How about Sprite?"

"Okay."

He hurried away, and in moments he was back with a cold can that sported a straw sticking out of it. "Here you go."

"Thanks." She sipped her soda, watching as he turned on the TV to a news channel, volume low.

"Is this okay? Too loud?"

"It's fine. Sit down before you make my headache come back."

Giving her a sheepish grin, he situated himself on the sofa next to her, then tucked her under his arm, against his chest. Snuggling in, she curled up on her good side to avoid pressing on the stitches.

"I need a shower," she said.

"I'll help you take a bath later. You can't get your stitches wet." He kissed the top of her head. "I'll get your keys and run by your place this afternoon, grab you some clothes to stay a couple of days. We're both taking off work until I'm sure you're better."

"Oh, we are, are we?" She tried to sound annoyed at his high-handedness, but couldn't.

"Yes. No arguments from you."

"I'm assuming I'll stay in the guest room?"

"For now." His voice was laced with regret. "For Drew's benefit. According to him, his dad wasn't exactly discreet about the parade of women who stayed at their house, and I don't want him thinking that sort of behavior is to be expected from me as well. Even though what you and I have—what I *want* us to have—in no way resembles Brad's antics, it's just . . ."

"I know. You want to set a good example for him." She hugged him tight. "I think that's very admirable."

"I'm glad you think so, but it's damned hard—in more ways than one." His teasing tone was tinged with wry humor.

Daisy peeked at his lap and saw the hard ridge pressing against his zipper. "I can help you with that, big guy."

"No," he said ruefully. "I don't think moving around that much would be good for your recovery."

"I don't have to move much to do this."

Still leaning against him, she went to work on the button and zipper of his jeans. Then she pulled the material apart and smiled at his boxers. "SpongeBob?"

"Hey, I'm channeling my inner fun side." Grabbing his waistband, he worked them and the jeans down past his hips, and his erection poked at his belly. "And they were on sale."

"Hmm."

Grasping his cock, she pumped slowly, loving the feel of his velvety length. His moans sent a thrill of satisfaction through her that she could reduce him to a mass of quivering need with nothing more than a simple touch.

His head hit the back of the sofa and his lips parted in bliss as she stroked him. Up and down, his hips following her motion, seeking more. Using her thumb, she smeared droplets of pre-cum over the purple head, then stroked down to his balls, squeezing the sac, and up again. Faster and faster she jerked him until he groaned, stiffening impossibly hard in her hand, and shot ropes of creamy white over her fingers.

"God, I needed that." He blew out a breath, and looked at her. "What about you?"

"I'm fine. I wanted to make you feel good."

"You always do that, sugar." He kissed her deeply, then stroked her cheek. "Tired?"

"Some."

"Would you like me to help you get cleaned up now?"

"That would be great."

After hitching up his jeans and boxers, he led her to the master bathroom and ran a nice hot bath for her as she undressed. Then he helped her into the tub and knelt beside it.

"I can bathe myself," she said. "I'm not an invalid."

"I know that, but humor me. I enjoy taking care of you. Besides, you can't get your stitches wet."

With a sigh, she gave herself to his tender care, and she had to admit he was very good at it. His hands were gentle as he soaped her skin, cleaning her abraded palms and kissing bruises she hadn't even realized she'd obtained in the struggle with Len. Then he supported her head as she leaned back, and got her hair wet before soaping the tresses, too.

"I love your hair," he murmured. "It's like spun sunlight."

"Thank you. I come from a family of natural blondes, and I used to spend a lot of time wishing it was a more interesting color," she mused.

"I know several women who would hate you for saying that." His lips turned up.

"By high school, I learned not to. When I got older, I finally started to appreciate being different."

"Are we still talking about hair? Lean back." He began to rinse carefully, avoiding her head injury.

"I suppose not." After he was finished rinsing, she sat up. "I was always a tomboy, and I hated girly girls. I wasn't delicate and I didn't want to pretend to be. I was happy climbing trees, jumping creeks on our bikes, catching frogs."

"Playing cops and robbers?"

She smiled. "Yeah. And I never stopped."

"I think you turned out just the way you were supposed to."

"I can't imagine it's any parent's dream for his or her daughter to be a police officer. Well, it certainly wasn't for my dad at first. I told you some about my relationship with him when we worked that last case together. He's proud of me now, in his way."

"What did he want you to be?"

"A teacher, or some 'normal' career for a woman to enter. Sexist, but safe in his view."

"My dad wanted me to be a businessman like him one day." He gave a laugh. "I couldn't imagine anything more horrible than wheeling and dealing, always crunching numbers or marketing the newest ideas. Might as well shoot me."

She shivered. "Don't say that." He had been shot last year and had come damned close to dying. She never wanted to be that afraid again.

"Sorry." He changed the subject. "Ready to get dried off?"

Nodding, she stood. He wrapped her in a thick towel and patted her dry, then did the same with her long hair, mindful of the stitches. Then he had her sit in a chair while he gently brushed out the tangles and blew her hair dry.

At last, he cut off the dryer. "All done."

"It takes a while. Maybe I should just cut it all off really short."

"Only if you want to see a grown man cry."

She laughed at his fake pout. "No worries, for now."

He gave her a T-shirt of his that was too big, but it would work for taking a nap. Showing her into the guest room, he turned down the covers and tucked her in.

"Will you be okay while I go get you some clothes and things?"

"I'll be fine. I'm just going to take a nap, not run around the block."

"All right. But I'll be back soon, and Drew will be home in a bit, too, if you need anything."

"Go, you, before you give me a bigger headache."

"Smartass."

After giving her a sweet kiss on the lips, he left, pulling the door shut behind him. She snuggled in and drifted for a while, basking in his care and obvious feelings for her.

Maybe this thing between them had a chance after all. If only she could be sure.

She must've dozed, because the next thing she knew, she heard a noise and opened her eyes to see that Shane was sneaking into the guest room. And he was wearing only a towel.

She smiled at the delicious sight. "I'm guessing Drew's not home from school?"

"Nope. Tommy picked him up for me, and he's staying over there for a while."

"Those two are becoming awfully chummy, aren't they?"

"I'm not complaining. That boy needs all the positive role models he can get." He stalked closer, then crawled onto the bed with her. "I'm not feeling like anybody's role model right now. In fact, I'm feeling rather naughty. I wish your head wasn't hurt."

"My noggin is much better, thank you." She eyed his spectacular form. All those sleek muscles were just begging for her hands and her lips. "I think you should take care of me before I burst into flames."

"We can't have that. But are you sure?"

"Very much so." She lifted his chin and kissed him. Searching at first, gentle. A sharp intake of breath betrayed his pleasure, then his spiky lashes swept down and his lips parted. He melted into her, holding her close, splaying his hands across her back.

Daisy wrapped her arms around his neck and deepened the kiss, exploring his mouth, savoring the taste of him. His spicy male scent mingled with the aroma of soap on his skin.

Her body heated in reaction to being pressed against Shane, who was almost naked, save for the towel. Her nipples tightened, and she imagined he must feel them through the thin old T-shirt, brushing against his smooth, bare chest. He broke the kiss and she rested a palm against his pounding heart.

"Babe, if we don't stop . . ." He sucked in a breath.

"Do you *want* to stop?"

"No." His gaze bored into hers, an intense gray storm. "Then don't."

"Daisy, you're hurt—"

"I'm more than okay, and I want you. Please."

Indecision warred with desire, then he stood. The towel had loosened so that it rode low on his hips, and the proof of his arousal had made a sizable tent underneath. A tantalizing thatch of dark hair peeked over the cloth.

"Take it off me, sugar."

The husky command sent a delicious shiver through her. She searched his handsome face for a trace of the laughing, teasing Shane she knew. This man wasn't him. Something dark and dangerous lurked behind his eyes, an eerie sense that the man about to make love to her wasn't Shane at all. Anticipation tingled along her spine, and an aching warmth unfurled between her thighs.

The towel slid off easily, and she let it drop to the bed. Oh, lord. He was two hundred pounds of naked, masculine perfection. Well, nearly perfect. A small circular scar on his abdomen marked where a bullet had come close to ending his life. Her world would have crumbled that day if it had.

His shaft jutted proudly at the apex of his muscled

thighs, daring her to touch . . . and she wasn't strong enough to resist. She curled her fingers around his velvety length, and he groaned.

Scooting closer, she slid her hand in a slow pumping motion, enjoying the way he sucked in his breath, body tightening in response. Emboldened, she cupped his sac, rubbing, enjoying the weight of it. She looked up at Shane, and the feral desire etched on his face scorched her to her toes.

"Do you want me?" he demanded.

"Yes," she managed.

"Sweetheart, I'm yours."

She dipped her head and tasted. The tip of him was fine silk, a salty pearl delight. She licked the drop away, then let her tongue explore the rest inch by inch. Tracing the ridge underneath, she worked her way to his balls and laved them. Shane buried his hands in her hair, careful of her head, and cried out.

"Oh! Oh, honey . . . Yes, yes!"

Daisy took him in her mouth, sucking deeply, relishing this feeling of power as he quivered. Shane's voice, hoarse with passion, brought her such pleasure.

"Oh, God, stop. Raise your arms."

She did, and he grabbed the edge of her T-shirt and yanked it over her head, baring her. Totally. Daisy had never liked sleeping in underwear, preferring freedom instead. Shane's face darkened and he growled low in his throat.

"Lie back."

Daisy settled on the pillows, watching him. He gripped her knees and spread her legs, moved between them, then released her.

"Wider," he coaxed. His hot gaze lifted to hers as she complied. "That's it, baby, let me see you, taste you. My turn."

He dipped his head and trailed the inside of her thigh with his tongue, until he found her center. Delicious shockwaves of erotic pleasure radiated through her limbs to her fingers and toes as he flicked her. She squirmed under him, craving more. More . . .

Shane laughed, a deep baritone sound of male satisfaction. "Like that, do you?"

"Yes!"

"Want more?"

"*Please* . . ."

With a low groan, he rose to his knees, lifting her hips in his strong hands as though she weighed no more than a feather. Only her shoulders rested on the bed. Though he supported her easily, she admired how the position emphasized the corded muscles in his chest and arms. He gazed down at her, lips turned up in a knowing half-smile, an expression oozing with raw sexuality.

When Shane spoke, his voice was a sensual caress. "I'm going to feast until you scream, sweet girl. Until you beg me to fuck you. And even then I won't stop unless I've tasted every last drop."

Words failed Daisy and her heart pounded. Shane was such a sexual creature. Never in her wildest, most torrid fantasies had she dared to dream that he might one day be hers. Even when they'd been together before, there had been doubt. That was fading away, almost to a distant memory. He brought her to him and nibbled gently, unraveling her thread by thread. The shock waves became warm pools, bathing her. His teeth grazed her again and again, heating her blood until she began to whimper.

"Oh, please!" She tugged at his hair, trying to pull him closer. He chuckled and answered her plea, fastening his mouth on her. A tidal wave of sensations carried her away in a languorous sea. He suckled, licked, and she gave herself to him completely. Tremors began to shake her as she watched him love her that way, the lamplight playing off his sable brown hair, his face buried in her soft folds. Giving and taking.

"Tell me what you want."

"You *know*."

"Say the words."

His sex talk was sending her over the edge, stripping her inhibitions. "Fuck me."

"Not yet. Come for me, sugar. That's it."

She came undone with a sharp cry, flew apart with the force of her orgasm, and he drank deeply, lapping her honey until she was certain he'd taken his fill. She was wrong. As she drifted back to earth, he lowered her to the bed once more, then covered her body with his. To her amazement, the feel of their naked skin pressed together rekindled the fire.

Shane brushed a strand of hair out of her face. "I can't get enough of you." He kissed her, a hard, possessive kiss, rich with their mingled sex. "Taste us? I'll carry the essence of you on my lips until the day I die."

Tears stung her eyes. "Oh, Shane—"

"Shh, sweetheart. Let me give you what we've both wanted for so long." Quickly, he rolled on a condom.

She gasped as he plunged inside her. Already slick

and wet from his attentions, she sheathed him smoothly. His rigid shaft impaled her, and she realized that he'd made his entry easier for her by pleasuring her first. His strong arms braced on either side of her head, he began to pump his hips, riding her in a slow grinding motion, his length stroking her sensitized bud.

"Ohhh." Wicked pleasure unfurled between her legs. He increased the tempo, slamming into her harder, faster. Wrapping her legs around his waist, she arched her back, allowing him to fill her as deeply as possible.

"Mine," he whispered against her. "Say it."

"Yes, *yours*. Shane," she said.

Relentless, he drove into her with long strokes. The fire consumed her, burning out of control until she met his thrusts with mindless abandon. She clung to his shoulders, nails digging into his skin, the rhythmic slap of their sweat-slickened bodies bringing her to the brink of climax.

"Daisy, baby, I can't stop—"

With a hoarse cry, Shane crushed her to his chest and buried himself to the hilt. The volcanic force of their release rocked them, and they remained locked together as the hot rush of his seed spilled into her. Spasms shook them in rolling waves that gradually gentled, leaving them trembling in each other's arms.

For several minutes neither of them made a move to separate. He seemed content to hold her, which was more than fine with Daisy. If she could, she'd keep him inside her forever.

"Wow," he breathed, smiling down at her.

The effect short-circuited her brain. With his too-long

brown hair falling into sparkling gray eyes, he was devastatingly handsome. And his gorgeous smile was genuine, all for her, just the way she'd always dreamed.

Please, please let the doubts stay away. Let him be mine.

"Yeah, wow," she smiled back.

He pressed a soft kiss to her forehead. "You're beautiful, Daisy. Inside and out. I'm just sorry I didn't take off my blinders a hell of a lot sooner. Months ago."

Her spirits soared. He'd said it before, but that she was finally beginning to believe him was a major victory. "Me, too."

Shane laughed, then slipped out of her and rolled to his back. A sharp sense of loss stabbed her with disappointment, but he pulled her with him, cradling her body against his. She sank into him with a contented sigh.

From the moment she'd first laid eyes on Shane years ago, she hadn't been able to shake the feeling, silly as it seemed, that this sexy man was hers. Or would be eventually. She'd clung to that feeling for years. That he only needed time to come to his senses. To see her as more than a friend and colleague.

Now that he had, she was damned afraid of something happening to ruin her happiness.

Carl Eastlake snapped the Sunday newspaper closed, curling his lip at yet another article lionizing the poor, tragic figure of Brad Cooper. What a friend, what a committed dad, what a supporter of charities, what a great all-around guy.

"What an insecure, aging asshole holdin' on to his

youth by chemical means," Carl said, laughing. "You bought the lie because you had the money."

On the table next to his coffee cup, his cell phone rang and he glanced at the display. Sanders, that pain in the ass. He picked up, already annoyed before the man said a word. "Yeah?"

"Carl, we gotta talk."

"No, we really don't. Just do your job and I'll do mine. End of story." Picking up a nearby pen, he began to doodle a stick figure in the margin of the newspaper. Just for grins he tried to make it look like Irvin Sanders, with glasses and a little goatee.

"No. I want a meeting face-to-face," Sanders insisted. "We have to work out the kinks in this thing before we broaden our client base. I insist. Otherwise, I may have to take my skills elsewhere."

"Is that so?" he inquired pleasantly. That alone should've been a clue, should've made the man leave town in the dead of night. "In that case, I'm all ears. I'm busy this coming week, so let's do a week from Thursday, the usual time and place. Call Johnson and tell him."

He wasn't that busy, but irritating Sanders made him happy. Without waiting for an answer, Carl ended the call and set the phone aside. Humming, he continued his doodling, finishing his artwork with a big X over the figure he'd drawn.

Stupid. Meddling. Fucker.

So hard to get good help these days, and all that shit. Sanders had been bitching about the product ever since the NFL star had dropped dead. Of course, two other clients had died since then. The papers just hadn't picked up on those, since they were nobodies. But they were nobodies with the money to buy the lie, and that's all Carl cared about.

So what if their illustrious clients were killed by their own stupidity? Who in the hell were they going to complain to? The law of averages ensured one simple thing.

There would always be one dumb-ass more than ready with the cash.

11

"So, what's the scoop on you and Daisy?"

Shane glanced at the office door beyond Taylor, making sure it was still firmly closed. His relationship with Daisy was now the worst-kept secret in the department, and he was surprised they hadn't been called in to Austin's office yet. He figured it was only a matter of time, though, and one of them would end up reassigned. Or worse.

Wouldn't that be fun?

He considered lying to his friend for about one second. "I guess the rumors are flying thick and fast, huh?"

"Uh, yeah," Taylor responded, arching a dark blond brow. "The question is, are they true? Don't put me off this time. I want an answer."

He sighed. "If you've heard we're going at it like rabbits and trying to figure out what exactly to label our status, then yes. All true."

"Jesus, when you decide to complicate your life, you really go balls to the wall. Has Rainey said anything to either of you?"

"Not yet, but I doubt it'll take him long once he decides this isn't going away."

"It's not? This is the real deal?"

"For me it is," he said. "But I hurt her pretty bad once before, and that's not something any woman forgets easily, especially Daisy."

"True. She doesn't strike me as the type to play games. Unlike Leslie."

"Ugh. Don't mention her name to me. I'm having a hard enough time trying to shake her off my trail as it is."

"She harassing you?"

"Not as such. She's not offering anything I didn't welcome before, so I can't really blame her."

"Which I'm sure thrills Daisy to no end. Where is she, by the way?"

"She went home. The captain put her on half-days for the week until her stitches come out and she gets a doctor's note. Of course, she insisted she was feeling well enough to work full shifts, but he put his foot down."

In fact, she'd gone to her home, not his. He wasn't very happy about it, but he had no real say in where she stayed. There was Drew to think of, too, and even though the boy said he was cool with Daisy staying there all the time if she wanted, he was determined to build a real family environment for them all. One based on love and commitment.

Even if his ideals twisted his libido into a pretzel in the process.

"Well, if anyone deserves to be happy, it's two of my favorite people," Taylor said. "I hope everything works out."

"Thanks. It's starting to look like it just might."

A knock sounded on the door, and the captain poked in his head. "Am I interrupting?"

Taylor turned in his chair and grinned. "Indeed you are. Come back later so we can continue to pretend to be extremely busy."

Austin snorted, pushing inside. "Listen up, slackers. We got a call from one of our informants. Claims he knows something about the body out on I-49. I need you two on this now, so get your lazy carcasses up and go talk to him."

Shane rose, checked his weapon in his holster, and grabbed his jacket. "On it, Cap. What's his name and where can we find him?"

"He's a street kid named Blake who likes to hang around down by the river, under the bridge. Petty thief with a rap sheet consisting mostly of misdemeanors for stealing food. Keeps his ear to the ground to give us tidbits so he can earn a little money for a meal without having to swipe it."

"Sounds like you know him pretty well," Taylor observed.

"He went to the high school, graduated last year right before his parents kicked him out. His parents were never stellar examples of kindness and understanding, but when he came out as gay, they came unglued."

Taylor practically growled. "That sucks. People like that shouldn't be allowed to breed."

Shane frowned. "He doesn't have friends he can stay with? Any other family?"

"Not that I've been able to learn, and, believe me, I've tried. He's not one to accept handouts, either."

"He'd rather steal than swallow his pride?" Taylor shook his head. "That's a teenager for you."

"I don't think it's pride so much as he's afraid. He

honestly doesn't trust very easily, so it's safer for him to keep to the shadows."

Until someone hurt him, or worse. They were all thinking it, Shane knew. "We'll touch base with him. And if we can get him to go to a church or the city shelter, we will."

"Good luck with that." The captain left, waving a hand, off to see to other business.

Shane and Taylor made their way out to Taylor's car, and Taylor headed in the direction of the old bridge. The kid was supposed to be waiting, but Shane was skeptical. Informants tended to be skittish, given their poor life expectancy if any of the criminals they were ratting on found out. If they caught a whiff of anything different or wrong, they vanished like smoke.

Downtown, they turned at the square and started down the road leading to the bridge. As they got closer, he kept an eye peeled for Blake. Shouldn't be tough to spot, as there wasn't anyone else in that area in the middle of the week and nearing sunset. How the boy had managed to survive the worst of the winter was beyond Shane. He shuddered to think of Drew in the same situation.

"There," Taylor said, pointing to the opposite bank. Just underneath the arch of the support beams, where the strong metal met the concrete pillars, stood a lone figure.

As the car drew closer and crossed to the other side, Shane lost sight of the boy for a few seconds. But as Taylor brought them around to park next to the riverbank, Blake stepped from the protective shadow of the bridge.

At somewhere around nineteen, he was smaller than

Drew. Slim and fragile-looking, as though he might shatter at a cross word, much less a fist or some other weapon. His jeans were dirty, his coat in tatters. His shoulder-length brown hair was tangled, and his eyes were huge in his face. Also brown, Shane saw as they approached. Big, sad doe eyes that had already seen the worst his world had to offer.

"I'm Detective Shane Ford, and this is my partner, Detective Taylor Kayne," he said in what he hoped was a pleasant tone. He showed the boy his badge, and Taylor did the same. "Our captain, Austin Rainey, sent us here to speak with you. Said you may have something interesting to tell us."

Some of the fear left the boy's face, but he was watchful. Not just of them, but of their surroundings. He scanned the entire area before relaxing some. "I heard these guys bragging last night outside by the Waterin' Hole. They didn't see me, 'cause I was around the side of the building."

"What were you doing there?"

The boy gave Taylor a sharp look. "Not selling my ass, if that's what you were thinking. I'm homeless, not stupid." He took a deep breath. "The manager there is cool, gives me a burger or sandwich when he's on shift in the evening. That's all."

"We believe you," Shane soothed. "What did the men say?"

"They were talking about the man that was found with the bullet in his head. Which isn't unusual, since stuff like that is big news. But these guys were saying how it was too bad he got his squeaky wheel greased, and the rest of them should keep their mouths shut and do their jobs. They were talking about receiving a shipment, taking their shit on the street. Here in town, specifically."

Excitement sparked along Shane's nerves. "You got a name, a time, or a place?"

"No names. But they set up a meet with the supplier for tonight, midnight, down by the dam where the barges go through."

"You mean the lock," Taylor clarified.

"Yeah."

Shane exchanged a look with his partner. "Shit."

The lock was in a state park not too many miles from where they were standing. The land around it was wide open, very few trees, with a swimming area and several parking lots for recreation seekers during the day. There was one road in and only that way out—and from the lock, anyone would be able to see them coming.

Anyone attempting to spy on the meeting would have to park and hike through brush. The terrain was rugged beyond the park, bordered by a sheer cliff. They'd chosen the perfect place to meet.

Which meant they'd have to get there first and hide somehow.

"Anything else you can tell us?" he asked.

The boy shook his head. "That's it. They didn't stay but a couple of minutes."

"They didn't see you?"

"If they had, I'd be floating facedown out there," he said, gesturing to the river.

Shane's stomach clenched. Reaching into his back pocket, he took out his wallet and removed one hundred twenty dollars—everything he had on him. Then he held it out to Blake. "Here. Get yourself a room and something to eat."

Eyeing the money, the boy swallowed hard. "This is way too much."

"It's not charity. What you told us could help get some dangerous criminals off the street and put their operation out of business. That money isn't nearly enough to compensate you for that and the risk you took."

"Okay. Thanks." His eyes were shiny as he folded the bills and shoved them in his jeans.

"Take this, too." Taylor extracted a business card and handed it to the boy. "This is my card, and it has my cell phone number on it. You decide you've had enough of the streets, you want an actual life, call me. I've got friends who can help you get a job, get on your feet."

"I don't know. I don't want to owe anyone." He looked uncertain.

"There's no shame in letting someone give you a boost. Hell, everyone has to start somewhere, right? How you pay those folks back is by doing a good job, being a good friend, and getting your life on track."

For a long moment, he stared at the card. Then pocketed it, too. "I'll think about it. Thanks."

"Call anytime, day or night. I mean that."

Blake gave them a small smile, then turned and started walking in the direction of town. Back across the bridge. Hopefully to find a motel room and be safe, at least for one night.

Shane's heart was heavy as he watched the boy go. "That Bambi thing he had going was not an act. We see some bad seeds in our line of work, but that's one of the good ones."

"God, that makes me sad," Taylor said quietly. "Makes me want to pummel somebody. How can anyone just throw away their own flesh and blood? I hope he calls."

"He was giving it some thought, I could tell."

"Hope so."

Shane walked with him back to the car. "What time do you think we should be at the park? Eleven?"

"You, my friend, have a family to get home to. Why don't you let me and Chris handle this one?"

He thought about that. It was a very tempting offer. But . . . "No. If I can help get the bastards who sold that poison to Brad, then that will give me and Drew something to celebrate. I'll call Tommy, have him pick Drew up. Those two are getting pretty tight, so I know neither of them will mind."

They got in the Chevelle, shut the doors. Taylor started toward town, and they crossed the bridge, passing Blake. The boy didn't acknowledge them as he walked, nor did they acknowledge him. Not when a mistake like that could be fatal to him.

"So how are we going to hide the car?" Taylor mused. "Even in the dark among the trees, the lights from the lock house will shine on the chrome and give us away."

He thought about that. "I've got an idea. Let's run over to the feed store."

"Say what?"

"Just trust me."

Sugarland Feed and Tractor Supply was on their way, not far off the square. When Taylor pulled up and parked, he shook his head. "I must have the nuttiest partner ever."

Ignoring him, Shane walked in and began looking

around for what he wanted. Any respectable feed store in this part of Tennessee had supplies for deer hunting. And in that area, he found what he wanted.

"Here we go." Grabbing a large package off the shelf, he showed it to his friend. "You were saying?"

"A camouflage tarp." His brows furrowed, then he got it. "To put over the car! You're a friggin' genius. What'd I tell you?"

"That's what I thought you said."

After Shane paid for their item, he stepped outside and called Tommy, who was glad to pinch-hit again. He hoped Drew wasn't feeling abandoned from being sent over there so much this past week, but from the boy's happy smiles whenever his brother-in-law came up, he didn't think so. It gave him peace of mind to know they had family next door with whom they shared a close relationship. Something Drew needed.

"We've got some time. What to grab something to eat at the diner?"

Shane's stomach grumbled. "Sounds good."

The diner on the square was one of those old-fashioned mom-and-pop joints with the best home cooking around, made from scratch. Nobody could touch their food, certainly not the chain restaurants with their premade crap.

He and Taylor found a table, and in minutes Taylor had ordered a burger and Shane the meat loaf special. Might as well be full if you had a late stakeout.

Pulling out his phone, he saw he had a text from Daisy. "I'm gonna make another call," he said, sliding from the booth. "Be right back."

"Do I get three guesses who it is?" His friend batted his eyelashes and made smooching noises.

"Shut up, idiot." He laughed in spite of himself. "You're gonna be next, and then we'll see who's making fun."

"No way, not me."

Shane walked outside and punched Daisy's contact button. After the third ring, she picked up.

"Hey, sexy. Are you home?"

"I wish. Taylor and I caught a break on one of my main cases. I can't say much on the cell, but you can probably guess which one."

"Ooh, I hope it pans out," she said, sounding excited. "You going to be late?"

"Looks like. Drew has to stay with Tommy and Shea again, not that he minds. I just wish I wasn't constantly shoving him out the door this week."

"Now, you know he doesn't feel that way at all. That boy and Tommy are like brothers already."

"I know. I'm the one taking it hard, and he probably hasn't given it a second thought."

"That's right. So stop worrying about him and focus on your job so you don't get hurt. Call me when you're done?"

"You'll be asleep by then, sugar. We're talking the wee hours, most likely."

"I'll sleep better once you call and tell me you and Taylor are okay."

He smiled. "All right. I can do that."

"Be safe."

"You know it."

They said goodbye and hung up. For the first time, it had hovered on Shane's lips to say *I love you*. It was a strange feeling, but good, too. After tonight, he was going to find a special time and place to let Daisy know exactly how he felt.

He just hoped she trusted him enough to return his feelings.

They got to the park early and Taylor backed the Chevelle into a stand of trees as far as he could. They were a bit close to the meeting site for comfort, but they were hidden in the shadows and they had a plan.

Working quickly, they spread out the tarp and draped it over the car to cover the whole vehicle. The material was a little short on the sides, the bottoms of the tires exposed, but other than that, it should do the trick. The shiny parts that would reflect in the lights were covered, and they should blend right in to the foliage.

Next Taylor took out his pocketknife and cut a hole in the material over the windshield, just enough of a long slit for them to see through. "That should do it."

"Now we wait."

Lifting the tarp on the passenger's side, Taylor crawled in and scooted over to the driver's spot. Shane followed and resumed his seat, then shut the door. They both lowered their windows, and then Shane readied the listening equipment they'd borrowed from the station. Checking his watch, he saw it was only eleven.

"So, did you always want to be a cop?"

Taylor groaned. "Why do you always want to play *This Is Your Life* when we're on stakeout?"

"Do we have anything else to do? Humor me."

His friend huffed. "No. I wanted to be an archaeologist. Okay?"

"Wow. That sounds really boring."

"I knew it! There's always something wrong with what I say."

"Not true. I merely said it sounded boring—to me. I'm sure digging around in the dirt for old dead shit is fascinating to some people."

"*Boring* people. You think that's me."

"I didn't say that."

"I'll have you know I'm completely fascinating when I want to be."

"Like when?"

His friend stumbled on that one. "Um, when I'm . . . tying up my lovers and spanking them until they squeal 'Daddy'! I'm not boring then," he said smugly.

"When you're *what*?" Shane's eyes widened, then he chuckled at his friend's grin. "You're a lying sack of shit, Kayne."

"On that one, *you'll* never know." He glanced at Shane. "So, same question."

"I don't know." He shrugged. "I guess as a teenager I wanted to be a rock star, but not being able to play or sing a note of music sort of hindered that dream."

"That might be a problem."

They shot the breeze for a while longer, then lapsed into silence as the time for the meeting approached. Both of them held binoculars, waiting. The tension slowly began to mount, as it always did when the rendezvous was close. At ten minutes until midnight, it appeared the wait was over. Headlights loomed, then were doused as the car approached.

An old four-door sedan drove into the lot, and Shane could see two men sitting in the front. They appeared to be waiting, most likely for the supplier. When the second car appeared, the familiar thrill of the unknown began to sing in his blood. The anticipation of the hunt.

Holding up his binoculars, he observed the second car park facing the first. A man in the second car got out, and he was alone. Shane noted he was on the beefy side, though not fat, and looked like he could hold his own in a fair fight—not that there was any such thing as a fair fight among their kind. He also had short hair, glasses, and a goatee. The most notable thing of all was the black leather bag he was carrying.

"Bingo," Taylor said in a low voice.

Thanks to the listening equipment, their voices came through pretty well.

"Whatcha got for us, man?" one of the pair asked, stepping out of the car.

"You know what. I got some grade-A Iron Man here. These babies work better than steroids and uppers combined. Ultimate performance enhancers."

"Except for the part where the clients are keeling over."

Goatee shrugged. "You want to apply for fuckin' FDA approval? Or should we get down to business?"

"No, man, we're cool."

"Now look at the product and exchange the money," Shane murmured.

Goatee sat his bag on the hood of the car while one

of the pair retrieved a similar bag, theirs blue. Each party unzipped their own bags and removed a packet for inspection. Goatee handed over a bundle that looked like a quart-sized Ziploc bag, and received a fistful of money to count. Leaning over, he did a quick check of the cash, while the two other men did the same with the drugs.

"Looks good," Goatee said. "We're done here, for now."

Then, they exchanged the gym bags.

"Gotcha," Taylor hissed. "Let's go!"

Reaching out his window, he yanked the tarp sideways and cranked the Chevelle at the same time. It started with a throaty roar and the headlights blasted the three men, freezing them like deer in front of a semi. Taylor peeled from their hiding place and the tarp fell away as they gained speed, closing the distance between them and the men.

Taylor hit the brakes and they threw open their doors, using them as cover.

"Police! Freeze!" Shane yelled. "Get on the ground!"

The suspects had a different plan. They scattered like cockroaches, diving for their respective vehicles. The two men threw their bag in the car and sped away, but Goatee was a bit more resourceful as he jumped in his car—he'd brought a gun to the party.

Popping several shots in their direction, he sped off after the first car. Shane dove back inside the Chevelle next to his partner as bullets pinged the body.

"Dammit, my car!"

Shane was barely upright before Taylor took off, tires screeching. Shane hung on, gritting his teeth as his partner swerved around the curves after the fleeing vehicles.

A high-speed chase through the Tennessee hills was a great way to end up plastered on the side of a rock face. The car careened dangerously, and the taillights of Goatee's car bobbed in and out of sight.

"Bump him!"

"I will if I can get close enough!"

On a straight stretch, his partner floored it and slammed into the back of the other car. The driver lurched to the side, almost lost control, but came out of the fishtail and sped ahead. Suddenly the bastard braked and made a hard right, heading in a new direction.

"Where does this road go?" Shane called.

"No idea!"

It was hard to hear with the noise of the chase, the wind whipping them through the open windows. The air was damned cold, too. But that was the least of their worries. The road was narrower here, the trees looming close on either side of them, reaching out with skeletal fingers as they flew by.

More dangerous curves, and Shane was turned around. It was so damned dark out here, without headlights they wouldn't be able to see their hands in front of their faces.

"Taylor, slow down," he urged. "We don't know where this goes."

"He's getting away!"

"He could be leading us into a—"

Suddenly the car in front of them swerved hard to the left, almost losing control in the process. But as it made the turn, Shane had a split second to see that the road in front of them simply vanished—

And then the Chevelle was airborne for two horrible

heartbeats. He had time to yell a profanity, and the car dipped, hit the incline hard, nose down, bucked over the rough terrain for a few feet, and shot straight into the Cumberland River.

Shane hit the dashboard hard, the wind knocked from his lungs as spray blanketed the vehicle and came in through the windows. He didn't have time to register pain, only the shock of the impact just before the water stopped the forward motion of the car and began to rush in. Christ, it was ice cold. They had to get out now.

"Taylor?"

A groan sounded from beside him. He looked over and could just barely make out his partner beside him, trying to move.

"Come on, buddy! We've got to get moving!"

The freezing water was rapidly filling the inside, covering their legs. Moving upward. The situation was dire, and he grabbed Taylor under the arms, hauling him backward, thanking God that in this case, they hadn't been wearing seat belts. Probably the only time in his life he would've had that thought. Because he wouldn't have had time to work Taylor free.

Reaching back, he tried the door, but by now there was too much pressure to get it open. So he continued to struggle, getting himself out the window first, then grabbing his friend and pulling as hard as he could just as the vehicle went under.

Taylor was jerked from his grasp.

"Fuck!"

Don't panic. Not now.

Sucking in a deep breath, he held it and dove. Completely blind, he groped for his partner and managed to grab his shoulders. Then he worked to get him under the arms again and haul him backward. Through the window, and, after a few heart-pounding moments, to the surface.

Shane broke free, gasping for air. Coughing, he pulled them toward shore, which was farther than he'd thought it would be. The car had really flown and traveled out a ways before hydroplaning to a stop. But Shane got them to the bank and pounded his friend on the back. Taylor, thankfully, started hacking up a lung almost immediately. It was a beautiful sound.

"J-Jesus, I'm s-sorry," Taylor stammered with the cold. On his hands and knees, he was shivering.

"It's okay, buddy. I'll beat the hell out of you later. For now, we need to see if we can find help. Can you walk?"

"I think s-so."

"You bleeding anywhere?"

"Honestly, I c-can't tell."

"Me, either."

Gaining his feet took more effort than he would've thought. That's when he realized the pain from the impact was starting to make itself known. That and how very cold and wet he was, and how dangerous a situation they were still in.

If not from the bad guys coming back, then from shock and exposure.

Reaching down, he helped Taylor to stand and then made the guy lean on him for support as they climbed the bank and tried to find the road again. They were going by what scant moonlight was filtering through the thick trees, and it took forever to find the telltale crunch of dirt and gravel that meant they'd located the road.

By this time they were both shaking so hard their teeth were chattering. Belatedly, he realized his cell phone was still in his jeans, but a quick check of the display revealed the thing was ruined, as he'd expected. He stuck it back in his pocket. If they got out of this in one piece, he'd take it to the store and get a new one.

They must have trudged along the road for more than a half hour when Shane spotted lights ahead. Off the road to the right. He got his hopes up and he wasn't disappointed. Back in the trees at the end of an overgrown driveway was a small, worn frame house. One that was obviously occupied, going by the porch light that was left on. The residents were long asleep by now, but that was about to change.

"C-Come on," he urged Taylor. "A few m-more steps."

"O-kay."

At last they reached the little house and stumbled onto the front porch. Shane rang the doorbell and waited, fumbling his soaked wallet from his back pocket. When there was no movement from inside, he rang it again.

Finally there was a shuffle from the other side of the door. A pause, as though the person on the other side was inspecting the visitors. Shane held up his wallet, badge visible.

"S-Sugarland PD, Detectives F-Ford and Kayne. We n-need some help."

A chain unlatched and a bolt slid, then the door opened to reveal a slight, elderly man peering at them with a bemused expression. "The police? Out here?" He eyed them from head to toe. "Damn, boys. What happened to you?"

"C-can we t-tell you on the way to town?" Shane asked politely. "We seem t-to have driven our c-car into the river."

After inspecting Shane's badge more closely, he nodded. "Sure thing. Let me get my keys." He shook his head and walked off, muttering about crazy policemen driving around not knowing where the river was located. In moments he was back with his keys and a couple of blankets.

"To the hospital with you both. Even if ya think you're fine as can be, hurts can make themselves known later. You'll need to get checked out and claim workman's comp if you were on the job tonight, in case you have medical trouble later."

"Thank you, s-sir."

"Not a problem, son."

Shane hated to admit that the old man was right. Which meant he'd have to call Austin from the ER. In the middle of the damned night. Then that would mean also telling the captain—who'd been yanked out of his nice warm bed on a winter's night—how colossally they'd managed to fuck up a simple drug bust that would have brought them loads of glory.

This night was bound to get worse before it got better. Because then he'd have to call the woman he loved, as promised.

And tell her that he and Taylor had almost drowned.

12

Daisy started when the phone rang at 3:27 a.m.

She hadn't been sleeping, but tossing as the hours crawled by. Snatching it off the bedside table, she frowned at Austin's number on the screen. Then came the sudden ball of dread that hit her stomach like a rock.

"Hello, Cap?"

"No, sugar, it's me," Shane's tired voice said on the other end.

"Thank goodness! I thought it was Austin about to give me bad news. Why are you using his phone?"

"Because he let me borrow it. He's at the hospital with me and Taylor, and—"

"What!" Sitting up, she switched on the lamp and began searching for her sweats. "Are you at the ER?"

"Yes, but—"

"I'm on my way. Stay put," she ordered.

She hung up without giving him a chance to protest further. In less than five minutes she was wearing sweats, a T-shirt, tennis shoes, and her coat, and was jogging out the door. Those two, plus Chris, could get into more scrapes than any ten guys she knew. Not that she had room to talk after her brawl with Len.

On the drive over, she consoled herself that Shane had done the calling and not Austin. He had sounded tired, but otherwise fine. She hoped that was the case. But what about Taylor? Shane and his partner were tight, as partners tended to be. If anything bad had happened to him, Shane would go nuts.

Speculating drove her crazy, and she was nearing panic by the time she dashed into the ER and pulled her badge from her purse, demanding to see her man. She was immediately shown to an adjoining pair of cubicles, where Austin was leaning against the wall, yawning hugely.

"Cap! What happened?" she called, jogging up to him.

"Those two fucktards almost got themselves killed, that's what," he grumbled. "Your man's fine, just a little bruised, but Taylor's more banged up. He inhaled a lot of water, too."

She didn't know which issue to tackle first—that he knew about her and Shane, or Taylor's condition. She opted for the latter. *Coward.* "Water? How?"

"They staked out a drug deal we got on a tip, and the info turned out to be good. The supplier was meeting two pushers to offload a shipment of what we suspect is that new drug."

"The one that killed Brad Cooper?"

"And some other victims, too."

"Did they make an arrest?"

Austin gave a humorless laugh and rubbed his eyes.

"Not only did they *not* make an arrest, Taylor fell for an evasion maneuver while in pursuit and drove right off the road into the Cumberland."

"Oh, jeez," she breathed, glancing around the partition between the two cubicles. Shane was sitting perched on the edge of the exam table, and gave her a wan smile. Taylor appeared to be out like a light. She glanced back at Austin, "Thanks for the update, Cap."

Then she left him standing there and joined her guy. Since Austin already knew, there was no reason to hide their status. She wondered what action he would take, if any, but she wasn't going to worry about that. That would have been the very least of her concerns if something had happened to Shane.

"What on earth am I going to do with you?" she said softly, taking his face in her hands. She kissed him gently, mindful of any injuries he might have.

"That's my line. And it wasn't my fault." He grimaced. "Wasn't Taylor's either. We were trying to catch the suspect, and he pulled a classic evasion on us."

"Know thy battleground," she quipped.

"Definitely."

"Are they letting you both go home?"

"That's what the doctor said. He almost kept Taylor, but decided he could go, too, since he doesn't have a concussion. His concern was Taylor's lungs, but he gave him a shot of antibiotics to ward off an infection."

"Does he need a ride home?"

"Austin's taking him. He'll be okay."

"All right." She kissed him again, and then spotted their captain watching with a bemused expression. Blushing, she let go of Shane.

She sat in a chair and waited with him for almost twenty minutes, until the nurse came with their walking papers. Then they bid Taylor and the captain good night, and climbed in her car. Daisy started it up and pulled away.

"I'm taking you to my house, unless you have any objections."

"None. Drew is taken care of for the night, and I'm beat."

"Good. Then let's get you showered, dried, and warm."

"That sounds like heaven—right after being in your arms."

She smiled and thanked her lucky stars that he was safe.

What a difference a week made.

Daisy couldn't help but mull over the push-pull of their relationship. They'd been lovers, then he'd run. Fast and far. Then he wanted her back, but she wasn't ready. She had to learn to trust him again, and that process had taken a large step toward healing when he'd run to her side, then nursed her in the wake of that drunk's attack.

And now . . . Maybe, for the first time, she and Shane were in the same place. Together. It was a heady idea, and her heart beat a little faster. That this man could be hers, for keeps, was a dream she'd held dear for years. Long before he was aware she existed. She'd pined from afar, and from very near, and it seemed that wait might be over.

After poking around in her closet, she settled on a pair of dark jeans that hugged her butt just right, and a black V-neck cotton shirt that made her loose blond hair and eyes pop. There were two very good reasons she wanted to look her best at Tommy and Shea's party tonight, and Shane was one, of course. The other was going to give her great pleasure, in a completely different way.

This wasn't just a party including Tommy's buddies, but with Shane's friends in the department, too. Well, Leslie wasn't a friend, but she had managed to wrangle an invite from Tonio, the new cop. Poor sap. If he didn't know the score yet, he would. That woman had served more cops than McDonald's.

Happy, Daisy grabbed her purse and keys and hit the road. She was stopping by Shane's first so they could all go together. Shane, Drew, and herself, attending their first party as a family of sorts, and she was as nervous as she was excited. Since that first lunch where she'd visited Drew at school, she felt that they were slowly forging a connection, even if he was still a bit sullen. Tonight would be the first real test of their progress.

The boy had no memories of his mother. She couldn't fill that hole, but she could be a mentor. A strong female role model where he'd never had one. Far from being a burden, she considered it an honor. A chance to make a real difference, unlike with so many young lives that touched hers and vanished.

A short time later she arrived at Shane's place and trotted to the door. She knocked and waited until it opened—and then she practically drooled at the sight of him.

He wore black jeans and a blue long-sleeved shirt

that looked absolutely gorgeous with his sable hair and gray eyes. The shirt, stretched across his toned chest and tucked in at his belt, emphasized his lean waist. His legs went on forever, and he wore brown boots to complete the ensemble.

"Do I pass?"

"Mmm." She stepped into his arms. "Good enough to eat. Too bad we're going to be surrounded by people."

"Oh, I might know of one place we can sneak away to, if you're game." He gave her a feral grin, and she shivered in delight.

"Secluded?"

"Very. And if we're stealthy, no one will ever know."

"You can certainly persuade a girl to be naughty," she said, kissing his neck.

His grip tightened on her hips. "I do try. But only with you."

"Jesus, my eyes are burning," Drew said with his lip curled as he sauntered into the room. "Don't make me lose my appetite."

Shane kissed her on the lips, then shot Drew a half-smile, making an obvious attempt to lighten the boy's mood. "She's mine and I'm hers, and I plan for it to stay that way. Deal with it."

"Whatever."

"Kid," he warned.

"Sorry." But they all knew he wasn't. "Ready to go?"

They trooped to Shane's truck and got in, Daisy riding in the middle. In minutes they were at their destination, parking behind several other cars that were already there. The front door was open, so they went on in and found the party just getting started, people laughing and talking, a group of the guys already talking about teaming up for pool.

Tommy greeted them with a broad smile, hugging Daisy and then giving Drew a knuckle bump. "Hey, big guy. Guess what I bought yesterday?"

"What?" The boy looked interested, knowing it was probably good.

"The newest version of Xbox was on sale at Walmart, so I picked one up, along with all the goodies and a bunch of games."

"Awesome!" From his face, Tommy may as well have said he'd won ten million dollars. "Do you have the new *Call of Duty*?"

Shane intervened. "Drew, do you think that game is appropriate?"

The boy looked at him as though he'd taken leave of his senses. "You're kidding, right? You're the one who bought me the first version!"

A couple of cops from the station snickered, and one said, "He's got you there."

"Damn, that's right," Shane muttered. "Fine. But stay away from the ones that have nudity."

"Yes, sir." The boy bounced off behind Tommy like a puppy.

Shane grabbed his heart. "My God. He said the words and he wasn't even in trouble. The sky is falling."

"They can shock you once in a while," Austin commented, taking a sip of his beer.

Tonio Salvatore showed up at that moment, Leslie in tow. "Do you have kids, Cap?"

"No. I never was blessed with any. If you guys will excuse me?"

The group stared after him, and Tonio frowned, his handsome face concerned. "Did I say something wrong?"

"Don't worry about it," Shane told him. "He doesn't say a lot about the subject of kids or his wife. Best not to mention either of them around him."

"Good to know. Thanks."

Leslie noted Shane's proximity to Daisy, the protective way he stood near her, and sneered. "Looks like that's not the only thing we shouldn't mention around the captain. Wonder what he'd say about two of his favorites hooking up under his nose?"

Tonio shot her a look tinged with faint disgust. "My God, Leslie. If he was going to discipline anyone it would've been you, about fifteen badges ago."

The woman's mouth fell open as several of the guys laughed. "You asshole! You haven't even been here that long. You don't know a damned thing about me!"

"No, but it's kind of like Bigfoot. Everybody's heard of someone who's seen it."

Now they were hooting, but Leslie didn't seem to take the teasing in the spirit in which it was intended. Outraged, she marched out the door and slammed it hard.

"There goes your date, bro," Julian said with mock sadness. "You break our mama's heart by leaving San Antonio to move here, then you're in town only a few weeks and you're already pissing off your fellow cops."

"Just the ones who want in my pants." He winked. "I'm following in your footsteps."

Julian had been the horn dog of Fire Station Five before his wife, an attorney named Grace McKenna, had let him catch her. Grace also happened to be the sister of Kat Paxton, Six-Pack's wife.

Daisy was always amazed how the groups had ties and everyone was like a big, extended family. They teased and fought, and they'd pounce on anybody who messed with one of them. They were the best.

Shane wanted to shoot some pool, so Daisy went and watched for a while, chatting with some of the wives and girlfriends who'd come to the party. They were a nice group of women who knew how to have fun, and most of them knew Shea and each other. Daisy never felt like the odd woman out, though. She couldn't recall when she had such a good time.

After a while, she drifted to the spare bedroom where Tommy had set up Drew to play on the Xbox. She cracked the door and peeked in, and was about to leave when he called out.

"You can stay if you want."

That hesitant statement surprised her and made her happy, too. This was the first time he'd invited her company of his own volition. Whatever he said next, she'd consider a victory. Walking inside, she left the door open and sat on the bed next to him, watching for a few minutes as his character leaped around, blasted, and annihilated the enemy.

Suddenly he paused the game. "You love Shane, don't you?"

She hesitated, unsure how to answer without upsetting him. "Would that bother you if I did?"

"No. I'm not a little kid. I know how that stuff works."

She doubted that, considering his lack of a positive female influence. "Do you resent him spending time with me? Us getting closer?"

"No," he said. "Well, not so much anymore. It's good to see Shane happy. He's close to his sister, but there has to be more. Right?"

"I suppose so." She marveled at his grown-up outlook.

"Shane deserves a super girlfriend, and you're pretty cool, I guess."

She'd been given the keys to the kingdom. Somehow she knew the buck stopped with this boy, who was growing up too fast. Who needed so much. Had such love to give. He could have made their lives miserable, but instead he was trying to embrace what they were and could be.

"Thank you." She hugged him. "You're pretty cool yourself."

"Hey, wanna play?"

She started to say no. But then she realized this invite was one more olive branch. How many times had he heard the word *no* at his house? That his dad was too busy? That he had guests to entertain?

"I'd love to." The beaming smile she received was her reward for giving exactly the right answer.

That's how Shane found them—whooping and hurling insults at each other about who was going to get splattered next. He came in and flopped down beside them, watching.

"How's the party?" she asked him.

"In full swing." His eyes warmed. "I thought I'd see if you wanted to go for a little walk with me."

She looked at Drew. "Do you mind?"

"Nah, go ahead. I'm good."

"I think Tommy mentioned he was coming to kick your butt in a bit," Shane teased.

"He can try. I'm undefeated!" The boy went back to playing.

Shane took her hand. "Come with me."

She told Drew goodbye, and he just waved without looking up. She let her lover lead her through the crowd, outside to the deck where grilling was underway. Night was falling, the stars peeking out as they made their way down the deck steps and toward the back of the Skylers' property, by the river.

"The day was pretty, but it's getting chilly," she noted.

"Don't worry, I'll keep you warm." His grin told her he'd very much enjoy doing it, too.

"Where are we going?"

"You'll see. I don't want to spoil the surprise."

"Why do I get the feeling you planned this?"

"Because you're a smart woman and you know me well. I'm devious when I want something, and I'll stop at nothing to get it."

"And what do you want?"

"You have to ask?" Stopping, he pulled her into his arms. "I want you."

His mouth took hers in a deep kiss. Not rough and bruising. Slow and sensual, the type of kiss that heats the body from head to toe. That binds the heart and refuses to let go. It was more than lust, more than desire. This was Shane, wanting her as a man wants his woman, and not just for sex. This was a connection so powerful and sweet, it defied words.

When he withdrew, he brushed a tendril of hair from her face and stared into her eyes for the longest moment. Like he wanted to take her into himself and never forget a single feature of her face. And she shivered at the knowledge that tonight—right now—meant a turning point in their relationship. For the good.

Taking her hand again, he led her along the bank, keeping to the trees. He kept a firm hold so she wouldn't stumble, until at last he reached a clearing in the trees near a deserted stretch of river. They stopped and he pointed.

"Just down there, up the bank from the water, is a cave. It's part of a system that runs all through this part of the county, intersecting with the river at several points. That particular cave is one where years ago, some hikers found the remains of a Native American. The remains went to a museum, but there are paintings still on the walls."

She waited, listening to the chirp of night birds, knowing he had more to say. That he was going somewhere with the lesson. The night took on a surreal quality. Haunting. Beautiful.

"I spend a lot of time on the river, especially at dawn and dusk. Did you know that if you listen very closely, you can hear their chants, the drumbeats floating over the water?"

She shivered, but not in fear.

"I've heard them, and it always makes me feel so at peace. They had a life here, too. They hunted, fought, loved, and died. They were family. That's why I built here, because of that sense of peace and belonging; times like this when I feel I'm part of something much bigger than myself, and that maybe a hundred years from now, someone else will stand right here, a couple perhaps, beginning their lives in such a special place. And wondering about the people who were here before."

"About us," she said softly. She began to understand what he was saying.

"This is our place now, but we only get to borrow it for a while. Nothing lasts forever, except the memory of love. People will come and go, like they've done since the beginning of the world, but the impression we leave will last for those who want to stop and really listen."

Facing her, he cupped her face in his hands. "This place is special to me, and I wanted to share it with the most special lady in my world. The only woman I'll ever want again." He sucked in a deep breath as her heart melted. "I love you, Daisy. I love you so damned much. My heart and everything I am is yours. Please believe that."

He kissed her again, and the truth wound around her. She knew that at last, he was hers. Truly, really hers.

"Don't run from me again," she whispered. "I can't take it. Not from you."

"Never, baby. Never again."

"I love you, too. I have for so long." Tears streamed down her face, and she held on to him.

"I'm so sorry I hurt you," he said hoarsely. "Please say you forgive me."

"I forgive you, and I love you. I want us."

"God, me, too. Come with me." Grabbing her hand, he led them to the clearing. Now she could see a tent, a large-sized one pitched in seclusion, far from everyone.

"You set this up for us." More tears flowed, happy ones. She wiped at her face.

"Earlier today, I came down here. Brought the tent and bedding. The others won't miss us for a while, and we'll get back before they take much notice. But I wanted not just to sneak away with you, but to create a memory we can share always."

He led her inside and lit the Coleman lamp that was sitting on a box next to a pile of bedding. A nice, warm glow, not too bright, enveloped the tent.

"Nobody will see us?"

"We're out of view of everyone here, even if a boater should come along in the dark. But I doubt that would happen."

She smiled. "Are you planning to ravage me?"

"Better—I'm going to make sweet love to you." He pulled her close. "I want to celebrate you being mine."

"And you're mine."

"Forever."

He set about making good on his promise, pulling her shirt over her head, then unclasping her bra to slip it off. Being bared to him, with nothing but canvas separating them from the night around them, made her feel sort of . . . free. As though they were making love the way it was intended in the beginning, with nothing but the heavens to witness them.

Never before had sex felt like an extension of love. Now she understood the difference, and she'd never be able to settle for less again. With Shane, she had faith that he would hold her and care for her. And she would return it to him.

Bending his head, he suckled her nipples, nibbling

each one with his teeth, hardening them to sensitized points. He pleasured each one to his satisfaction, leaving her arching into him. Needing more.

"So beautiful, my baby."

Her shoes and jeans went next, along with her silky black panties, leaving her naked before him. Heat bloomed between her thighs as she worked on the buttons of his shirt, exposing his smooth chest to her hungry gaze. Running her palms down his chest and abdomen, she thrilled at his shudder. He wanted as much as she did.

He pulled off his boots, then she got his jeans undone and worked them down. His erection popped free and he kicked his clothes aside, drinking her in.

They came together with slow hunger, the heat building into its own entity. A living force that drew them together, stoked the flames into steady fire. Not the frantic coupling of lust, but the pure joining of love, deep and true.

He lowered her to the bedding and she found it soft, inviting. He'd seen to her comfort, thought of everything. He hovered over her, kissed down her tummy. But instead of leaving her on her back, this time he gently urged her onto her stomach and spread her legs. Lying between them, he licked her sex, laving, sending tendrils of excitement coiling through her nerve endings. Parting the tender flesh, he feasted on her, giving her every ounce of his attention. Taking her to the peak.

Then he got up and pulled her to her hands and knees. She'd never felt so exposed, or so completely owned, in a wonderful way. She was his.

Two fingers dipped into her sex, began to pump into

her channel. She loved the way he prepared her, taking such care. She moaned, wiggled back into his touch.

"Like that, baby?"

"Yes, please . . ."

"Make love to you? That's what I'm doing."

"I need you inside me," she begged.

"I'll always be inside you," he whispered, rolling protection on his cock. "Always."

And then he was pushing his length inside, stretching her so full. She'd never felt anything as incredible as Shane loving her with all his soul.

Grasping her hips, he thrust deep, moving so slowly at first. Driving her insane with the fire licking her womb, her sex. Then he sat back, taking her with him so that her back was pressed to his chest and belly, his cock still buried inside her.

She gasped in pleasure. She'd never made love in such a decadent position. So intimate, every possible inch of their skin touching, her lover surrounding her. In this man's arms, she was higher than she'd ever been. His cock buried deep inside, there had been nothing like this, ever.

Because he loved her. And she loved him.

He began to move, thrusting up into her tight sheath. Holding her close to his heart, he loved her as no man ever had, or ever would again. Kept her safe and sheltered.

Her Shane. Her love.

The tide began to sweep her out of control and she cried out, her sex clasping him as her orgasm rocked her to the core. He quickly followed, shooting his release deep into her, warming the core of her, to the fiber of her being.

How long they remained in their embrace, she didn't know. But she heard his breathy declarations of love, reveled in his kisses on her neck and shoulder. They remained even after he'd softened, basking in the glow of what was certain.

"We should go back," she said reluctantly. "I'm sure they're eating burgers by now, and are fully aware that our walk lasted a lot longer than a mere stroll."

He chuckled. "Damn, you're right. But maybe Drew's still wrapped up in the Xbox and hasn't noticed."

She turned and made a face at him. "Do not mention our boy while we're naked and stuck together."

"Sorry." Suddenly, he squeezed her tight. "You said *our* boy."

"Well, he is. I love him, Shane," she said honestly, moving off his lap to face him. "He's such a good guy, and he's going to grow into an incredible man because of you and Tommy."

"Brad too. And you. I've noticed how you two are starting to bond."

She smiled. "We are, and I think things are going to start looking up for him. For all of us."

"I believe you're right, sugar."

Moving to the box holding up the lamp, he retrieved a small pack of wet wipes and a hand towel. He began to clean her up, then himself, doing so as if it was the most precious task in the world. He had thought of everything.

As they dressed, she regretted having to leave. She wished they could stay all night without anyone panicking or wondering where they'd gone. As if reading her mind, he smiled.

"We'll come back. I promise."

"I'm going to hold you to that."

"I expect you will." He winked.

He doused the lamp and turned on a flashlight he'd stowed beside it. As they started back through the dark, she held tight to Shane's hand, even though he wouldn't let her fall.

She trusted that now. Trusted Shane.

Now that she'd found love, no one was ever going to take that from them.

Carl paced the living room, yelling into the phone at Irvin.

"Yes, I'm keeping our meeting, you dumb fuck! We've got even more to talk about, don't we?"

"Come on, Carl! It's not my fault the cops showed up the other night. I have no clue how they found out about the drop, unless one of those morons decided to tell them," the man insisted. "They were questioning the product right before the cavalry came. Don't you think that's suspicious?"

"Everyone, even you, is suspect when it comes to screwups like this. You're the one who started questioning the product to start with, so I suggest you get your head in the game and start observing your damned surroundings. I got no patience for shit like this, and you're going to find yourself out of a job before you know it."

Meaning retired, permanently. They both knew it.

"I'm sorry! I'll be more careful from now on. But we do have to discuss the stuff, and you know it. The formula is flawed, nothing near the success it could be if only—"

"What, you want to go legit?" He snorted. "That'll happen. You're just a washed-up scientist with a rap sheet. You could invent the cure for cancer and nobody would give you the time of day."

Silence. Then, "Fuck you, Carl. I know what we've got here and it does have real potential. Black market or not, we could go global with this. There are countries begging for drugs like this, with nowhere near the tough drug laws as the States, or they aren't enforced. Screw thousands per drop—we could be raking in millions."

It was a thought guaranteed to make even Carl sit up and take notice. But they didn't have the manpower to spread that broad without tying in with some very dangerous pros. Men so powerful even Carl shuddered at the thought of doing business with them. No, in that situation, Carl would be the grunt again. The nobody.

That was not going to happen.

"I'll think about it," he lied.

They hung up, and Carl knew the man's fate was sealed. He'd get the formula in the hands of someone who'd do what he was damned well told and wouldn't dream with stars in his eyes.

Stars fell, and so did dreamers.

Only the ruthless survived. And Carl was nothing if not a survivor.

13

"Another crappy day at Hicksville High."

Leaning against a tree at the park near campus, Drew took a drag from the cigarette Ty had given him. He hated the taste, but it made him feel good to do even one small thing he shouldn't. Like he had some sort of control over his life, even when he didn't.

"Doesn't have to be." Ty gave him a grin.

"Man, I can't skip again. I've already gotten into enough hot water with Shane as it is."

"Screw him. He's such an uptight ass—"

"Don't talk about him like that," Drew snapped. "He takes good care of me, and he loves me. Which is more than you can say for *your* old man. And you're the one who said you wished your dad was more like him!" Even though he still hadn't met Carl, he knew that much from Ty.

Thoughts of his own dad, dead and buried, hit Drew hard. That happened a lot, and he couldn't help but think if he'd been a better son, his dad would still be alive. Sickness churned in his gut.

The barb he'd almost forgotten about hit the target, and Ty made a face. "True that. I'll be seventeen in three weeks, and he won't even front me the money to buy a broken-down piece of crap. And I can't get what passes for a lame-ass job in this town without a car! I'm hosed either way."

"How does he afford nice stuff like the Escalade, anyhow? What the hell does he do all day?"

"I don't know, but whatever it is, I want in on the action." Ty narrowed his dark eyes. "I think it's past time we find out."

"We?"

"Sure. It'll be an adventure," he suggested slyly. "Then when we catch him, he'll have to cut us in on the action."

"I doubt I want any part of what he's up to. But I wouldn't mind knowing, just for kicks." He thought of Shane's suspicions about Carl and Johnson. The strange smell that had been lingering in Johnson's empty barn as they'd painted the outside.

What if he could help make up for the trouble he'd caused Shane?

"What're we waitin' for, then? Let's play detective." He smirked. "Maybe that'll earn me some brownie points with your cop."

"Not unless you plan to tell him what's going on."

"Depends on whether my old man cooperates. You're not going to say anything to Shane, are you?"

"No," he lied. If he saw Carl doing something illegal, he would do exactly that. Even if he got himself in more trouble because of skipping school. "I'm just curious. Besides, I wouldn't be going if you hadn't asked."

"Good. Now all we need is a ride."

"To where?"

"Johnson's place, for starters. Dad's been spending a lot of time with the jerk."

Drew groaned. "You're determined to get us shot by that psycho, aren't you? The last thing I want to do is come within a mile of him ever again."

"We're not going to do anything but watch, I promise. He won't see us."

"Like he wasn't supposed to see us before?"

"That was different. This time we'll stay hidden, and if my dad doesn't show, we'll scout around the area some."

"So, who are we getting this ride from?"

"I've got it covered."

Ty walked toward the school building and Drew followed, thinking he had to stop trailing wherever his friend led, like a stupid cow. If he found something useful to report to Shane, he'd do it, sort of as a favor to the man he'd treated like crap for the past few weeks. If not, he'd start distancing himself from Ty. The guy was a little off, took too many risks that made Drew uncomfortable.

"Hey, Alan!"

Drew jogged to catch up with Ty. "Are you crazy?" he hissed. "You're asking that dickweed for a ride?"

"Relax. He's a dickweed with a car, and one who enjoys bucking the rules. He'll play."

The jock stopped his trek into the building to arch a brow at their approach. "If it isn't our resident felons in training. What do you want?"

"We need a ride out to Ferris Road," Ty said. "Like, now."

That earned a smirk. "Cuttin' class, huh? What makes you think I'll help?"

"Because I can pay you in weed, that's why."

Weed? Shit. He definitely had to cut Ty loose as a friend.

"I don't do drugs, creeplet. But I got nothin' to do in first period, so sure. Why not?" Alan strode for his car, an old Camaro that he was always tinkering with.

Drew couldn't help but admire it aloud. "Sweet ride."

The boy cut him a surprised look. "Thanks. I saved for two years to buy it, and I work on it when I can."

"You have a job?"

"At H. G. Hill, over on Main," he said, referring to the local grocery store. "Why? Does that surprise you?"

"Just asking." Who knew the snarky jock was such a hard worker? Actually, it did surprise him a bit. Almost as much as the jock's softened attitude toward him.

They didn't speak much on the way out to Ferris Road. When Alan turned onto the road, he pulled over. "Here you go. You didn't get a ride from me, dumbasses."

Ty slid out first. Drew was about to follow him when Alan gripped his wrist to stop him. Drew gave him a questioning look, and the other boy lowered his voice.

"Ditch that little creep before he ends up getting you in bigger shit than you can get out of."

"What do you care? I thought you hated my guts."

"Nah. I just had this idea of who I thought you'd be," he admitted. "A spoiled rich brat who'd strut around acting like you were better than everyone else. Then I invited you to sit with us that day, and you threw my olive branch back in my face."

Drew blushed. "Sorry about that. I had a lot of shit going on in my head."

"I realized that, after I thought about it. I was wrong about you and I'm not proud of it. Just like you're wrong if you think Ty Eastlake is your friend. He's bad news, and so is his dad. Think about it."

"I will. Thanks."

The jock shot him a smile and he returned it. Drew got out of the car, mulling that over. Alan, the guy who was such an ass to him on his first day, might actually make a much better friend. Weird.

"What were you two talking about?" Ty asked suspiciously, watching Alan turn the car around and head back to town.

"Nothing. He was just giving me some crap about being a spoiled rich kid." He didn't feel bad about lying, and, thankfully, Ty bought it.

"You are a spoiled rich kid. In fact, you could buy us both a set of wheels and it wouldn't even put a dent in your green."

He tried to make it sound like a joke, but Drew knew he wasn't. Right then and there, he understood why Ty hung around him—the money. He wanted to sponge, and all this time he'd been buttering Drew up, getting his hooks in deeper and deeper, pretending to be a friend. Maybe he even hoped Drew would fund him and his dad in whatever scheme the man had going.

He was on to the prick now. He should just walk back to town, but he really wanted to see what was going on with Ty's dad and Johnson. If he could help Shane with his case, it might go a long way toward easing the guilt he felt about how badly he'd treated the man.

Not to mention easing the agony in his chest over what had happened to his own dad. The guilt over how he could've prevented it by telling someone what he knew. The pain never left him, but maybe he could make up for everything.

So he followed Ty, once again, for what he swore was the last time.

Shane's cell phone rang at 10:15 a.m. He was poring over case notes, barely into his second cup of coffee, and groaned at the intrusion. If he didn't get calls every ten minutes, he might get some work done.

Checking the display, he saw a number he didn't recognize. In his line of work, that was annoying but not unusual, so he answered. "Hello?"

"Hello, this is Marylyn Estes, and I'm the registrar at Sugarland High. May I speak to Shane Ford?"

"That's me, Mrs. Estes. How can I help you?"

"Mr. Ford, I'm calling to check on Drew's absences from school," she said in a concerned voice.

A chill went through him. "His what?"

"His absences. He's missed first period four times and seventh period six times, most of those on the same days. He's had excessive tardies in the period after lunch as well. I know he's turned in written notes from you excusing him, but—"

"No, I haven't written Drew a single note excusing him from *any* missed school time. If he's given the school notes, they're forgeries. I had no idea he was skipping."

Fuck! I swear to God—

"That's what we were afraid of," she said with a sigh. "I just wanted to find out whether the absences were legitimate. Nobody thought too much of them at first because of the terrible tragedy he's been through, plus he's such a polite boy and always came back with a note. But when they continued and he didn't show up today, we decided to check and make you aware this was happening."

"He's not there now?"

"No. And his grades are suffering, because he's not turning in the work he's missed."

What in the hell is that boy thinking?

"Oh, believe me, he *will* turn that in," Shane said, seething. "Whether or not the teachers will allow him late credit is up to them. And he'll be punished at home for skipping and forging my name."

"I hate that Drew is in trouble, because he really is such a nice young man who's just very lost right now," she said sincerely. "But I agree he's at the point where he needs intervention. We appreciate your support, Mr. Ford."

"Do you think counseling would help? I've suggested it and he didn't want to go, but I'm thinking I've made a mistake in not insisting."

"Legally, I can't tell you to seek outside professional counseling for him. But if it were *my* child . . ." She left it hanging.

"Thank you, Mrs. Estes. I'll be looking into it."

"You're very welcome. His first-, fourth-, and seventh-period teachers will be contacting you. Is there anything else I can answer for you?"

"Not at the moment, but I appreciate the call."

After hanging up, Shane slumped at his desk. That's where Daisy found him some minutes later.

"What's wrong?" she asked, sitting in a chair next to him.

"Drew's been skipping school almost as frequently as he changes underwear, and he's been forging my name on the absence notes. He's skipping now, in fact, which is why they called me."

"Oh no. What are we going to do?"

He blinked at her. "We?"

"I think of him as mine, too," she said with a soft smile. "I love him *and* his new father, so of course it's *we*."

He gave her a smile. "You don't know how good that makes me feel. Drew and I are lucky to have you, sugar."

"I wish I could kiss you, but that might cause a stir."

"Not as much as you think, since I'm pretty sure Taylor and Chris have managed to blab our status to everyone who wasn't at the party or already in the loop." Leslie was less than happy, but he wisely refrained from saying so.

"Still. We don't know what's going to happen with our jobs since we blew the No Dating Other Cops rule out of the water."

"Yeah, but they can fire me if they want. I'm rich, remember?" He gave her a wan smile.

"You'd wither and die within a year without detective work, and you know it. But don't worry; it won't come to that. I'd resign first."

She would, too. But he wouldn't let her, so they'd figure out something.

"What are you going to do about Drew?"

"I'm going home to wait for him to show up. Then I'm going to ground his ass, and have a long talk with him doing most of the listening. I'm going to take over driving him to and from school, and I'll sit in every one of his damned classes with him if I have to. Then he's going to counseling—period. I know you always think I'm being too hard on him, but—"

"No, I don't. I think you're doing exactly the right thing."

"Really?"

"Yes. I think I'm too easy, and I always stick up for him when he needs a firmer hand. I promise to support you more from now on."

He didn't think he could love her more. "I don't think you're too easy. He needs that with you one-on-one, but I appreciate you backing me. If we're gonna do this family thing, we have to present a united front."

"I agree."

He stole a quick kiss, anyway, earning a few good-natured comments from around them. Standing, he shrugged on his jacket over his holster. "I'll call you later."

"Please do. I want to know he's home safe."

"Dinner at my house?"

"Sounds good, but I'll cook. I have a feeling both of my men will need some mothering by then."

"I have a feeling you're right."

A short time later, he wasn't at all surprised to arrive home to an empty house. Pacing, he prepared for a long wait.

"There's nothing going on," Drew said. Not even a leaf was moving on Johnson's place. "It's obvious he's not home. Why don't we head back to town?"

"I've got a better idea. There's an old moonshine distillery not far from here, in the hills. There's a cabin, too, about a hundred yards from it where the old timers used to live while they made their hooch."

"I don't know . . ."

"The place is so cool! Think of it as a history lesson," Ty said. "I'll bet you've never seen anything like it, and there's always old stuff lying around."

"What, like actual hooch?"

"No, stupid. That's all gone. But there's jugs and some leftover equipment. Once I found a big knife and a button from a Confederate coat in the dirt."

"That's cool." He had to admit that sounded interesting. "I've heard of people finding Civil War artifacts all over this part of Tennessee, but I've never found any myself."

"Then come on. It's not like we'd make it back in time for school, anyhow."

He agreed with some trepidation, but Ty was right. They wouldn't make it back for school, and this was the last time he was doing this, anyway. Might as well see if he could find something interesting, since staking out Johnson's place had been a bust. He was still disappointed about that. He'd wanted to make Shane proud.

The hike was longer than he'd expected, but since it was in the general direction of town instead of away from it, the walk home from the distillery wouldn't take as long. Just when he was about to accuse Ty of making it up, the place came into view.

The distillery was sitting in a copse of trees and nearly overgrown with weeds. Drew wasn't sure how the contraption worked, exactly, except that there were a bunch of barrel things, trays where the liquid must've run, and a spout where the finished product finally emerged to be bottled.

"Awesome," he said, checking out the setup. It was like stepping into another world. "I can't imagine living up here, working day after day making moonshine for the money to survive. I've read that it was a whole sub-culture that was accepted among hill people."

"It still is, in some places. I saw a special about it on cable. The groups are so tight-knit and dangerous, even the FBI and DEA can't get in to close 'em down."

"I imagine today it's a lot higher-tech than this."

"For sure."

They kicked around some, poking about the remains. There wasn't much there in the way of souvenirs, so they eventually moved on, ambling in the direction of the cabin Ty mentioned. They both kept an eye open for arrowheads, which were abundant if you had a sharp eye and knew what to look for. Drew didn't have a ton of practice, though, and didn't find anything. But neither did Ty.

Both of them forgot all about exploring when they topped the last hill and found the cabin. Because it wasn't empty—three cars were parked haphazardly around it. There didn't appear to be anyone outside, which meant they were inside.

"Stay down," Ty said, pulling him behind the trees.

"Isn't that your dad's SUV?" He eyed the black Escalade, a terrible urge to get the hell out of there kick-starting his nerves.

"Yeah. And that's Johnson's truck." Ty pointed to an old red Chevy. "I don't know who the third one belongs to."

"Me, either. Ty, let's go. Whatever they're doing, we don't need to know." So much for being a hero.

"Screw that! This is my chance to get in on whatever game my old man has going. You don't have to worry about where your next dime is comin' from, but the rest of us have to survive." The boy practically sneered the last sentence. "Leave if you want, pussy."

Drew hesitated. He really, really wanted to bolt. But he couldn't, in good conscience, leave without knowing Ty was safe. Even if the guy was a dick. "I'll go with you to look, but then we're ghosting out of here. All right? And when you confront your dad, I was never here."

The other boy thought about it. "Deal."

There are times in a man's life, he'd heard, when he should listen *very* closely to the little voice in his head screaming *You're about to do something really freaking stupid!* In some form or another, Shane had been attempting to drill that message into his thick skull for weeks. But sometimes a man has to make that final, awful error before the message truly hits home for good.

As they crept forward, and Drew heard the vicious argument taking place inside, he had a feeling that *this* was that final error.

Ty crouched behind the Escalade and motioned Drew forward. Gritting his teeth, Drew dashed from his tree to his friend hunkering low. Ty pointed to the side of the cabin to a window, indicating that was their destination.

"No, they'll spot us! This is close enough."

"We need to hear what's going on and see who the third person is."

"*You* need to, not me."

The boy went, anyway, and Drew silently cursed. The

shithead was going to get them killed. But if he could bring something to Shane after all . . ..

He got moving and squatted under the window next to Ty. The voices could be heard pretty clearly from here, and there wasn't a lot of doubt what the ruckus was about.

"I'll tell you both the same thing Holstead told you," a man shouted. "That shit is totally unstable. We can't successfully market a product and keep it under the radar when it starts killing off our customers right and left! We have to perfect the formula if we have a prayer of establishing a business long term."

"That's not Johnson," Drew whispered.

"Not my dad, either."

So it was the third, unknown man.

Another man countered angrily, "Fuck the long term! We're making boatloads of money *now*. So what if a few spoiled, rich athletes are dumb enough to take the stuff and drop dead? They deserve exactly what they get." That wasn't Johnson, so it must be Carl Eastlake.

And his voice sounded too damned familiar. Then what Carl said hit Drew, and he felt lightheaded. An awful truth was taking shape in his mind, but he had to know for sure.

As the two men continued to verbally duke it out, Drew took a chance. He raised his head to peer over the ledge and through the window. Beside him, Ty did the same.

Johnson was standing off to the side, merely watching the heated debate. However, it was the sight of Carl Eastlake that rooted Drew to the ground in spellbound horror.

Oh, my God. God, no. This man, Ty's dad—Carl was the one who . . .

Just then, Carl became tired of arguing. Suddenly, he pulled a huge gun from the waistband of his jeans and pointed it at the third man's forehead. "I guess you didn't learn your lesson from Holstead when he decided to be the squeaky wheel. This conversation is over."

One pop, the gun jerking in Carl's hand, and a red spot bloomed right between the man's eyes. Brains and blood splattered all over the table behind the victim, and Johnson simply moved out of the way as their former partner slumped to the floor.

"Shit, shit!" Drew staggered backward, unable to tear his horrified gaze away.

"Fuck!" Ty shouted, standing up.

Which immediately gained Carl's attention, his murderous gaze fixing on the two boys at the window. "Ty!" he shouted. "Get your scrawny ass in here, boy."

Ty lit out in the direction of the woods, not even stopping to see if Drew was behind him. Drew was hot on his heels, running faster than he ever had in his life. He was convinced he'd feel a bullet tear through his body any second, ending his life as fast as that of the man in the cabin. Either that, or his heart would explode from pure terror and he'd drop like a stone. As dead as his father.

His dad, whom Carl had killed with his drugs and pretty promises to an aging NFL star. Of playing stronger. Regaining his edge over guys who were younger and faster.

They ran through the woods, taking the most direct route all the way to town. Drew wasn't sure how long they'd been running, but his sides were heaving and his lungs burning as if he'd swallowed hot coals by the time they stopped in the parking lot behind Hardee's.

"He's gonna kill me," Drew panted between breaths, bracing his shaking hands on his knees.

"He won't." Ty was struggling for breath, too. "I won't tell him who you are. I swear."

"But he recognized me."

"What do you mean? From where?"

"My dad's house. He fucking sold my dad drugs."

"Shit! Okay, look, you didn't rat him out for that. I'll convince him you won't tell about this."

"I'm a goddamn *murder witness*!"

"Fuck, man, let me think," Ty said between gritted teeth, running his hands through his hair. "Okay, here's the deal. You can't tell, because you knew your dad was doing drugs and didn't do anything about it—you're, like, an accessory."

Drew flinched from the pain. "It *is* just as much my fault. I suspected what was going on, but I never told anyone, not even Shane."

Ty took a few more breaths. "I'll explain it to the old man, and he'll let it slide."

"OK." Drew wasn't so sure. That didn't sound right. But his mind was in complete chaos and he couldn't think right now. Grief, ragged and raw, was threatening to rise and suffocate him. Swallow him whole. "I gotta go home."

"I'll call you later. Have your cell handy."

"Sure."

He turned and left. Walked forever on shaking legs,

the image of his dad, dead on the floor of his office, meshing with the memory of Carl shooting that man between the eyes. So much death and destruction.

For money. For ego.

Drew could've talked to his dad. Could've helped him. Should have.

Didn't.

Those agonizing thoughts chased around and around in his tormented brain. Seizing him with an iron grip until he couldn't think anymore.

He could never say a word. Never. He could not face what he'd done.

He'd let his own father die.

Shane paced until he couldn't anymore. Then he settled on the sofa and flipped channels until the front door opened.

Daisy walked in, looking around. "He's still not home?"

"No. I've called his cell a dozen times, but he must have it turned off."

She came to sit by him, wrapping her arms around him. "He'll be home soon. In the meantime, can I get you a beer?"

He thought about it. "Just one. I want to be lucid when he gets home. After he and I talk, we'll revisit that idea."

Melting into her, he kissed her long and passionately, giving in to his need to touch her. Hold her close. She healed him by just being near, and he couldn't get enough. Slipping a hand behind her head, he grasped the tie of her conservative ponytail and worked it off, then raked the strands free. He loved it down.

"There. Much better."

She smiled. "Let me get that beer, then I'll change and start dinner. Anything you're craving?"

"Besides you? Let me think . . . Nope."

"Charmer."

"Does that mean I'll get lucky, then?"

She winked. "Maybe."

He watched her go, mood lifted some. He liked having her here, liked that she'd moved in some of her things even though they were still living separately, for Drew's sake. Drew was more receptive, too, ever since the cookout at Tommy and Shea's place. If they could just get the boy on the right path, things would be looking up for them as a family.

Daisy returned, handing him the beer, then padded off. He thanked her as she left and sipped his beer, eventually letting his eyes close, drifting some as he heard pleasant cooking sounds coming from the kitchen. Good smells were coming from there when at last the door opened.

Across the room, he saw Drew step into the foyer and just stand there staring at him. Shane set his almost-empty beer on the coffee table and stood.

"We need to talk."

The boy shuffled in, the slump in his posture telling Shane he knew he'd finally been busted. He said nothing, waiting. Shane noted his face was so pale he looked like he'd had the flu for a week. He certainly didn't look like a young man who'd enjoyed skipping school.

"Where's your backpack?"

His eyes widened as though he hadn't given it a single thought all day. "I'm not sure. I think I left it in a friend's car."

"You think? What friend?"

"Alan."

"All right. You'll get it back from him tomorrow." He paused, letting the boy stew for a long minute. "The school called today. Any idea what they had to say?"

Tucking his hands in his front pockets, Drew nodded. "They told you about me."

"What about you?" He was determined to make the boy state what he'd done.

"I—I skipped school."

"Not just once."

"A few times," he mumbled. Then he did the strangest thing—he walked to the window and slowly, carefully pulled back the curtains. Peered outside. He remained perfectly still.

Shane frowned. "What are you doing?"

Drew jumped back as if he'd been startled by the sound of Shane's voice. "Sorry."

"Why is your hand shaking?" His eyes narrowed. "What have you been doing all day?"

"Just kicking around town, hanging out with Ty. Nothing special."

Ty. That name made him cringe. "Hanging out doing what? Smoking dope?"

"No! I—I'd never do drugs after . . ." The boy trailed off, tears welling in his eyes. "I wouldn't."

Damn it. "I had to ask because I'm worried about you." Daisy came into the room and sat in a nearby chair, silently lending her support just by being there.

"I'm fine," the boy said. "I'm not going to cut classes anymore. I've learned my lesson."

"In one day? You've been skipping since you came to stay with me, you've been gone all damned day long, and suddenly you've learned your lesson?"

"I have!"

"Something happened today," he said with absolute certainty. "What's going on, Drew? Did you boys get into more trouble? Is Frank Johnson hassling you?"

"No! We weren't doing anything but messing around, and time got away from us—that's all!"

The boy was lying. Shane exchanged a glance with Daisy and knew she had the same opinion. They were both good cops, but she was even better at reading kids than he was. And this one was scared, hiding something. It wasn't Shane he was scared of, either, he was positive.

"I think I should go have another talk with Carl Eastlake. See if he can shed any light on where you boys were today."

Drew's face drained of color. "Please don't talk to him," he said in a choked voice. "He— he's mean. He'll beat Ty if you go over there with any more complaints about us. A-and I'm not going to be hanging out with him anymore, so it doesn't matter."

A half-truth. He smelled it. Drew reeked of fear. *What in God's name is going on?*

"All right," he allowed. "We'll talk more later about exactly where you went and what you did today. For now, I think it won't come as any great shock to find out you're grounded. Indefinitely. Am I correct?"

"Yes, sir."

"Next, either Daisy or I will be driving you to school

and picking you up for the foreseeable future. No off-campus lunch, either. Possibly until the end of the school year."

"Yes, sir."

"Last, if I have to sit in every one of your classes with you to make sure you attend, your teachers will not have a problem with that. Is that going to be necessary?"

"No, sir."

"Tomorrow you will go to every one of them and gather all of your makeup work. Prepare to spend the next couple of weeks getting caught up."

His head bobbed. "Okay."

"Do you have anything else to say for yourself?"

"Just that I'm really sorry," he said hoarsely. "This is all my fault. Everything."

Shane could tell he wasn't just talking about cutting school. But he couldn't imagine what on earth had happened to make Drew act this way.

"I guess that's it for now, then. Go to your room until it's time for dinner, and no TV."

Hanging his head, the young man walked away. Shane's heart hurt watching him go.

"I'm proud of you," Daisy said, standing to wrap him in a hug. "You handled that like a strong dad who was in control."

"Thanks." He took comfort in her warmth, as much as he could. "But there's something really wrong, sugar. He's scared of something."

"I agree. I thought he was going to pass out when you mentioned talking to Carl Eastlake."

"You think he beats his son?"

"From his rap sheet and what I know of him and Ty, it's a strong possibility."

"There's a special place in hell for anyone who beats their child. I'd love to pin something lasting on him that'll put him away for good."

"We'll figure it out. For tonight, why don't we all have a quiet dinner and let Drew process everything? Maybe after he's had a day to think, he'll be ready to talk tomorrow."

"I hope so."

Shane had a horrible feeling in his gut that tomorrow might be far too late.

14

Shane dropped Drew off at school the next morning and watched the boy walk all the way inside.

He still hadn't opened up. Nor did he eat breakfast. He was like a ghost, moving through the house, in danger of vanishing into mist.

Turning toward the diner on the square, Shane decided to grab a cup of coffee and a breakfast sandwich to go.

Looked like he was going to need the pick-me-up.

Drew's head went all swimmy and he braced a hand against a locker. He hadn't slept all night, and his mind was still a scrambled mess. The trouble at school and the consequences Shane had leveled barely registered.

He'd seen Carl Eastlake kill a man. In cold blood.

Shot dead. Right between the eyes.

The red hole in the man's forehead, the blood and brain matter bursting through the back of his skull like a hammer smashing a melon, were forever ingrained. Stuck in a constant loop that he couldn't escape.

Drew had seen Carl do it, and had seen him deal

drugs, too. He could link Carl to enough criminal activity to put him away for life, maybe even get him the death penalty for the shooting. It didn't matter that Ty had called last night with the promised assurances.

The man was going to kill him.

Even though Drew was just as guilty of his own dad's death, he was going to have to tell Shane. There was no other way out. Shane was a cop. He'd know what to do.

This afternoon, Drew would spill everything. In truth, it would be a relief to get it all off his chest.

"Oh, hey," a voice said. He looked over to see Alan standing beside him. "I've got your backpack in my car. I wasn't sure if you'd be here and I didn't want to carry it around if you weren't, so I left it in there."

"Sure, that's fine." He couldn't seem to think what else to say.

Alan eyed him. "Dude, are you stoned or something?"

"No, just tired. Can we go get my backpack?"

"Here." Digging in his pocket, he handed Drew his car keys. "Get it yourself. I've got a test to make up before first period and I'm late. Just give 'em back to me in English."

"Okay, thanks."

Alan disappeared down the hallway, leaving Drew alone. Despite their rocky start, it seemed like he might be an okay guy. Funny that Alan had believed Drew's biggest problem was being a rich brat.

If only he knew.

Slipping out a side exit, Drew headed around the building toward the back parking lot where Alan always parked his Camaro. He had plenty of time to get the backpack and haul his butt inside for his first class. He wasn't going to disappoint Shane again.

He stepped around the corner and noticed a dark blue van parked next to the curb. He'd never seen it before, but it wasn't unusual to see all sorts of vehicles at the school. Probably delivering something.

Just as he passed the van, the door slid open. A man leaped from inside, straight at him, holding something white in his hand.

He barely had a second to register Carl and then the man was on him, one strong arm wrapping around his throat, the other reaching around to his face.

"No! Get off me!" Reacting instantly, he brought his foot down hard on the man's instep as Shane had once taught him. Carl grunted in pain, but Drew was off balance and it wasn't enough to make him let go.

The white thing was smashed over his face, and he realized it was a cloth. A foul-smelling chemical assaulted his sinuses and made his head spin. Frantically he reached for his phone, but it fell from his nerveless fingers and hit the curb, skittering away.

"Nice of you to show, kid. Saved me the trouble of havin' to follow you, waitin' for my chance," Carl gloated. "I appreciate that."

The inside of the dirty van was the last thing Drew saw before everything went dark.

Shane was sitting at his desk when his cell phone rang at 10:10. After yesterday, he now recognized the number and immediately tensed in dread.

"Hello?"

"Mr. Ford, this is Marylyn Estes again from the high school," she began.

"Mrs. Estes, what can I do for you?" *Please, if that boy has any sense . . .*

"I'm so sorry, Mr. Ford, but I'm afraid Drew didn't show up for first period again. His teacher came to the office right after class was over to let us know."

He sat bolt upright. "That's impossible," he growled. "I had a long talk with Drew last night and he was truly sorry for his actions. He promised me he'd attend from now on, and I know he was telling me the truth."

Wasn't he? Could he have imagined Drew's sincerity?

"I understand how frustrating this is, believe me. I've worked for the school for years, and I know how easily they forget promises like that when temptation steps in."

He considered that. Had just been thinking it himself, but . . .

"Not with Drew," he said with conviction. "I watched him walk into the building myself. He was there and promised he'd stay. He wouldn't lie, not after last night."

"Well, he *was* here," she conceded. "When we asked around, one of the students said he gave Drew the keys to his car because Drew's backpack was inside. Apparently, Drew went out to the car and didn't return."

Oh, God. Something was wrong. He knew it had to do with why Drew was so upset last night.

"Nobody recalls seeing him outside after that?"

"None we've spoken to. I think it's possible he simply skipped as he's done before, many times."

Fear rose and his stomach lurched. "Possible, but I don't think so. Please call me if he does show up."

"Will do."

Shane had his coat on and was about to rush out to search the streets for Drew when none other than Carl Eastlake materialized in the doorway. As he came to stand in front of his desk, it took every ounce of restraint not to vent his anger and fear on the man he was quickly coming to loathe.

"Eastlake," he said evenly. "How can I help you?"

"I got a call from the school and Ty is missing. Thought you might know something about that, since our two have been out makin' mischief most every day." He eyed Shane coolly. "Ty mentioned you're a cop. Fancy that, huh?"

Shane didn't answer as he studied the man. He noted fresh scrapes on the knuckles of his right hand and a scratch on his neck. "Been in a fight recently?"

"Yeah, bar fight last night." He grinned. "I love a good scrape."

Lying bastard. The scratches were too recent to be from last night. He decided to play along. "No, I haven't seen the boys. I was going to ask you the same thing."

"Well, I want to file a report on Ty. I'm tired of that kid disappearing whenever he pleases."

That didn't make sense on so many levels. "You know we can't file a report for a missing person before forty-eight hours has passed, unless there's been an abduction. Then we can do an Amber Alert."

"Huh. That's a stupid rule, the forty-eight hours thing. Guess I'll have to come back, then."

"But he'll probably be home by then," Shane pointed out. "Doesn't he always show eventually?"

"I have a feelin' he won't this time," Carl said.

The casual way he said it chilled Shane's blood. There was no reason for the man to report Ty missing—unless he had firm cause to know for sure the kid wouldn't return. Before he could respond, Carl gestured to the picture on Shane's desk.

"Good-lookin' boy. Real shame about his daddy."

Shane held his temper. Barely. The man sounded anything but sorry. "Yes, it was tough on everyone."

"Yeah, I imagine it was hard to play second daddy to a dead NFL star's son."

"Where did you hear that?" he asked, anger mounting. His efforts at raising Drew were none of the bastard's business, and the oily tone grated on his nerves.

"Easy, Detective. I read the papers, same as everybody else. Plus our boys have gotten tight. Word gets around." The man's grin was unnerving.

He didn't give Carl the satisfaction of reacting further. "Right. In any case, I haven't seen them. If I do run across Ty, I'll have him call you."

"Thanks. You do that." With a wink, the man turned and left.

"What the heck was that all about?" Daisy asked, stepping inside the office.

"That's what I'd like to know. He wanted to file a missing-person report on Ty because he didn't show at school this morning."

"What? Don't tell me they skipped again!"

"Drew was there, but he went out to a friend's car to retrieve his backpack and never returned."

"I was so sure you'd gotten through to him last night," she said in disbelief, plopping into a chair.

"I did, I'm sure of it. Something isn't right, and every instinct is telling me that Eastlake bastard is in the middle of it. He was acting weird, and he had scrapes on his knuckles and a scratch on his face. And he didn't really act that concerned about Ty at all."

"You think he was fishing?"

"Yeah. He remarked on Drew's picture, and the way he talked about him gave me chills."

"Well, he's a creepy man in general. He's always like that."

"This felt different."

"So, what do we do now?"

"Let's hit the street and see if we can turn up any witnesses who've seen Drew since this morning. If you want to go with me, that is."

"I wouldn't be anywhere else."

Thank God for this woman. He loved her so.

Jesus, his head was splitting.

Consciousness returned painfully, each movement he attempted jarring his brain. Drew groaned, wondering what the hell had run over him. Then he realized he was lying on a cold, dirty floor. What . . .

"Wakey, wakey," a man's voice sang.

Cracking his eyes open, he saw a blurry face hovering over him. A face that gradually cleared and became Carl's hated visage. "The fuck?"

Then he remembered. Carl had done bad things. Blown a man's head off.

"Nice of you to join us. Isn't it, son?" he asked, addressing someone else in the room.

Drew followed the man's gaze and swallowed hard.

This was the same cabin as yesterday, Drew noted. The body of the man Carl had killed was gone, but the stains on the table and floor remained. It made him sick.

His former friend was sitting at the blood-spattered table next to Frank, his lip split, eye blackened. Ty had obviously been crying and looked petrified. He was no longer the cocky kid who wanted in on whatever Daddy was doing. Unlike Drew, he wasn't bound. The look he sent Drew was filled with very real remorse.

And Drew understood that he was about to be made into an example for Ty. They were going to kill him.

His fears were confirmed when Carl turned to Ty. "Stand up, boy." Ty did, shaking visibly. "You said you wanted into the family business. Fine. You got it. But first, you have to prove you're man enough to do what needs to be done."

"Please," Ty whispered. "I don't want to anymore. Let Drew go. I told you he wouldn't say anything." That earned him a backhand across the face, and his head snapped to the side.

"First lesson: you gotta *discourage* people who poke their noses in our business. You following me?"

Ty nodded, wiping his bloody lip.

"Good."

From the table, he retrieved a knife and handed it to Ty. Then the bastard walked to where Drew was huddled on the floor, yanked him up, and dragged him to a wooden chair he pulled from the table into the center of the floor. He shoved Drew roughly into it.

"Now cut him," he ordered Ty. "Make the rich brat bleed."

"No," he protested, eyes wide. "I can't!"

"Cut him or I'll use that knife on *you*."

He meant what he said, and there wasn't any doubt about it. He'd cut his own son for not following orders. Drew met Ty's gaze and gave him a slight nod. It was okay. Ty had to do what he had to do, and hopefully he could drag it out until help arrived, as slim a hope as that seemed.

Trembling from head to toe and gripping the knife, Ty stood in front of him. It seemed they stared at each other forever, the atmosphere in the room thick with the murderous greed of the men in it. Men who would teach a boy to become a killer. They were pure evil.

"Do it!"

At Carl's yell, Ty slashed downward, slicing Drew's right forearm. Drew cried out in surprise even though he'd anticipated it. Christ, it hurt. The gash burned and blood immediately began to soak the flannel shirt he'd worn to school just that morning.

The shirt he'd be wearing when he died.

Carl and Frank were laughing, calling Ty a chip off the old block. Ty stumbled back, and Drew began to shake.

He couldn't believe his life was going to end, just like his dad's. All because of this bastard. The truth finally settled in: it wasn't Drew's fault at all that his dad had gotten mixed up with these creeps. But now he was going to pay, unless someone found and rescued him.

Shane! Please come get me.

He'd given the man nothing but grief, and now he'd do anything for a second chance. Closing his eyes, he begged whatever higher power might be listening for just one more.

I won't waste it this time. I'll love my new family and cherish every day I have with them, for the rest of my life. I promise.

If he made it through this alive, it was one promise he fully intended to keep.

Daisy had never seen Shane so strung out. Not even in the aftermath of Brad's death.

Drew meant the world to him, and if anything bad happened to that boy, she knew Shane would fall to pieces. They had to locate him soon.

But he was nowhere to be found. They checked all the usual spots—down by the river, all the local parks and fast-food hangouts, even the boys' houses. Carl's SUV wasn't home, which they found interesting. Somehow she didn't think Carl was out frantically searching for Ty.

When they'd exhausted the obvious possibilities, Shane was practically pulling out his hair. "What now? I can't file a report either, even though I know something is wrong! Why the hell didn't I push him until he opened up last night? Why didn't I keep him home today until he talked to me?"

She put a hand on his thigh as he drove. "We're going to find him. He's going to be okay." She prayed that was true. "We may not be able to officially file, but we can talk this out. Something tells me the answer is in front of us. And we have friends who can pull strings."

He took a deep breath. "Right. Tell me what to do, honey. I can't think."

"Let's go back to the station and run down what we know. Talk it out like we would any case."

"Okay."

When they arrived, they went inside and beckoned to Chris and Taylor to join them. Curious, the detectives followed them straight into Shane's office, where she closed the door behind them and brought everyone up to speed. She told them Drew was missing, and about his weird behavior of late. That he was edgy and afraid. Then about his disappearance and Carl's earlier visit.

Chris piped up with an idea. "Okay, here's what we do. Let's bring in a dry-erase board and diagram this out with all the players."

"Great idea," Daisy said.

"I'll get it." Taylor ducked out, moving quickly. In less than five minutes, he returned, rolling in the large white dry-erase board from the conference room. It barely fit in Shane's small office, but it worked.

Chris picked up a marker and began to draw stick figures, labeling each one. "We'll start with Drew and his dad," he said, placing the two figures on the bottom half of the board.

"Why Brad?" Taylor asked.

"Because all Drew's troubles start with his death." Chris shot his cousin an apologetic look, but Shane agreed with him.

"That's true."

Chris continued. "So, after his dad passed away, Drew came here and these all became important people who provided his foundation." Next, underneath Drew, he added figures labeled with the names of Shane, Daisy, Tommy, Shea, and himself. "That about right?"

"Looks good," Shane said.

"All right. Now, above him, let's add people who've

become a part of his life, whether friends or not." Above Drew, he added Ty and Carl. "Who else?"

Shane spoke up. "Frank Johnson. Both boys had to repaint his property."

"Got it. And?"

"A kid named Alan," Daisy interjected. "He knows Drew, but I'm not sure how well."

Chris added Alan out to the side. "Is that all?"

The assembled group perused the figures. No one could think of anyone else.

Chris went on. "Now, let's start connecting these folks and make a nice little spider web of who all knows who. From the bottom up."

"Drew and Brad."

Chris made the line connecting them. Then the rest as they were given to him.

"Drew and Ty."

"Ty and Carl."

"Carl and Frank."

"Carl, Frank, and both boys."

"Carl, Frank, and *us*," Shane said slowly. "We've been trying to hang them for years."

"Well, we've got a nasty pattern emerging here," Taylor said thoughtfully. "But we're missing something. What's the missing link?"

"We're missing a connection to *Brad*, not Drew." Shane's voice rose in excitement. "Brad connects to Sugarland before his death. That guy in the ditch off I-49, Larry Holstead, was connected to the drug that killed Brad. Holstead had traces of it on his clothing."

Chris caught the thread, twirling the marker in his fingers. "Meaning what? Who's missing?"

Daisy gasped in sudden realization. "What's missing is where that drug originated! We need Brad's dealer in the diagram!"

The color drained from Shane's face. "Jesus. Good thinking, sugar."

Quickly, Chris scribbled in that figure next to Brad, then added a connecting line to Carl and Frank with a question mark above it. "Is this possible? Does this mystery drug dealer connect with *all* of our characters in Sugarland, including Holstead?"

"Whoever he is, if we're on the right track, he sure as hell completes the missing link," Shane breathed. Then he ran a hand through his hair, mussing it. "My God, I never gave a thought to Brad's dealer. I need the surveillance video from his estate. Who's going with me?"

Daisy and Chris immediately volunteered to accompany him, while Taylor reluctantly agreed to remain on stand-by. In minutes the trio was on the road, Shane driving. The trip to the estate seemed to take forever, especially when they were so hopeful of turning up an important clue. As Shane finally pulled up to the gate and punched in the security code, they were all on edge.

"Jeez, I can't believe the kid inherited this," Chris murmured.

Driving through, Shane glanced at his cousin. "Wealth and fame ain't all it's cracked up to be. Brad left behind a grieving son who has no use for all of this, and who would much rather have his dad back."

"Sorry. It's just overwhelming to see it up close."

"No worries. Most people react like that."

"What are you and Drew going to do with this place?"

"That's Drew's decision to make when he gets older.

In the meantime, the groundskeepers maintain it. Personally, I'd like to see him sell it someday and purchase something else that's just his."

He parked around back, near the garage, and used his key to enter a back door near the kitchen. They waited as he jogged off to disable the security alarm, and Daisy goggled at the place. Her living room and bedroom would both fit in the huge kitchen. It struck her as kind of sad, the idea of Drew and his dad rattling around alone in a place this big. It appeared to be more of a showplace than a home.

Her opinion didn't change when Shane returned and led them through the living room to the large study. The interior was about as warm and inviting as a museum, and Shane must've caught her expression of confusion and distaste.

"This isn't who Brad was," he said quietly. "It's what he thought he wanted."

"That makes sense. I don't feel the man you loved like a brother in this house."

"He was never here."

Shane began a search of the office, beginning in the cabinet where the surveillance equipment was set up on shelves. The small monitors showed the live feed from several cameras positioned around the exterior of the house. There were none inside.

Next he opened a set of doors underneath the monitors where cases of DVDs were stored. As he flipped through them, he cursed anxiously. "Dammit! The ones for the weeks leading up to Brad's death are missing."

"The lead detective from the case probably has them," Chris suggested. "Can you call him?"

"Yeah. It's just an extra step I'd hoped to avoid." Reluctantly, he placed the call and stepped from the office.

Daisy and Chris milled around while Shane spoke urgently on the phone, explaining the situation in as few words as possible. He seemed to have a bit of difficulty convincing the other cop to let them take a look, since they weren't sure they had an official case on their end to warrant it. But in the end, the man relented.

"He's going to let us come in and look at the feed," Shane told them. "But only because he's been trying to identify some people on the tapes and he's hoping I might know them. Maybe it's a long shot, but it's all we've got."

Shane reset the alarm, locked the door, and they left. Daisy was silently glad to be gone from the mansion and its lingering pall. Now that Drew had moved all his belongings to Shane's, she hoped not to return in the near future.

Detective Lacey was waiting for them when they arrived and showed them into a room with a player and monitor. He was a nice enough man, professional but not so tight his ass squeaked when he walked. He didn't have to show them a damned thing, but was smart enough to realize playing well in the sandbox frequently gained rewards.

"I don't know what use this will be," he began, seating himself in a rolling chair in front of the monitor. They took up chairs flanking him. "Our focus, of course, is the drug angle. We want the seller behind bars, and so does the media. I've narrowed down the feed to a few shots of visitors we couldn't identify."

He started playing the clips, giving them a verbal rundown. "Most appear harmless, but we know better than to assume based on appearances. Here's one." The feed showed a skinny kid placing a flyer on the front door. "This was a onetime visit. Anybody know him?"

They all shook their heads.

"He's probably nothing. Just a kid who slipped through the gate, which is interesting, but I think he just placed the flyer so he could brag to his friends he'd been on an NFL star's estate. Next one."

They went through several. The footage showed a stream of visitors, all innocuous. A pizza delivery guy from Drew's favorite place. The grounds people, whom Shane verified were OK. A worker from the power company. A cable man. A preacher.

"I didn't think Brad was religious," Chris said, squinting at the screen. "Hey, am I seeing things or is that . . ."

"Fuck me!" Shane burst out. "It's Eastlake!"

"Who?" Lacey asked, eyes lighting up.

"Carl Eastlake, a scumbag we've been trying to bag for years," Shane snarled.

"Why the hell is he dressed like a preacher?"

Shane waved a hand at the video. "It's not like he would want to risk showing up frequently at a famous NFL player's home looking like a drug dealer. He's got to be the one who was supplying Brad with that shit. We're finally going to get that fucker."

"Maybe, but even though he shows up on the feed many times, the vids aren't solid proof he was selling." Lacey was practically vibrating with anticipation, though.

"I don't need proof he was selling to tear him apart." Shane's fist banged on the counter. "It all makes sense now, why Drew has been acting so weird. Why he was so damned scared last night when I mentioned I might talk to Eastlake about him and Ty skipping school."

"Catch me up," Lacey said.

"Drew had to have seen Eastlake come and go from the house, and he's not stupid. He must have known the man was his dad's dealer. Drew's been having all these mood swings, having trouble coming to terms with his dad's death."

"He's been feeling guilty," Daisy realized. Her heart broke for him. "He feels responsible for not telling anyone that his dad was using. That poor baby."

Shane picked up the thread. "Then he moves in with me and meets Ty at school. The two become friends. But Carl is never home, so it takes time for their paths to cross. When they do meet—and now I believe that's what took place yesterday when they skipped school— he's terrified. And Carl instantly knows Drew has made him. The boy is now a threat to him. A witness."

"Now he and Ty are missing," Chris muttered. "Jesus Christ. I suggest we track Drew's phone, ASAP."

"That asshole has my boy, and when I catch him, he's going to wish he'd never been born."

The cold rage in Shane's stormy eyes made Daisy shiver.

Carl had better run. Because there was nowhere in the world he could hide from Shane.

15

Chris's suggestion was a good one.

Shane paced his own department's conference room, agonizing over how long it was taking to track a damned cell phone. So they wouldn't have to get permission from the brass and delay things, the obvious answer was to use the TrackMyPhone app to locate his boy fast.

But Chris's face as he approached didn't signify good news. Shane loped out of the conference room to meet him.

"Cuz, it's not good." Pulling out a familiar phone with a patriotic rubber cover, Chris looked grim. "We found it in the back parking lot at the high school."

He stared at the device, at first not comprehending the magnitude of how very bad this was. The phone wasn't with Drew; it had been left behind. No doubt at the scene of his abduction. An animalistic roar erupted from his chest and he turned, picked up a chair, and sent it flying. It crashed into a desk, and three nearby officers scattered. He was reaching for another, might have torn the station apart, if it hadn't been for Daisy.

"Honey," she whispered. "This won't help him. The only way we'll save him is if you keep your head."

Arrested, he stared at her. She was a calm river in the storm that had been his life since Brad's death. Regardless of the stares it gained them, she cupped his face in her hands. And placed a very sweet, gentle kiss right on his lips.

Gradually, the world began to make sense again. Until he was centered. Had a purpose—to protect his family. He'd sworn he would, and he would not rest until Drew was safe. Giving Daisy a kiss in return, he walked over and righted the chair, muttering apologies to the officers he'd startled.

Chris got his attention again. "I was about to tell you that the cap approved tracing Ty and Carl's phones. We'll turn up something soon, buddy. Try not to worry."

Easier said than done. But he was glad the guys were on it, because he was useless at the moment. Now he knew firsthand why there were rules forbidding coworkers who were life partners from being on the same shift. Even working for the same department was discouraged for this very reason; when loved ones intersect with the job, cases could get messy. It's why he was never paired with his cousin, unless it absolutely couldn't be avoided.

Drew wasn't his coworker, but he was family. An innocent who'd had the misfortune to intersect with one of their cases. Daisy was family, too, in every way that mattered.

"Shane," Taylor called. He and Chris were jogging toward him, waving a paper. "We've got a location on Carl's phone. It was tracked to a location east of town, in the hills not far from Frank Johnson's place."

The captain was right behind them. "You four go, but be careful. Carl and Frank could be together, and they're like rattlers when they're cornered. Neither of them are the type to take prisoners or to let themselves be brought in on felony charges that'll put them away for good. I don't give two shits about them, but I won't have my best detectives getting hurt."

"Thanks, Cap. We'll take care." Shane managed a smile at him. They were damned lucky to have the man as their superior. If he didn't go and have a heart attack on them from the stress in his life, they'd be doubly blessed.

They took two of the department's SUVs. One was to escort what the others hoped would be their prisoners, though Shane didn't much care if Carl survived to be arrested. The other was for retrieving Drew and Ty. Taylor rode with Shane. The man was his partner, and even if he'd rather be with Daisy, he wouldn't jeopardize their case by not following procedure.

"Isn't there an old distillery and a cabin out here?" Shane asked, glancing at Taylor, who was driving.

"Yes. The signal seems to be coming from that area. There's not much else around, so that would be my bet."

"If Carl does have them, I can't believe he was stupid enough to think he wouldn't get caught."

"He's that arrogant," Taylor mused. "I doubt he was planning on us figuring out that he was connected to Drew and Brad. That will be his downfall."

"Oh, he's going down all right. I just pray he doesn't take my son with him."

Taylor glanced at him. "You really think of him as yours, don't you?"

"He *is* mine," he said fiercely. "I've known him since he was a baby. I've changed his diapers, taken him to ball games. Fixed his skinned knees. I've loved him and taken care of him while Brad was off making a name for himself, for as long as I can remember. Hell, since I was younger than Drew is now."

"I keep forgetting Brad was something like eight years older than you."

"Yeah. When I was Drew's age, Drew was three years old. He's always been my little buddy, and now he's my son. I'm going to kill Carl Eastlake for trying to take him from me."

"I'll pretend I didn't hear that last part."

When they turned onto Ferris Road and got close to their destination, Taylor pulled over, killed the lights, and shut off the ignition. They'd go in quiet, scope out the situation.

The four of them moved as a unit, keeping to the road as they neared the cabin, then veering off and making the final approach through the brush. They'd have to be extra careful, since it was only late afternoon, the cover of darkness still a couple of hours away.

As the cabin came into view, it was obvious from the two vehicles parked beside it that someone was there.

"That's Frank's truck," Shane said in a low voice, pointing. Then he studied the blue van. "I've never seen that other vehicle before."

It was a large utility-style vehicle with blacked-out windows. Side door. No plates. Perfect for abducting someone from a parking lot. His blood pressure rose.

Shane palmed his gun and gestured between himself

and Taylor. "We'll get a look inside, see what's going on in there."

"We'll take the back," Chris said. He and Daisy palmed their weapons as well.

Before they left to circle around, Daisy looked at Shane in worry. "Be safe. *Everybody*," she amended.

Forcing his thoughts to calm, Shane led the way to the side of the cabin. It was slow going, creeping from tree to tree, since there wasn't a thing in between to mask their presence. The last few yards to the cabin were totally exposed, and he gritted his teeth as they crouched low and took off.

He didn't take a deep breath until they reached their destination without raising a shout of alarm. Just then, the sound of a tear-filled voice reached his ears, and his heart lurched.

"Please don't!"

He'd know that voice anywhere. Drew was in real trouble, and they needed to act fast. He and Taylor exchanged a grim look. They had to get a glimpse of everyone's position and who was armed and with what, before busting in there.

Shane carefully rose. What he saw froze his heart. Drew was slumped in a rickety chair in the middle of the floor, one sleeve of his shirt wet and dark. Frank was holding a bloodied knife, while Carl stood to one side, egging on Ty.

Because Ty had a gun trained on Drew's forehead.

"Christ almighty," Taylor whispered from beside him.

Carl was shouting at Ty, a wicked gleam in his eyes. "He knows too much! Do you want me to go to jail for selling that shit to his daddy? It won't matter that Mr. High and Mighty Football Star wanted more and more drugs to keep himself going! Oh no—they'll blame me!"

"I d-don't want to," Ty wailed, gun shaking dangerously in his hands. "He won't say anything, I promise!"

"Of course he will, stupid! Shoot him!" Carl barked.

"Let's move," Shane hissed. As he ran, he signaled to Chris at the back, who nodded and disappeared around the corner.

He kept his cool enough to slow down and tread quietly on the front porch, but only just. Carl's berating of Ty was ratcheting up in volume, and the kid was bound to break any second. If that happened—

No. He wouldn't allow it.

Shane and Taylor positioned themselves on either side of the door, and Shane pointed to himself. He'd go in first. Counting off with his fingers, he made his move on three, stepping out and kicking the door with all his strength. The wood splintered and rocketed inward, banging hard against the wall and stunning the group inside.

"Sugarland PD! Drop your weapons!" he yelled, training his SIG on the most imminent threat: Ty.

The boy swung around with the gun in hand, tear-stained face the portrait of horror. His weapon was trained in Shane's general direction, but he was like a statue.

"Drop it, Ty!" Taylor yelled.

Carl was livid. "Shoot his ass!"

Just as Ty started to lower the weapon, Carl grabbed it from his hand, and Frank chose that moment to launch the knife in his hand at Taylor.

All hell broke loose. A crash sounded from the back as Chris and Daisy charged in. Shane and Carl took aim at each other, Shane's enemy getting his shot off a split second earlier. He felt a punch in his left side and grunted, dropping to his knees as Drew screamed his name. Carl flew backward, crimson blooming on his chest, and fell to the floor on his back. He didn't move again.

Frank made a dive for Carl's weapon, but Chris was on him before he could reach it, tackling the bastard to the floor. He wrenched the man's hands behind his back and slapped the cuffs on him.

The burn was making itself known in Shane's side, just above his belt, spreading along with the blood starting to soak his shirt and pants. But his sole thought was getting to Drew. His son, who was terrified.

"Shane!"

"You're going to be OK," he said as he reached his boy. "It's over."

"Y-you found m-me."

"I did. I'll always find you, even when you don't want me to." He tried to smile, but winced as he reached for the knife on the floor. He was becoming light-headed, but that wasn't going to stop him from cutting those damned ropes from his boy's wrists and ankles.

"That asshole sh-shot you," Drew said, breath hitching.

"I've had worse," he said truthfully. But not by much, though it wouldn't help the boy to know that.

Making short work of the bonds, he tossed the blade aside and helped Drew remove them. The second he was free, the boy was in his arms on the floor, shaking uncontrollably. Shane held him tight, barely aware of Daisy attempting to soothe Ty.

"Thank God," he said hoarsely. "I was so afraid we'd be too late."

"Ty wouldn't have done it. But Carl would have if you hadn't found me."

Shane wasn't convinced the other boy wouldn't have caved, but it no longer mattered. "I've got you, son. It's okay now."

"I was going to tell you about Carl, after school. I'm sorry—"

"Shh. We'll talk about it later."

"This is my fault!"

"No, it's not. None of this is your fault. Do you hear me?" It wounded his soul to hear the boy blame himself for the transgressions of men who had known better.

His vision began to blur, and his heart pounded as he struggled to breathe through the pain. Suddenly Chris was at his side, urging him to lie down.

"Come on, cuz. Hang tight. We've got an ambulance on the way."

Flat on his back, he blinked, trying to remain conscious. Vaguely he registered other voices, more officers arriving. Frank was hauled away, but he couldn't tell by whom. Faces hovered above him, drawn with worry.

He tried to point. "Get Drew's arm checked."

"I'm okay." The boy gave him a watery smile. "Just a scratch."

Daisy gripped his hand, beautiful eyes filled with tears. "I love you."

"Love you, too. Gonna be fine," he whispered. That's all he could manage. His tongue felt heavy, his body weighted with bricks. He wanted to stay awake, but it was becoming impossible.

"Shane?" Drew's frantic plea came from far away. "You can't leave me, too! Please stay with me! I need you!"

He wasn't going anywhere. But the words wouldn't form.

The cabin, the people he loved most, disappeared as he was plunged into darkness.

When Shane passed out, Drew started to cry.

"No," he moaned, shaking the man they both loved.

Daisy wrapped her arms around the boy, pulled him back and held him close. "The paramedics are here. Let's move back so they can help him."

Chris helped her wrestle the boy from Shane's side, but they didn't go far. Just enough so that the men rushing through the door had room to tend him.

Right away, she recognized the men—and one woman— as Tommy's old teammates at Fire Station Five. Captain Howard Paxton stomped in, cursing when he saw who the injured officer was. He stood to the side, out of the way, with Eve Marshall and Julian Salvatore, Tonio's brother, while Clay Montana and Zack Knight crouched by Shane and went to work.

Both men snapped on latex gloves and murmured to each other in quiet tones. Clay checked his patient's blood pressure and spoke calmly.

"Pressure's dipping."

He started an IV as Zack cut Shane's shirt in half to reveal his blood-soaked torso, then set about cleaning it and applying what Daisy assumed was some sort of pressure bandage.

"Let's get him out of here," Zack said.

As they eased him onto a backboard and lifted him onto a gurney, Daisy's pulse hammered in her throat. He was too still, lashes resting on his pale cheeks. A couple of the men were trying to reassure her and Drew that he'd be all right, but it wasn't much comfort. The medics couldn't hide the fact that they were in a hurry to get him to the hospital, that Shane was losing too much blood. She wouldn't feel better until she saw him awake and on the mend.

She and Drew trailed the gurney out the door, but she held the boy back when he tried to climb into the ambulance. "No. We need to stay out of their way. I'll drive you, and we'll get you checked out while they're making Shane better. All right?"

Zack slammed the ambulance doors shut behind Julian and nodded to the group. "We'll take him to Sterling," he said. Then he hopped into the driver's seat and started the vehicle.

Drew stared at the ambulance as it rumbled off, taking the man they loved with it. The boy looked about five seconds from collapse.

"Come on," she said, hugging his shoulders. "The quicker we see about that cut on your arm, the quicker we can find out about Shane."

"Yeah." He swallowed hard. "OK."

"You guys got it here?" she called to the captain, who'd arrived on the scene.

He waved her off. "Go on. I'll be along when I can to check on Ford."

The others expressed similar sentiments, and Chris tossed her a set of keys to the SUV he'd driven on the way. She guided Drew to the vehicle and helped him in before getting in on her own side and starting it up. The boy was silent, pale and shaken, as they rode. The ER would dress his injuries, but the wounds on his heart and soul would take much longer.

"Shane's right," she said. "None of this was your fault."

"I should've told Shane about Dad," he whispered. "I saw that creep, Carl, in our house a lot, dressed up like a stupid preacher. But I knew a freak like him wasn't pushing religion. I didn't know what to do, so I waited, thinking Dad would stop doing the drugs on his own. I thought, *If he doesn't, I'll tell Shane.* But I waited too long."

Daisy blinked back tears. Poor boy, to carry that burden. "Neither of you had any way of knowing those drugs were so dangerous. They were supposed to be performance enhancing and undetectable by routine drug screening. Even when training camp started, your dad likely wouldn't have stopped. He was looking to extend his career and he made a bad decision. He didn't know they were lying about their product. But he made his choice to take the risk, Drew."

"I still wish . . ." His voice broke, and he rested his head against the window.

Reaching over, she gripped his hand. "I know."

"Carl murdered a man in that cabin yesterday," he said quietly.

"What?" She glanced back and forth between him and the road.

"Yeah. Did you notice all that dried blood on the table and floor? It's not mine. When we skipped yesterday, we came out here to see what Carl was doing. He and Frank were in there with a third guy. They were arguing about the drugs. The third man was saying that the drug was defective and needed to be improved before any more hit the street. Carl shot him between the eyes, then spotted us watching, and we ran."

"So that's why he was after you. God, kid, you almost got yourself killed!"

"I know it was stupid. And I was dumb to think Ty could talk him out of hurting me." He paused. "Carl also mentioned killing someone named Holstead. Frank was in on that, too."

"Well, Carl's dead and we've got Frank now, thanks to you." Drew was a credible witness and would have to take the stand, most likely. But it would make their case even more airtight.

They rode in silence for a few minutes. Then suddenly the boy sat up. "There's something else. I think I might have an idea where they were making the drugs."

"You do? Where?"

"When we painted Frank's barn, there was a weird smell coming from inside. We poked around in there and didn't see much, but I keep thinking maybe we missed something. Maybe he stashed them out of sight."

She smiled at him. "That's good work, kid. We'll definitely get a warrant and check it out. Hey, you might make a great detective someday."

He smiled a little at that. "Maybe. It might be cool to help put assholes in prison, like you guys do. I think Dad would like that."

She wiped at a tear. "I know he would, kiddo."

In the ER, the doctor and nurse, once they were finally available to see Drew, took good care of his arm. Shane had already been rushed into surgery, and most of the staff was with him. Another doctor had to be called in.

The cut on Drew's arm was deep enough to need stitches, but the injury wouldn't leave lasting damage, save for a scar. The teen endured the stitches like a man, not even flinching. Daisy was proud of him, but didn't embarrass him by gushing overmuch.

Once they were finished, they were ushered to a smaller, private waiting room, where the families of more critical victims were placed away from prying eyes. That in itself set her nerves on edge, fear spiking. She tried to hide it from Drew, who was slumped in a chair, exhausted, and thought she was managing pretty well.

"Sit down. You're making me crazy."

Or not. "Sorry." She flopped down beside him with a sigh.

Soon after, cops began to trickle in as word got out that one of their own was down. They made small talk, and the tension rose. Tommy and Shea arrived next, both of them making a beeline straight for her and Drew. Daisy could tell how afraid they were, but they reined it in for the teen's sake. More than three hours had passed by the time Austin, Taylor, Chris, and even the newbie, Tonio Salvatore, were able to break away and join everyone.

The clock barely seemed to move.

Then the door swung open and a doctor stepped inside. "Is this the . . . family of Shane Ford?" he asked, brows raised at the number of people in the room.

"Yes!" several cops loudly agreed.

Daisy, Drew, Shea, and Tommy were ushered to the front of the group, and Shea acted as their spokesperson. "Dr. Chen, hello."

"Nurse Skyler," he said in surprise. "It's good to see you, though not under these circumstances."

"Thank you. I'm Shane's sister, and everyone else here is just as much his family as I am. How is he?" she asked in a tremulous voice.

The doctor adjusted his glasses and nodded. "Mr. Ford lost a lot of blood and gave us a bit of a scare in surgery when his pressure dipped dangerously low. We had to fish out the bullet, staunch the internal bleeding, and give him two and a half pints of blood. That said, no major organs were hit. He came through after a couple of bumps, and, barring infection, I'm confident he's going to recover well."

Daisy's knees sagged with relief. Drew wrapped her in an ecstatic hug, and there was a collective murmur in the room as everyone exclaimed their relief.

"He's in recovery now, but he should be moved to a room in ICU shortly. I expect he'll be there a day or two, then he'll be ready for a regular room."

"How long will he have to stay here?" Daisy asked anxiously.

"I'd guess a week, but maybe he'll get out sooner if he's a good boy." The doc winked, and some of the group laughed in relief. "A nurse will let you all know his room number once he's settled in. I'll be by to check on him later tonight."

With that, he left. Daisy realized she and Drew were still clinging to each other, so she led him back to their seats.

"I *told* you he was gonna be OK," the teen said, giving her a mock look of superiority.

She couldn't help but laugh. "Right. I guess I should listen to you, huh?"

"You know it. Daisy?"

"Hmm?"

Suddenly he grew serious. "I never thought I wanted a mom, but since it looks like I'm going to get one, anyway, I'm glad it's you."

Tears pricked her eyes as she smiled, reaching out to push a lock of dark hair from his eyes. "And I'm glad you're my kid. You're a pretty great guy, and I love you."

Blushing, he smiled. "You, too."

"I'm a great guy?"

He snorted. "Yeah, whatever."

"I thought Shane erased that word from your vocabulary, young man."

"Nah. I'm a work in progress, and he's got a long way to go."

"I'm pretty sure he's not going to mind at all."

"True that. I *am* pretty awesome."

Laughing, she smacked his shoulder. Both of her men were awesome, and she couldn't wait to get started on their lives together.

As soon as Shane got back on his feet.

Shane came awake slowly.

Soft sounds penetrated the cotton in his head. A beeping noise. Shuffling. But wherever he was, it was quiet. He was lying in a comfortable, warm bed. Though when he tried to move a bit, there was a pinch in his side.

He sucked in a breath because of the pain, and that hurt even more.

"Easy," a sweet voice said. "Don't wiggle around."

"Daisy?"

"It's me, sweetie. How do you feel?"

"Like I've been sat on by an elephant."

That earned a giggle. "Not quite. Do you remember what happened?"

He thought about it. Gradually, the memory came back. "Carl shot me. Is the fucker dead?"

"As a doornail. You killed him."

"Good riddance." Finally he was able to open his eyes. It took a couple of minutes to focus on Daisy's face, and when he did, he managed a smile. She looked beautiful, if a little tired, blond hair down around her shoulders, the way he loved it. "Hey."

"Hey, yourself." Leaning over, she kissed him on the lips. "I'm glad you're back."

"Me, too. Or I will be when I get out of here." He surveyed the rest of the room. There were flowers and balloons. Nice. "Where's Drew? Is he OK?"

"He's totally fine," she assured him. "He went down to the cafeteria with Shea. He stayed with Tommy and your sister last night, and they convinced him to stay home from school today. But he's determined to go back tomorrow and catch up on the work he missed."

"He is? Did an alien invade his body?" She just laughed. "How long have I been here?"

"The shooting was yesterday. You slept all night and most of today."

"Damn. I lost twenty-four hours. Could've been worse, I suppose."

"Much." She hesitated, and he waited, knowing she had something important on her mind. "Drew told me what he'd been so scared about the night before he disappeared, and we were right. It was Carl."

"I knew it!" He tried to sit up, but fell back, groaning. She fussed over him for a minute before he shook his head. "Go on, tell me."

"When the boys cut class, they found Carl and Frank at the cabin with a third man. The third guy argued about the drug being defective, and Carl mentioned killing Larry Holstead. Then he shot the third man between the eyes. Both boys saw the killing, and then Carl spotted them and gave chase. They got away, but that's why Drew was so frightened when he came in."

He stared at her, the truth washing over him. "My God. I lectured him about classes and his grades. I grounded him, and he'd just seen a murder. He knew Carl was going to come after him! What kind of father am I?"

"A good one." Clasping one of his hands, she kissed his fingers. "You said what any dad would have with the information you had."

"I knew something was terribly wrong. If I had just pushed him harder for the truth, he wouldn't have been in danger yesterday."

"Listen, you and that boy are driving me crazy with your self-blame," she said, arching a brow. "You're both going to have to learn that there are circumstances you can't control. You don't have a crystal ball to see the future and know exactly what to do. So give yourselves a break, please."

"I will if he will," a voice said from the doorway.

Shane smiled when he saw Drew walk straight toward him. "Come here, kid."

Drew wrapped him in a careful hug, then let him go and took a vacated chair by the bed while Shea did the same.

"Cool to see you awake," the teen said, smiling. "I thought you were going to sleep all day."

"I still might. Injured man's prerogative."

"I guess you don't want to hear another apology?"

"You guessed right. There have been enough regrets to go around, and it's time to move forward. Don't you agree?"

"For sure."

Shea stood, perhaps sensing they needed time together, and kissed Shane's cheek. "I'm going to run some errands now that you're awake. Love you, bro."

"You too, sis."

After she was gone, Shane studied Daisy and Drew before addressing the boy. "I want to talk to you about something, Drew. This isn't the ideal place and time, but . . . I need to know how you feel about the three of us becoming a family."

The words hung there, and Drew looked between them in apparent surprise. "Why would I have a problem with that? What, like I didn't think that's where you guys were going?"

"I don't know, but I thought if you weren't ready for that, if you just wanted it to be you and me for a while, then that's how we'll do it."

Daisy agreed. "We want what's best for you. We'll wait until you're ready."

"You guys would really do that for me, wouldn't you?

Just put your lives on hold because you love me." He said it with a strange sort of wonder, as though nobody had ever put him first.

In a way, Shane knew Brad hadn't put his son first in many years. As close as they all had been, that was an inescapable truth.

"We would. You're our first priority."

For a few seconds, the boy looked like he was going to cry. After a long moment, he composed himself and grinned. "I want you both to be happy, and I'm totally cool with the hot cop chick moving in with us. Just sayin'."

Shane couldn't help but laugh. "Good. But she's my hot cop, and don't forget it."

"Guess that means you're getting married?"

"If Daisy will have me, nothing would make me happier."

Her eyes widened. "Is that a proposal?"

"Like I said, it's not the ideal place, and I don't have a ring hidden in my hospital gown, but yes. Will you marry me, Daisy Callahan?"

"Yes, I will!" She leaned over, giving him a thorough kiss. The look in her eyes promised much more the moment he was well enough to handle it.

"Awesome." The boy bit his lip. The twinkle in his eyes before he spoke suggested he already knew the answer. "So, since we're all happy campers, am I still grounded?"

"For skipping school almost a dozen times? Uh, that's a big ten-four."

"Damn. Guess I still can't drive the Mustang?"

"Not until you manage something quite a bit above a two-point-zero GPA."

"Had to ask."

"For all the good it did. Have fun during house arrest while I'm home recuperating and being grumpy."

The boy rolled his eyes. "Whatever."

"Dammit, Drew—"

"Hey, he's a work in progress," Daisy said, and gave Drew a wink.

Giving up, Shane settled back and closed his eyes. But he was smiling as he pictured his family. Their future together.

He was a damned lucky man.

A little over a week later, Shane was parked in his own easy chair. It was wonderful to be home, even if his family fussing over him was bound to get old eventually.

Daisy had taken off a few days to play nurse, with Austin's blessing. The captain had said the brass wouldn't make a huge fuss about them working for the police department—but they could *not* work calls together any longer, for everyone's safety. They were being lenient, and Shane was grateful. As for now? He couldn't wait until he could play doctor with his honey. Damn, he was so horny he hurt—another pain to add to the list.

Just then, the key turned in the front door and she rushed in, holding two grocery sacks. "Hey, handsome! How are you doing? Everything okay while I was gone?"

"You were only gone an hour," he pointed out, adjusting his blanket over his hard-on. "What trouble could I get into?"

"Plenty, knowing you."

He gave her a pout. "Not fair. Trouble just finds me."

"Then you and Drew have that in common."

"Oh, crap. What's he done this time?"

"Nothing. That I know of. But I guess we'll find out when he gets home from school in a couple of hours."

"That's reassuring."

"Seriously, I do have some news," she told him, perching on the arm of the sofa close to him. "Ty has moved to Texas to live with an aunt. Turns out she's wanted Ty to come live with her for years and has never been able to get him away from Carl. He said he'd call Drew with his new address and phone number."

"Fabulous." He grimaced. "I feel bad for the boy, really. He can't help the way he was raised. But I'm not sorry that he won't be an influence over Drew anymore."

"I don't think he would have, anyway. Drew told me he'd already decided not to spend so much time with him anymore. In fact, he's been mentioning Alan quite a bit."

"That's good. New friends are what he needs."

"Found out something else: Drew was right. The drugs had been manufactured in Frank's barn, but after the boys pulled that stunt with the spray paint, he and Carl moved them to a warehouse in Nashville. Taylor and Chris found the address in some of Carl's papers and passed it to the Nashville PD. Lacey and his team made the find there. Stuff had a street value of millions, or would have if the formula had ever been perfected. That knowledge died with Holstead and the goateed man from the cabin, Irvin Sanders."

"Goateed?" he mused. "That would be our supplier who got away when we took our dunk in the river. Sounds like they cut off their noses."

"Yep. Frank's the only one left to take the rap, so he's

singing loud, giving up their ring of sellers on the street, hoping for a deal."

"Good luck with that." Shifting, he tried to be discreet about reaching under his blanket to shift the erection straining at his sleep pants.

"Are you mining for gold under there?" She grinned wickedly.

"Damn, baby. You know I'm going crazy," he grumped. "We haven't had sex for *days*."

"Because someone went and got his ass shot and has to recover."

"It's not my ass that hurts. It's a little more toward the starboard side." With that, he flung the blanket off his lap to reveal the large tent poking at the front of his flannels.

"Oh, my. That does look uncomfortable. But while the spirit is willing, the flesh is wounded." She pointed at the area on his side where his bandage and staples were hidden under his shirt.

Grabbing her hand, he pressed her palm to the ridge of his cock and ground against it. "Some of the flesh isn't wounded at all. I need you. I'm dying here. Please, sugar?"

Finally relenting, thank God, she started to work down his pants. "All right. Only if we go slowly. One twinge, and we're done."

It would take a lot more than a twinge to stop him. Especially when she finished exposing his stiff cock, then tossed aside his pants. Then she scooted off him to remove her clothes, baring every inch of creamy skin to his gaze. Her shining blond hair cascaded around her shoulders, and her rosy nipples begged to be sucked. He wanted those long thighs straddling him, too.

"Climb on top of me. There's plenty of room."

"I will. But first . . ."

Kneeling between his legs, she spread his knees and grasped his erection. Lowered her head and began to lave the leaking tip. He sucked in a breath, watching her sweet mouth work him. Those pretty lips. Her mouth felt like hot velvet when she took him in, began to suck.

"Jesus, yes."

Holding the back of her head, he guided her up and down on his shaft. Loving the tingles that skittered from his cock down to his balls. They tightened, and he knew he had to stop.

"Gonna come if you don't stop." Gently, he urged her off. "Climb on and fuck me, sugar."

She straddled his lap, and he positioned his cock at her entrance. They both groaned in pleasure as she slid down, taking him inside her. She began to move, almost too carefully, driving him insane.

"Faster, honey. You won't hurt me."

He didn't care if she did. He needed this badly. She increased the tempo and he tried to thrust, but only managed a few pumps before his side protested. So he let her take control, and she was so damned sexy riding him. His own goddess to keep forever.

His cock slid in and out, the slick heat bringing him closer and closer to the edge. Too soon, the familiar quickening began in his groin and became fire that shot through his balls and cock.

"Shit! Yes, baby!"

His release hit hard and he shot into her, filling her up. Arms around his neck, she tightened around his cock with a cry, following him in orgasm. They floated for a few minutes, coming down from the high. It was so fantastic, being together with her. Here in what would be their home.

He kissed her lips. "You're amazing."

"You're the one who's injured." Gingerly, she felt his bandage to make sure he was okay.

"Tell that to Mr. Happy." She giggled. "When are you going to make an honest man of me? If we don't set a date soon, I'm going to be tempted to move you in, anyway, and risk scarring our boy for life."

"Oh, I doubt he'd be all that affected, at least in a bad way." She kissed him thoroughly. "But you're right. When do you want to do the deed?"

"Tomorrow?"

"A bit soon. How about next month?"

"Really?" he asked hopefully. "You won't need more time to get all that stuff together that women do? Whatever that is."

He had no clue, except from Tommy and Shea's wedding, and he hadn't had to do anything but pick up his tux and show up. And get Tommy drunk at his bachelor party the night before, of course.

"No, it's not like I have a big family. I don't want anything fancy, either. Just a small wedding and a party afterward here with our family and friends."

"Whatever you want, sugar. I just want your big day to be special."

"I can't think of anything more special than becoming the wife of the man I love."

"You look very pleased with yourself, future Mrs. Ford."

"I am. I scored the most dedicated bachelor in town, and I'm not about to let him go."

"Escape is something I'm not interested in, I assure you. I'll never run from you or our love again."

"Prove it." She wiggled on his lap.

Since she'd reawakened the beast, he smiled and set about doing just that once again.

He'd prove to her that nobody made him happier and that he'd cherish her forever.

Daisy and his son. The two people he was born to love and protect.

Shane and his family were complete, at last.

About the Author

Bestselling author **Jo Davis** is the author of the popular Firefighters of Station Five series, written as Jo Davis, and the dark, sexy paranormal series Alpha Pack, written as J.D. Tyler. *Primal Law*, the first book in her Alpha Pack series, is the winner of the National Reader's Choice Award in Paranormal. She has also been a multiple finalist in the Colorado Romance Writers Award of Excellence and a finalist for the Bookseller's Best Award, has captured the HOLT Medallion Award of Merit, and has been a two-time nominee for the Australian Romance Readers Award in romantic suspense. She's had one book optioned for a major motion picture.

Connect Online

www.jodavis.net

Turn the page for the a special preview
of the next book in the
Sugarland Blue series,

Hot Pursuit

Coming from Signet Eclipse
in December 2013.

God help me, I'm only twenty-eight. Too young to die.

Taylor Kayne bolted upright in bed, bathed in sweat, heart beating a sharp, painful rhythm against his sternum. The ghost sensation of cold steel pressed into the back of his head slowly evaporated, bringing him to wakefulness. Once, the real-life incident that spurred the nightmare had been nicely suppressed and compartmentalized in a tight little box in his brain, but lately it descended with alarming frequency.

Delayed PTSD. Wouldn't that tidbit give the Sugarland PD's shrink an orgasm?

Shane Ford, Taylor's partner in Homicide, would be shocked, too. Shane knew the story of what had happened four years ago, but had no idea the past was riding Taylor hard. Driving him to lose sleep, affecting his appetite, costing him focus at work. And nobody could find out, especially Shane.

Why the hell was this happening *now*, when his life was mostly together?

Pushing from bed, he stood and shook it off, one more time. One more day. He could do this.

Glancing at the clock, he grimaced. Just shy of five thirty in the morning. Jesus, that sucked. But since he'd skipped his run for the last few days, he might as well take advantage of the extra hour before he had to get ready for work. He knew he'd feel better once he got his blood pumping, but lately it had been damn hard to get motivated.

"Get your ass moving, slacker," he muttered to himself.

In less than two minutes, he was dressed in jogging pants, a T-shirt, and tennis shoes. Sucking in a deep breath, he headed downstairs and out the front door, locking it behind him and then hanging the spare key on a cord around his neck. After tucking the key under his shirt, he started off.

Settling into a brisk pace, he regulated his breathing and enjoyed the feeling of stretching neglected muscles, his soles hitting the pavement. He loved to run. He wasn't a fitness nut, not even close, but the fresh air was good for him. Helped him clear his head. Especially in the early summer like now, before the weather turned too hot.

As always, he admired the older homes in his neighborhood, with their tidy yards and beds full of flowers. He had a healthy competition going with the neighbors on his street, trying to outdo one another on who could cultivate the best yard. They even held a yearly contest at their block party. Shane liked giving him shit about that. *Sue me. I like plants and flowers, and I'm social.*

Whatever. Focusing on his home gave him something to do to take his mind off his lonely single status for a while. Besides, ladies loved that sort of shit, right? When he found the One, she'd admire his botanical handiwork and realize she'd found the *perfect man*. The idea made him smirk at his own idiocy.

He was so into his thoughts, the steady pounding of his feet on the asphalt, that he didn't register the whine of an approaching engine. Acceleration.

Not until it was almost too late.

Out of habit, he glanced over his shoulder—and his eyes widened. A black pickup truck was barreling down on him and swerving in his direction. Twisting his body, he dove for a row of hedges just as the bumper of the truck clipped his left side. The shock of the impact barely had a second to register, and then he was flying over the bushes. He hit the ground hard, skidding, one knee and an arm taking the brunt. Coming to a stop, he rolled to sit up, half-expecting the truck to burst right through the hedges and mow him down.

At the sound of the vehicle squealing around the corner, he let out a sigh of relief and sat there, pushing a shaking hand through his hair.

"Shit!"

Sharp pain began to make itself known, and he inspected the damage. His right forearm was scraped, bloody, and dirty, but once it was cleaned it wouldn't be too bad. The laceration across his kneecap might be more problematic. Probing it, he hissed a breath. The cut was nasty, and he was bleeding like a stuck pig. It was a tricky spot for stitches, though, so he'd just have to tend it as best he could.

Getting to his feet was more difficult than he expected. He was already hurting all over, getting stiff. Of course, there was nobody around on this quiet street to help him, and he hadn't brought his cell phone. He'd jogged about four miles, and he was looking at a painful walk home. He was going to be late to the station.

He started off, wincing with every slow step. His body was throbbing everywhere, so to occupy his mind, he tried to focus on what he recalled about the truck.

The vehicle was black. Completely. Tinted windows that were beyond legal. Thinking harder, he realized it was a Ford. Newer model, from the grille and logo. He hadn't been able to get a glimpse of the driver or the plates. As for who might hold a big enough grudge to try to run him down? Fuck, he'd been a cop since he was twenty-one. That list would take all day to compile.

That was all he had, and it wasn't much.

The walk home took over half an hour. By the time he limped up the porch steps, he wanted nothing more than to crawl back into bed and give the finger to this whole day. Instead, he took a hot shower, paying special attention to getting the dirt out of his scrapes and the cut on his knee. It hurt like shit, and he knew he'd feel worse tomorrow. Joy.

Once out of the shower, he toweled off and gathered some first-aid supplies, then sat on the toilet lid. The arm could wait. His knee was still bleeding like a bitch, and he doused it with antiseptic. Several gauze pads later, the bleeding had slowed, and he closed the laceration as best as he could, using some wound glue he'd bought at the drugstore a while back. It worked okay, and he bandaged and taped his knee for good measure. He'd have to watch that wound for infection.

There wasn't much he could do for the scraped-up arm. He hit it with antiseptic as well, downed a couple of ibuprofen, then hobbled into the bedroom and spotted the time. Just after seven. Before getting dressed, he had to make a call. Picking up his cell, he sat on the bed, brought up his contacts, and punched the number.

Shane answered on the second ring. "Hey, what's up?"

"I'm going to be a little late, half hour or so. I, um, had an incident."

"What kind of incident? What happened?" He could hear the concern in his partner's voice.

"Truck tried to turn me into road kill while I was out running this morning."

"On purpose?"

"Yeah."

"Fuck. You okay?"

"I'm fine, just moving slow. Scraped my arm and cut my knee after he hit me—"

"The bastard actually *hit* you?" his friend barked. "Why the hell aren't you in the ER getting checked out?"

"Calm down, partner. Like I said, it's not that bad. I got clipped by the bumper, is all." He cut Shane off before the man could get started again. "After I get there, I'm going to file a report so the guys on patrol can watch for the truck. Black Ford."

"The one with the fucking *dent* in the front."

He had to smile. "That'll be the one."

"I'm already at the station. I'll give them a heads-up so they can go ahead and start looking," he said, an angry edge to his words.

"Thanks, man."

"You need a ride? I can send a squad."

"No, I'm good." The last thing he wanted was to call even more attention to his situation.

"All right. Take your time and I'll see you soon."

Ending the call, Taylor went to the closet and chose an acceptable pair of jeans that were comfortable. Then he lingered over the shirts. A short-sleeved one would be better because it wouldn't rub on the scrapes, but then he'd have to field questions all day from people who hadn't heard about this morning. Debating, he settled on a dark, long-sleeved cotton shirt that would hide the wounds and any dots of blood that might seep through.

Once he was dressed, putting on his shoes was an effort. Amazing how fast the body became bruised and sore. Good thing he was going in to the station—if he sat around here much longer, he might never move again.

Downstairs in the kitchen, he settled on coffee and half a toasted bagel. He needed something in his stomach, and he couldn't live without his daily jolt of caffeine. Especially today. He carried both with him and eyed his new Challenger before climbing in.

He loved muscle cars, and this was a really cool one. But he missed his old Chevelle, which had been fucked up a few weeks ago when Shane and he had taken a dip—car and all—into the Cumberland River while in pursuit of a suspect. The car was currently sitting alone and forlorn in Christian Ford's big garage out back of his house. Chris was Shane's cousin and a fellow Homicide detective, having recently transferred in from Texas. The three of them tinkered on fixing the Chevelle when they had time, and Taylor had the extra cash, which wasn't often.

God, he missed that car.

The Challenger started with a throaty roar, which he

had to admit was pretty butch. Too bad he couldn't enjoy driving it today, with his knee screaming every time he switched from the gas to the brake. Maybe he should've accepted the ride. Too late now.

He made it to the station and was thankfully able to give his report with little fanfare. Apparently, Shane had told only those who needed to know: their captain, Austin Rainey, and a couple of uniforms. He had no doubt that the entire department would know within the hour, but at least he was able to have some breathing room. A few minutes later, he limped into his partner's office and closed the door.

Shane looked up from some papers, giving him a half-smile. "Hey. He must've winged you good."

"For sure. No point in sitting around at home, though."

"You might reconsider tomorrow, when it's worse."

"We'll see." He wouldn't call in sick unless he was on his deathbed, and they both knew it.

Shane just shook his head. "Tell me exactly what happened."

Taylor spent the next few minutes giving his partner the rundown, though there wasn't much to tell. They went back through some of their most recent cases to try to form a list of who might still carry enough of a grudge to commit attempted murder, but although there were several candidates, none was that strong.

Taylor tried to get comfortable in his chair, wincing as he squirmed. "Most of them are in prison or dead. And the ones that are out . . . I can come up with a list as long as my arm of who would run me over if they had the chance, but . . ." He frowned.

"What?"

"This had a different feel. Nothing I can put my finger on, just intuition."

"Like he was waiting for the opportunity?"

"Exactly. I've got no proof, though."

"You and I both know people kill for two main reasons—passion or money." His partner eyed him. "Which one do you fit?"

Taylor snorted. "Since I'm not loaded, I'm guessing passion. And there're all kinds of passion-motived killings. Specifically hate, when it comes to cops."

Unbidden, his nightmare intruded. Viciously, he shoved it into its box.

"Okay. Someone you, or we, arrested, then."

"Maybe." Rubbing his eyes, Taylor let out a tired breath. "Can we talk about this later? It might not even happen again."

"Sure."

Somehow, Taylor didn't really believe that. A chill slithered down his spine, telling him this was only the start. Could be his overwrought, stressed mind, but it didn't seem likely that was all there was to it.

A knock interrupted his thoughts, and Captain Rainey stepped into Shane's office. "We've got a body at the Sugarland Motel. Caller reported the sound of a gunshot, and Jenkins found the guy shot between the eyes."

Shane stood, groaning. "And let me guess. It's our turn."

"Yep." The captain looked at Taylor. "You up for this?"

"I'm here, aren't I? If I was going to laze around, I'd stay home."

Rainey grinned. "That's the spirit. Now, go get fucking busy." Turning, the captain strolled out, whistling.

"He's all heart," Shane said, making a face.

"At least he's in a good mood today. Wonder what's up with that."

Their captain was having serious marital problems—as in going down the tubes, permanently. He'd been tired and haggard the past few months, and they had all been worried about his health. Today, however, he had a spring in his step.

"No clue, but let's not rock the boat."

Taylor rose with some difficulty and stiffly followed his partner out the door. Turning down Shane's offer to drive, he slid behind the wheel, and they were off.

On the way, he thought he saw a black truck in traffic, three cars behind. Then it turned and was gone.

As though nearly being run over wasn't enough, the corpse with the neat little hole in the center of its forehead turned out to be a harbinger.

A sign of a shit storm heading his way.

Taylor stood next to Shane as both of them studied the dead man sprawled faceup on the floor. His salt-and-pepper hair was surrounded by a sticky pool of blood congealing on the industrial-grade carpet, and his expression was vaguely surprised.

"Who the hell was the poor bastard?" Taylor muttered. "And why did he get popped here of all places?"

Shane snorted. "He could've had the decency to get his ass killed in Nashville, out of our jurisdiction."

Taylor rolled his eyes at his partner's crappy joke.

"You know what I meant."

"Yeah."

Both of them glanced around the small motel room,

but there wasn't much to see. At least on the surface. Carefully stepping around the body, Taylor noted some clothes hanging in the closet next to the bathroom.

"Another suit, a couple of pairs of jeans, and three polo shirts." He peered into the bathroom. "A shaving kit in there. That's all."

"Got a small leather carryall on the table containing underwear and socks. A plane ticket, too, round-trip from LAX to Nashville International and back. Looks like he arrived yesterday, was supposed to fly back in three days. Car keys and his wallet beside the bag." Shane left the leather trifold sitting on the dresser and flipped it open with the edge of one latex-covered finger. "Max Griffin, born December 12, 1946. San Diego address."

Taylor's heart gave a lurch. He stared at Shane, his friend unaware of his sudden chill. *It means nothing. San Diego is not Los Angeles. They're two different cities, 121 miles apart, almost a two-hour drive.*

"Interesting," he managed. "So the car outside is his rental. He was here for a specific reason, but there's no evidence of what that might've been."

"Not yet." Turning, Shane yelled out the open door to the officer who'd arrived first on the scene. "Jenk!"

Aaron Jenkins, their new hire at the department, stuck his head in the door. "Yes, sir?"

"Take these and open that rental. See if you can find anything inside to give us a clue why our dead guy was in town." Shane tossed him the car keys, and the kid caught them one-handed. "Be careful about touching stuff."

"On it!" His boy-next-door face lit up at the prospect of helping with the investigation.

As Jenkins ducked out again, Taylor chuckled. "Damn, were we ever that young and green?"

"Probably, once upon a time." His partner quirked his mouth in a half-smile. "Do you ever wish you could go back to your early twenties?"

"For the wild social life and the hot young bod? Sure. For being the low cop on the totem pole again? Not so much."

"True."

"Though my bod is *still* hot."

"If that's what you want to tell yourself, old man."

"Says he who turns the big three-0 next week," Taylor shot back. "I'm only two years older than you."

"Just fucking with you."

"When are you not?"

In truth, Taylor gave as good as he got when it came to his partner. Shane and he had worked in Homicide together for over four years, since Taylor had moved to Sugarland, Tennessee, from Los Angeles. His mind shied away from the disaster that had prompted his move, and he focused on how content he was here, among people he liked and respected.

Shane and he might trade barbs, but it was all in good fun. His partner had become one of his best friends, and he'd do just about anything for the man. He had no doubt the feeling was mutual.

"Nothing much in the car, sir," Jenk said, stepping into the room. "Just some fast-food wrappers and a map. Isn't that odd?"

"What's that?" Shane asked.

"Well, who uses a paper road map anymore, right? Most people use their smartphones or a GPS, especially if they're traveling alone. Hard to read an old-fashioned map when you're driving."

That gave Taylor's partner pause. "You're right, though sometimes people prefer the old way of doing things. Reading a smartphone while driving alone would be just as tough." He sighed. "Come to think of it, we didn't find a phone at all. Good work."

The kid beamed at the praise. Taylor suppressed a grin and was about to play razz the rookie when Medical Examiner Laura Eden arrived, along with the police department's forensics unit.

The room got crowded, so Jenk, Taylor, and Shane moved outside to let the others process the scene. There wasn't much to find, and in less than an hour, Eden was giving them the short version.

"No surprises. Well, not counting the man with the bullet in his brain," she said drily. "Based on the blood splatter, this is indeed the murder scene. Mr. Griffin was shot in the forehead at point-blank range with a smaller-caliber handgun. Nothing much to bag except a couple of hairs and some other fibers."

"They finding any prints?" Taylor asked.

The striking brunette arched a brow. "In a motel room? Seriously, Detective?"

His face heated. "Right." How stupid of him. Not to mention it sucked to sound like an idiot in front of a gorgeous woman who'd turned him down flat for a dinner date. Twice.

"Anyhow, I'd say he's been dead for about an hour and a half. That's all I know, but I'll send you what I've got when I know more."

Taylor cleared his throat. "We about done here, then?"

Shane nodded, running a hand through his longish brown hair. "Yep. Thanks, Laura."

"No problem. See you, guys."

It kind of smarted how she just went back inside without a backward glance, all cool professionalism. His partner must've noticed something in his expression as they walked to Taylor's car, because he couldn't resist making a comment.

"It's not you, buddy. *You're* the one who told me she had a thing for the captain."

"Yeah, I know," he grumped as he slid behind the wheel. "Why do women always want the guy who's not available?"

"They're twisted like that, my friend. Well, not all of them." Shane buckled his seat belt. "Just find a different horse to bet on than Laura."

"Easy for you to say. You snagged a fine woman, and you've got a great kid."

A dopey smile split his friend's face. "I did, didn't I? I'm a lucky SOB."

I will not be jealous. I'm happy for him.

He was, truly. Shane and his new wife, Daisy, had been through hell and so had Shane's seventeen-year-old godson, Drew Cooper. Being colleagues at the police department had been a minor obstacle for the couple compared to their other troubles, especially helping Drew deal with the trauma of his father's death. Then there were the awful secrets Drew had been keeping and the danger those secrets had brought into their lives.

But it was over now, and the three of them were forging a new life together.

"Hey, you're a great guy," Shane said, sensing the dip

in his mood. "You're going to find a fantastic lady who loves everything about you. You're funny and easygoing, and you're a good friend to everyone who knows you."

"Is this the part where we hug?"

"Shut up, asswipe."

But he laughed, and Taylor couldn't help but be a little cheered as he pulled out of the parking lot.

Maybe this day would take a turn for the better after all.

Max is dead! Oh, God.

Cara Evans pulled the baseball cap low on her head and watched the activity from her hiding place in the park across the street from the Sugarland Motel. Angrily, she swiped away the tears that refused to quit falling. Just as she'd done for the past four goddamned years.

Max had come to town, looking for Cara. Then he'd phoned, urging her in a hushed voice to meet him at the motel. Why had he come to her? Especially now, after all this time? Who killed him, and why? His visit could be related to her sister's murder. Or their father's estate. Any number of things. But the answers to those questions had died with Max in that awful room.

One thing for sure—the murdering asshole would pay for snuffing out the life of a good man. The only person she had still counted as a friend in the entire sorry world. Leaning her head against the rough bark of the tree, she gave up and let the tears flow. For several long moments, she allowed herself to grieve, barely aware of the sounds of activity across the street. Gradually, however, she gained a measure of control. Her fingers tightened around a solid object she'd forgotten about.

Max's iPhone.

She'd be in a fuck ton of trouble if and when the cops thought to track its whereabouts. It would be hard to explain her presence in Max's room and why she'd lifted the device. Harder still to convince them that she hadn't killed him, that he'd been dead when she arrived. But she planned to get rid of the phone. As soon as she took a peek to try to determine why he had wanted to see her so badly. Why he had possibly died for it.

Voices across the motel's parking lot snared her attention. Peering around the tree, she saw two men in plain clothes emerge from the room. Detectives, from the glint of the shields hooked to their belts at the waist. She'd been too stricken with panic and raw grief to pay attention when they had arrived, so she studied them now.

Both were tall, but the brown-haired one was taller and leaner than the other. The man who was presumably his partner was maybe an inch or two shorter and more muscular. Golden blond hair just covered his ears, layered in a loose, casual style with some wisps of bangs falling into what looked from here to be quite a handsome face—

Recognition hit her like a baseball bat to the head, and though she'd half-expected him to show up, she felt sick. If not for the tree, she would have tumbled to the ground.

Taylor Kayne. Untouchable. Man's man. Lauded hero.

"Fucking lying murderer," she whispered, rage welling in her chest. Despair, rotten and black, clogged her throat.

Once again, Kayne was smack in the middle of the hell that was her life. That suited her fine, though. Because the bastard probably didn't know Cara had come to Sugarland or even have a clue who she was in the first place. He sure as hell didn't know that he was the reason she was here. Or that she knew where he worked, lived, ate, shopped, jogged.

But he would find out soon. She was biding her time, waiting for the perfect moment. Then she'd spring her trap. Force him to spill every last filthy secret that should have corroded his guts by now.

Detective Taylor Kayne was going to confess to murdering her sister.

And then Cara would exact long-awaited sweet revenge.

ALSO AVAILABLE
FROM

JO DAVIS

Line of Fire
The Firefighters of Station Five

To his fellow firemen, Tommy Skyler has it all. But the golden boy of Station Five hides a private pain. He was once a star quarterback until tragedy derailed his dream. Since then, he's struggled with his choices—including his decision to become a firefighter. His one ray of light is from beautiful nurse Shea Ford. When a dangerous rescue lands Tommy in the ER, what better opportunity to win her over? But when a conspiracy culminates in deadly arson, Tommy realizes that a ruthless enemy is closing in, threatening to destroy the couple's love—and their lives.

Available wherever books are sold or at
penguin.com

facebook.com/LoveAlwaysBooks

PRAISE FOR THE FIREFIGHTERS OF STATION FIVE SERIES

Ride the Fire

"The perfect blend of romance and suspense. Neither element overshadows the other. Jo Davis creates a great combination of romance, steamy love scenes with mystery and suspense mixed in. I was pulled right into the book, and before I knew it, the last page was turned. I wasn't ready to let go."　　　　　—Fiction Vixen Book Reviews

"Once again, Jo Davis has rocked it in this series!"
　　　　　—Night Owl Reviews

"Jo Davis continues her steamy, heat-packed romantic suspense stories with *Ride the Fire*. This book is a great blend of hot romance with suspenseful, well-plotted action."
　　　　　—Fresh Fiction

Line of Fire

"Grab a fan and settle in for one heck of a smoking-hot read. . . . Fiery-hot love scenes and a look inside the twisted mind of a killer make *Line of Fire* stand out. Add in the behind-the-scenes look at the other characters and I could read this book over and over!"
　　　　　—Joyfully Reviewed

"Full of romance and steamy love scenes with a splash of mystery and suspense. This combination had me eager to turn the page and left me wanting more. The love scenes were scorching hot!"
　　　　　—Fiction Vixen Book Reviews

continued . . .

Hidden Fire

"Surprisingly sweet and superhot . . . one of the best heroes I've read in a long time. If you want a hot firefighter in your room for the night, grab a copy and tuck right in with no regrets. Four hearts." —The Romance Reader

"A fast-paced romantic suspense thriller."
—The Best Reviews

Under Fire

"Four stars! A totally entertaining experience."
—*Romantic Times*

"Scorching-hot kisses, smoldering sex, and explosive passion make *Under Fire* a must read! Experience the flames of *Under Fire*!" —Joyfully Reviewed

"Exhilarating [with] a two-hundred-proof heat duet . . . a strong entry [and] a terrific, action-packed thriller."
—*Midwest Book Review*

Trial by Fire

"A five-alarm read . . . riveting, sensual."
—Beyond Her Book